*To: Marj —*
*Many happy journeys...*
*Kileen Prather*
*Oct 2014*

# JOURNEY BECKONS

## By

## Kileen Prather

ISBN: 978-1-934666-56-2

Cover Design by Summer R. Morris
Layout Design by Stephanie Reynolds

Published and distributed by:
High-Pitched Hum Publishing
321 15<sup>th</sup> Street North
Jacksonville Beach, Florida 32250

Contact High-Pitched Hum Publishing at
www.highpitchedhum.net

Contact author Kileen Prather at
www.kileenprather.com

This is a work of fiction. The literary perceptions and insights are based on the author's experience. All names and places not historical, characters and incidents are either products of the author's imagination or are used fictitiously.

High-Pitched Hum
Publishing

I would like to dedicate this to my friends, Jan and Joe, who have helped me along this Journey. And to my son, Frank, who made so much possible.

# Chapter One

Cassie gazed thoughtfully out the window of her apartment overlooking Seattle's Elliott Bay to the hill that was the Queen Anne district in the distance. The condo had glass patio windows with two balconies facing the south and west sides of the city. In the daytime she often watched the parasailers gliding by her balcony with the surreal Mount Rainier to the southeast standing like a sentinel guarding the city.

Spending several months in Seattle had been one of the best things that had ever happened to her. Cassie recalled telling her children she did not anticipate any drastic changes to her life and yet summering here in this city was something she never imagined in her wildest dreams. Although she knew her time there would end all too quickly, for a little while she would be able to leave the sadness behind.

Cassie was living in the popular Belltown section of the city. Her apartment complex, named Harbor View, had panoramic vistas of Puget Sound and the Olympic Mountains to the west as well as spectacular sunsets each evening.

Many of the buildings in Belltown had murals painted on the walls and Cassie enjoyed looking at them as she walked to the Market Place or over to the Seattle Center complex where the Space Needle was located. She was living halfway between the two areas and spent a lot of time walking through the downtown. Cassie enjoyed watching all the different people, from the homeless to the street musicians as well as the tourists and wealthy, who all contributed to giving this city such a vibrant atmosphere.

Recently turned fifty-two and newly retired after twenty five years as a high school history teacher, Cassie wondered where the next phase of her life would take her. At one time she had looked forward to retiring and traveling as often as money would allow but now had mixed feelings about leaving teaching. Life had a peculiar way of changing when you least expected it.

Turning from the window, Cassie walked across the room toward a mirror by the front door. As she glanced at her profile, she began reflecting on her life and how she came to be in Seattle for the summer.

Her short brown hair showed only traces of gray and her green eyes seemed to sparkle. Many people often commented on their color. Her friend, Jane, had often told Cassie that her eyes reminded her of the green color seen in the Caribbean Sea. Jane was always going off somewhere in the world. When she returned and told Cassie of her adventures, it made Cassie even more anxious than ever to travel.

Cassie was medium height and a size twelve. As she aged, she had to work at maintaining her weight. Although she used to complain about making time for exercise, she realized it was also important to her mental health. Not only did it help her keep weight in line, but Cassie had discovered it was the best way to work off her stress.

Cassie and her husband Jim lived in New Brighton, Minnesota, a suburb of Minneapolis. The Minneapolis area had many lakes and Cassie felt a peace, which was better than taking a tranquilizer, as she walked various routes around her neighborhood on her daily jaunts. As she strolled around the different lakes, she never grew tired of watching the waves lapping against the shore. Naturally, the waves were much bigger on the days a strong wind was blowing.

Cassie and her husband had been married for thirty-one years. Six years before, Jim had been diagnosed with diabetes.

He had a job working for Hennepin County but had enough years to retire. Even though Jim had laughed at the diagnosis, he took early retirement and sat at home bemoaning his fate.

The doctor tried to convince him that even though much of his illness could be traced to his family history, he could still control the progression and severe side effects of the disease if he took care of himself. Jim, ignoring the doctor's warnings, had continued to smoke and eat as he pleased. As a result, a year later, Jim had circulatory problems with his leg and had to have his right leg removed up to his knee. Naturally, Jim had spiraled into depression over his condition, especially since he felt he could never drive again.

Cassie tried to remain positive and keep Jim upbeat but he had just ignored her and continued to smoke while spending his days complaining about how his life was now over. He refused to participate in physical therapy or any other exercise and he angrily refused any depression medication the doctor felt would help him.

As Jim put on weight from just sitting around all day and because of some side effects from the medications he was taking, intimacy between them became nonexistent. His doctor told Cassie he could switch some of the doses or try different drugs but Jim was so depressed by his situation, he would try nothing to better his condition. He told the doctor if the medications he was now using were taking care of his problems he did not want to try switching. Cassie had a feeling he wanted to punish her because of his health conditions.

Cassie worried what would happen the next school year when she was officially retired and spent all day at home. She did not want to think about a life without purpose. Jim was always putting her down when she was at home and Cassie realized he was jealous of her health. However, Cassie knew Jim could do a lot more if he adopted a more positive outlook on his life.

Jim was sixty-two years old and collecting social security disability as well as his retirement money. Their house was paid for and they had managed to save a lot of Cassie's salary over the years and had invested their money. With both of their retirement and investment incomes, they would have enough money to live comfortably and even travel occasionally. They had talked about traveling for years but now Cassie knew Jim did not want to go anywhere. He had lost all his zest for living.

Cassie kept telling him that he should come to her school and volunteer a couple of times a week. There was always a need for volunteers at her school and she thought it would help him feel good about himself again. But Jim preferred sitting in front of the television all day complaining about how life had not treated him fairly.

Cassie had always believed she would be married forever and this had been reinforced by her religious upbringing. Besides, somehow it did not seem right to leave Jim in his condition, even though she had to endure extreme loneliness for the last few years.

Jim no longer talked about the future and never said much of anything to Cassie except to inquire about meals or complain about his health problems. Because he spent most of his time alone in the den, Cassie felt she was living virtually alone in their house even though Jim was physically living there.

Cassie told Dr. George, their physician and family friend that her life was manageable but when her blood pressure became extremely high, he had become quite concerned. The doctor knew stress was causing the elevated blood pressure and told Cassie she needed to take a break from the situation or she would not be around much longer to take care of Jim.

The couple's children, Kit and Gray, had no real idea how difficult it was for Cassie to live with Jim. They were horrified when they came over to visit their dad and Cassie told them about Doctor George's recommendations. Both of the children were married and living their own lives. Even though they lived fairly close in nearby suburbs, Cassie knew they did not notice how bad her conditions were at home. They were either in denial or they felt ignoring the situation would make it not seem so bad. Basically, they were so wrapped up in their own lives, they assumed their parents would just deal with their problems.

"I hope you're not planning on getting a divorce, mom. Dad needs you and it wouldn't be fair to leave him now," Kit told Cassie as she paced in the kitchen.

*I wonder when things can be fair for me,* Cassie thought to herself, remembering how the doctor had insisted she take a break from her care giving.

"I'm not planning on divorcing your dad," Cassie responded. "I just thought it might help me to get away for awhile, although that would involve a separation from your dad for the summer. I'm not sure where I would go or what I would do but I need to start thinking about a temporary change from this intolerable living situation."

"Well who would take care of dad if you went away?" her son Gray asked surprised.

"I don't know what I am going to do. I do know the doctor told me if I don't take a break from your father, I may not be around much longer to take care of him at all."

"I just don't understand why Doctor George won't give you some blood pressure pills like he gives dad," Kit replied.

"I don't want to take medication if I don't need it. Besides, blood pressure medicine can't help when stress is the problem. Don't worry, I don't plan to do anything drastic with my life," Cassie told the two of them.

They left shaking their heads thinking their mother needed to forget the doctor's advice. Cassie felt so beaten down by her family. It was as if everyone had a right to live their own lives anyway they pleased except for her. It was hard to express what she was feeling and deep down she knew no one wanted to hear it. As long as she said nothing and continued to hold all her thoughts in, everyone around her could remain calm and happy.

Somehow, Cassie knew she needed to focus on her own needs for awhile so she could continue to be there for her family. The problem was they could not accept that she needed time to herself. She felt that she was living in a world of dreams that might have been. Presently, all she could see ahead of her were long years of incredible loneliness as a combination nurse and mother to her husband.

Cassie did not want to become an empty and bitter person because of her situation. She always had an upbeat attitude towards life. Even when negative situations arose, Cassie looked for the positive side.

Jane, Cassie's friend, also helped to keep her focused positively. She had brassy red hair and laughing blue eyes that seemed to fit her personality. Jane had been divorced for several years and seemed to find fulfillment in her travels. She met wonderful people from all over and kept in contact with them. Jane's husband George had been unfaithful and since she had left him, she cultivated many men friends but she had never let anyone get close to her again.

Jane kept reiterating that she could not remember the last time Jim had said something nice or even smiled at Cassie. They had been friends a long time and Jane was extremely concerned about the mental and physical health of her friend. She knew Jim had been a little selfish, expecting Cassie to be the "perfect wife." Jane felt Jim took for granted that Cassie would always be around for him while not giving any support in return.

Despite that, the marriage seemed to work for them and Jane always thought they were good together. However, Jim's selfishness had gone over the top as far as Jane was concerned. She felt Jim needed a wake-up call if their marriage was to survive.

Cassie realized she had created this "monster" by catering to Jim. There was a time when he had been willing to help with work around the house when she needed something done. Now, Jim was too depressed to do anything but wallow in self pity. Cassie knew that continuing to live in this manner was no longer an option.

Living such an emotionally negative and empty life for so many years was taking a toll on her. Cassie was beginning to agree with Jane's assessment and feared it might be too late for her marriage to be salvaged.

How to turn things around was something she grappled with every day. When she had asked Jim to go with her to talk to a counselor about their life together, he laughed at the suggestion.

After Jim refused to go for marriage counseling, Cassie knew something inside of her had died. She felt no joy except when she was teaching. She could not believe Jim did not see how miserable she felt. But, then she realized Jim could not see anything except his own unhappiness.

Although her situation seemed hopeless, Cassie recognized that their life had to change if they were going to stay together.

# Chapter Two

Mid-April finally arrived with Easter rapidly approaching. Cassie liked it when Easter fell later because there was a feeling of spring in the air. The new season seemed to be a time of hope. Summer was just around the corner and, of course, everywhere Cassie looked, love was in the air, especially among the students. It seemed a perfect time of new beginnings, since the long winter was finally over.

The hopeful atmosphere did not seem to extend to Cassie's house. Jim's depression was getting worse and she was at a loss as to what to do about it. In another month and a half school would be over, and although she was officially retiring, Cassie was considering substitute teaching the next year just to get out of the house and having a break from her husband.

Subbing was something she was not really looking forward to. She actually just wanted to walk away totally from the school scene when she retired and do some community volunteering. Cassie knew substitute teaching would be a good excuse for not staying at home with Jim. She hated not having any direction in her life and knew there was no way she could sit around the house all day as Jim did. All thoughts of doing any traveling seemed out of the question at that point.

The most frustrating aspect was that Jim did just fine during the day while she was at school. He slept in and could get dressed and fix his meals while she was gone. However, as soon as she walked in the door, he needed a drink and this done and that to be taken care of until she could not even sit down for five minutes. Cassie was afraid that her life would continue in just that way if she did not get out of the house on a regular basis in the fall.

She had even started taking her walks after work around her school before going home. A couple of times she came home to change her clothes but before she could go out the door, Jim began demanding she do something for him and she had ended up not having time to walk. She tried to explain that she needed to exercise but he had laid such a guilt trip on her for being away from him all day, she ended up helping him with what he wanted.

The second time that occurred, Cassie realized she would have to walk before going home. Jim never questioned what time she got home. He just needed her undivided attention the minute she walked in the door. She had tried again to talk to her daughter about her dad but once again Kit just ignored her plight.

Cassie was hoping Kit would come over one day a week to spend some time with her father so she could have some free time. However, Kit was going through problems with her job and told her mother she was just too busy to help. Cassie watched her race out the door to meet her husband for dinner and a movie.

Cassie just sighed after their talk. It appeared Jim was not the only selfish person in the family. She knew if she could not get Kit to come over one day a week to give her a break, there was probably no use in even bringing it up with Gray.

And she hated asking Gray knowing his circumstances. Kit's job did not have the set hours like her brother's and she had a lot more free time than Gray. Cassie did not think it would be too heavy of a burden on Kit to come over one afternoon a week to give her mother a chance to get out and away from the stress.

Gray was an accountant and he and his wife Karen had recently started their own business. She knew they were at work by 7:00 a.m. and did not get home until after 9:00 p.m. most nights. Of all the people in their family Cassie knew Karen, her daughter-in-law, understood better than her own children and would have helped if she had the time.

Karen's mother had suffered a stroke shortly after her husband retired and being devoted to his wife he had taken care of her for three years. Karen had lived at home while attending college helping her father as much as possible.

After graduating from college, Karen took a job with a company that expected her to put in long hours. It was there that she had met Gray. For the first year they dated, they only went out on Saturday nights. Besides working long hours, Karen's weekends were devoted to helping her dad buying groceries, cleaning the house, and preparing meals so dinners could be just warmed up during the week.

One morning Karen's father simply did not wake up. The family doctor said he died from a massive heart attack in his sleep. Karen was convinced the stress of caring for her mother had led to the heart condition which eventually had killed him.

Karen's mother was told of her husband's death and the morning after the funeral she died in her sleep like her husband. Realizing her mother no longer wanted to live without her husband, she had just let go.

Karen was shell shocked. It had been expected that her mother might die but in less than a week Karen had to make arrangements for two funerals.

Cassie knew Karen felt a lot of empathy for her situation and would constantly ask how she was doing and if she needed any help. But Cassie felt guilty asking Karen to help when she was so busy with the new business and this made Kit's rebuff and denial even harder to bear.

Cassie always thanked Karen for her offer but pointed out Jim was much more self-sufficient than Karen's mother had been. For the present, Cassie was stuck and knew she had to let go of the anger she sometimes felt towards her children.

As she walked in the door returning from her day of teaching on the Thursday before Good Friday, Cassie heard Jim yelling for her. She tried to control the anger welling up in her and started thinking instead about the Easter Sunday dinner she would be preparing for the family.

As she took her coat off Jim's voice was farther away than usual. Through a haze, Cassie saw Jim come around the corner in his wheelchair with an empty glass in his hand. As the room began spinning out of control she was wondering why Jim could not get his own drink as she fell into a swirling black void.

Cassie did not remember anything else. The next conscious thing she heard was Jane and Kit, with voices raised, having what sounded like an argument in the next room. As she came to, she realized she was not at home. It appeared she was in a hospital bed. She could tell Kit was upset by the tone she was using.

Cassie heard Kit tell Jane that all her mother needed was a new doctor. "If Doctor George had given mother blood pressure medication like he should have, we wouldn't have had to call 911 and she wouldn't be in the hospital right now. She needs to have some pills or something to help her deal with her problems so she won't get sick like this again."

"Don't you understand? Your mother may die if she continues to live with the stress she's been enduring for the last few years?" Jane told Kit in exasperation. "Look at what happened to Karen's father."

"There's no use arguing about this," Cassie heard Gray say. "Mom and dad's problems are different that Karen's parents. Let's wait and see what the doctor says. Mother's blood pressure is back in the normal range and Doctor George said she'll be all right tonight. Personally, I think we should all go home since mother is no longer in any danger and deal with this situation tomorrow. I know Dad is sleeping by now but shouldn't one of us look in on him tonight, Kit?"

"I told Dad I would call him if anything changed. He'll be all right tonight. I'll go over in the morning and fix him some breakfast before coming to the hospital."

Jane was extremely upset by the whole situation but realized the children were afraid of what had happened to their mother and were avoiding how to deal with the situation since they were not sure what the future might hold. Their mother had always been there to fix every difficult problem and now she was the problem. Kit and Gray just were not sure how to deal with this new situation.

Memories of Karen's parents had Gray feeling pretty shaken but he was afraid to admit it. Not knowing what to do about the situation, Gray thought maybe Kit was right; if his mother started some kind of blood pressure medications she would be fine again.

Jane did not want the children to get upset with her when she did not have any answers at this point. However, she did have an idea and knew she would be making a call when she got home. She was hoping for an answer before coming to the hospital the next day. Maybe she could help resolve this situation to everyone's satisfaction. Well at least to Cassie's satisfaction.

Cassie pretended to be sleeping when she heard the three of them come in and take one last look at her before going home for the night. As she drifted back to sleep she wondered who would fix Easter dinner. Then she realized that she really did not care.

# Chapter Three

The next morning, Cassie woke early when the nurses came in to check her blood pressure and the IV that had been inserted in her left hand to keep her hydrated. She wondered how anyone could get any decent rest in a hospital with all the hustle and bustle that was constantly going on around the place.

At 9:00 a.m. Dr. George came into see her. He wanted a chance to talk to her before her family arrived. "Good morning, Cassie, how are you feeling today?"

"I'm feeling much better, Doctor George."

"Cassie, I'm going to keep you in the hospital until Tuesday. Since it is Good Friday, only essential tests will be run today and I need to rule out the possibility that you might have some other serious health problems. I'll schedule you for tests first thing Monday morning."

The doctor knew Cassie could go home on Saturday for the weekend but he thought she would be better off resting in the hospital away from the stress of her home life. He knew how Jim was treating her and now she had her children adding to her stress.

"You might be able to go home later in the afternoon on Monday, but you might feel more rested waiting until Tuesday morning. We can talk about that Monday afternoon after I get the preliminary results back. I'll be honest with you, Cassie. I don't think we are going to find anything physically wrong with you. I believe your condition is caused by the stressful conditions you are living under at home."

Cassie was relieved. "Well, if it's only stress I should be able to deal with it."

"Cassie, don't think of it as only stress. Stress is very damaging. Many physical illnesses can be attributed to stress. I want you to take me seriously. The type of stress you're living under can and will kill you if you continue as you are. You'll recall what happened to Karen's father."

Tears welled up in Cassie's eyes. "But doctor what can I do? Jim just laughs at me when I say I feel stressed. And, I've asked him to go to counseling but he has refused."

"From everything you've told me and what I know of Jim, I realize you won't be able to change him at this point in time. Cassie, don't worry right now. I want you to rest and relax while you're in here. I'll talk to your family when they come to visit today and I wanted you to know what I plan to tell them. They'll resist what I have to say, Cassie. People today feel that there is always some kind of magic pill to take that will make you feel better. Your family will insist you get a second opinion."

"I trust you, Doctor George."

"Cassie, believe me, if you want a second opinion I will not take it personally. At present I think the best thing to do is to run some tests to rule out any serious health problems. After we get the results back, if you are in good physical condition we can discuss other solutions. And, if you do want a second opinion there are some specialists I could suggest."

Cassie felt reassured by her doctor's words. "Unless you find something physically wrong with me I don't want a second opinion Dr. George. I have always been comfortable with any diagnosis you've made. I really believe Jim likely wouldn't have lost his leg if he had taken your advice in the first place."

"It makes me sad to say that is definitely true, Cassie. And you need to understand I don't believe he has any right to make you feel guilty for choices he has made. You have done everything you could to keep him healthy and he has chosen his unhealthy lifestyle instead."

"I guess this means I won't be home to fix Easter dinner," Cassie said as she smiled at the doctor.

"I've already talked to your daughter about that, so don't worry, Cassie. I will be meeting with your family at 11:00. Your friend Jane called and I told her she should come and visit you anytime. I suspect that she is very good emotional support for you and Jane should be with you when your family comes in to see you after my talk. Maybe they'll be more reasonable in her presence."

Cassie thanked the doctor as he left her. As she lay there, she thought about what he had said. She knew Kit would be upset because she would view it as one more problem in her world. And she knew Jim would not believe a thing the doctor said. If the doctor did not find anything seriously wrong with her, Jim would just tell her to toughen up and get a grip.

Cassie realized she was almost at the end of her rope with Jim. She felt his resentment whenever she was around him. She did not want to hurt him but she knew he had to make changes if they were going to continue living together. And the doctor's talk had scared Cassie enough to make her realize that things had to change. Her health was just as important as Jim's.

Before long, Jane arrived with a bouquet of flowers and a wide smile on her face. Cassie chuckled at her grin. "You look like the cat that ate the canary, Jane."

"I have some news for you Cassie, but tell me what the doctor said first."

Cassie repeated the doctor's recommendations and also confided how her feelings for Jim were changing. Jane was shocked when she heard about Jim's leg.

"I guess I never realized he might have saved his leg if he had stopped the smoking."

"Cassie, I have a proposal for you and I don't want you to say "yes" or "no" right now. I just want you to promise me you'll think about it, okay?"

"Okay Jane."

"You remember my friend Sylvia I told you about who lives in Seattle?" Cassie nodded as Jane continued. "Anyway, she's going to Europe for the summer. She plans to leave right after Memorial Day and be gone until the first part of October. She has a wonderful apartment condo in downtown Seattle that overlooks Elliott Bay. She told me a couple of weeks ago she is looking for someone to stay in her place to watch over things and take care of her plants while she is gone."

"What does this have to do with me, Jane?"

"I called her last night when I got home from seeing you. She still hasn't found anyone trustworthy to look after her place. Please don't be upset with me, Cassie, but I told her you might be interested. I told her she could feel very safe about her things if you lived there."

At first Cassie was shocked. How could I be gone from Jim for so long she wondered? Aloud she said, "How could I possibly go away like that, Jane?"

Before Jane had a chance to answer Kit, Gray, & Jim came in and none of them looked very happy. Kit immediately repeated what Doctor George had told them. She was extremely upset and told her mother she thought the doctor should just give her some pills and release her from the hospital so Cassie could fix Easter dinner for everyone.

Cassie, with a little smile, just rolled her eyes at Jane. Then Jim started in. Cassie could almost feel her blood pressure rising as he spoke. He never even asked her how she felt and there were no flowers or little goodies from anyone in her family. He insisted she check herself out of the hospital immediately and come back on Monday as an outpatient for the tests. Then he told her he was beginning to wonder if they shouldn't find a new doctor—one who knew what he was doing.

Listening to Jim, Cassie became outraged. She had enough and finally exploded. "What do you want Jim? Shall I get rid of Doctor George and ignore his warning? If I ignore what he's telling me, I could end up with something worse happening, like you did. I don't intend to spend the rest of my life waiting on you hand and foot while you continue to live your life the way you want. And, I don't intend to get even sicker because I resent having to take care of you when it is apparent you couldn't care less about how I feel. You make bad choices, Jim, and I am not supposed to say anything or rock the boat. I also have a right to a life and I refuse to suffer in silence anymore because of your decisions."

Turning to her children she said, "And, Kit and Gray, I am tired of you two pretending nothing is wrong and that I just need to stay quiet and pretend life is great. You three come storming in here telling me what I'm supposed to do and you don't even ask me how I feel. All you want is for me not to upset your lifestyle in any way. I think the three of you better leave, now. You can all figure out what to do about Easter dinner yourselves, which is apparently the most important thing you care about at the moment. I plan to stay here and figure out what to do with the rest of my life"

Thinking Cassie was just stressed and did not really mean what she was saying Kit said, "Mom you don't really mean that. We only want what is best for you."

Cassie was close to tears and taking a deep breath said, "Kit, I asked you to come over and help one afternoon a week to give me some time for myself but you were too busy with your life. Well, I am too busy right now to listen to all of you telling me how I am supposed to live my life. I feel you don't want what's best for me, but what is best and most convenient for all of you. Please just go, now. We can discuss this further when I'm feeling better."

Jane had moved away from Cassie so that she was almost behind the opened bathroom door when Jim and the kids had entered the room. She was proud of Cassie for speaking up to her family. However, as she watched them file out, Jane wondered if anything Cassie had said had even sunk in.

After the three filed out, Jane came back to Cassie's bed. "You did the right thing, Cassie. You need to stand up to them. They will keep taking advantage of you and you will continue to be stressed if you don't make your feelings known to them. I hope you'll give Seattle some serious thought. It could be the best thing to ever happen to you. And who knows, maybe you're destined to go there."

"You're right, Jane. I will give Seattle serious consideration. I can't believe how thoughtless they all are. Maybe if I get away for those few months, my family will learn to appreciate me more. And, if not, at least it will give me some time to myself to think about what direction I want for my life after retirement. I think life in the Pacific Northwest this summer could be just what the doctor ordered."

Cassie had no idea that she was indeed about to embark on an exciting journey. She was about to discover that life could be more fulfilling than she could ever imagine.

# Chapter Four

Kit stopped in to see her mother on Saturday morning. Knowing her daughter had a lot of errands to run and things to do since it was the weekend, Cassie told her Jane planned to come and see her that afternoon and she did not need to stay. Instead she would look forward to the family visiting her the next day.

Kit seemed relieved she did not need to sit with her mother. Cassie could sense the strain between the two of them and was relieved when her daughter left shortly afterwards.

The day passed quickly and quietly. Cassie felt sinful just lying in bed reading a book with nothing to do. Jane stopped in for a short visit and told Cassie all about Sylvia's condo. She was afraid Cassie would not agree to go to Seattle and she was going to do anything she could to try and entice her to that wonderful city.

Cassie's family arrived at the hospital early the next afternoon. It was Easter Sunday and the children and their spouses had taken their father to Easter services and then to a family style restaurant for brunch. This time when they came in, Gray was carrying an Easter lily plant for his mother. Cassie began to wonder if maybe her agitation with them the day before had helped to change their thinking somewhat.

Cassie soon discovered she was mistaken. Before long, Jim began grumbling about Cassie staying in the hospital until Tuesday and Kit and Gray began bickering over who would take care of their dad until Cassie came home.

This time Cassie did not get upset nor say anything to them about their selfishness. Simply knowing there was hope for taking a break from all of them had helped to release her frustrations and kept her stress levels down.

She had almost convinced herself that she needed to stay in Minnesota for the summer but once the bickering started she realized nothing would change unless she went away. Cassie could hardly believe how she had swung from one way of thinking to the other so quickly. Of course, this was all based on the assumption that there was nothing physically wrong with her.

Before her family showed up, Doctor George stopped in briefly after his Easter services. She told him how she felt towards her children and also mentioned Jane's proposal to her for the summer.

"That's an excellent idea, Cassie. We'll wait until the tests come back but I really don't think we are going to find anything wrong with you. We seem to have your blood pressure under control and it's been running normal ever since you've been in here away from the stress and pressure of your home situation. If the test results are normal, with everything I know about you and Jim, I will be more convinced than ever that emotional stress is the cause of your illness. I think a four month break from your family would be just what the doctor ordered." The doctor was looking at Cassie with a broad smile.

Cassie had vacillated about going to Seattle for the summer but realized the doctor was right as she listened to her family bickering. She almost felt like she wasn't even in the same room as her family discussed what they should do about her situation.

When the discussion ran out of steam, Kit told Cassie they would all spend the afternoon with her. Cassie loved her family but knew she could not stand having them crowded around in her small hospital room all afternoon.

Very carefully, so she would not hurt their feelings, she explained that the doctor had been in and told her she needed to rest that afternoon before her tests the next morning. They all seemed relieved when Cassie told them about needing some quiet time and it wasn't long before they filed out.

Cassie realized as they left that Jim had said goodbye but had not even kissed her when he came in or when he had left. Suddenly, she knew her marriage was in serious jeopardy.

A few minutes after her family left, Jane popped in for a visit. Cassie told Jane everything that happened with the doctor and her family. When she finished, she took a deep breath, smiled and said, "Jane, call your friend, Sylvia. Tell her if she approves, I would be happy to stay in her condo as soon as I get out of school until she comes back the first of October."

"Oh, Cassie, that's wonderful! I know you are making the right decision. As soon as I get home I'll call Sylvia this afternoon and then I'll call you tonight to let you know what she thinks."

After Jane left, Cassie lay back on her pillow and thought about the decision she had just made as a sudden sense of relief flooded over her. She could not believe she had agreed to go to Seattle without giving it a second thought. Then she realized that if she had given it more thought she might have backed out.

Cassie could not believe how excited she was about her up and coming summer in Seattle. She almost felt like a college student, leaving home for the first time.

Cassie spent the rest of the afternoon reading and she had just finished dinner when the phone rang. Jane called to tell her Sylvia had been relieved and excited to know Cassie would stay in her place.

Jane's word on Cassie's reliability was all she needed. Sylvia asked Jane to have Cassie call her the following weekend when she knew the results of her tests, so they could firm up the details on her move there for the summer.

Cassie could not even imagine how she was going to tell Jim and her children. For the first time in months she felt the heaviness that had been weighing her down fading away. She fell asleep quickly and easily. When the nurse arrived with a sleeping pill she noticed the smile on her patient's face. Since Cassie was sound asleep, the nurse decided not to awaken her.

# Chapter Five

On Monday Cassie's tests did not start until almost 10:00 a.m. The tests for surgery patients always came first and it was a very strange feeling for Cassie to lie in bed with nothing to do. She knew by tomorrow that would change and decided to enjoy her "forced vacation."

It was close to 1:00 p.m. when Cassie finished the testing and was wheeled back to her room. The nurses brought her some soup and toast since she had missed the regular lunch time. She was a little tired from the tests and fell asleep after finishing her soup.

It was not until after 4:00 p.m. when Doctor George came to her room. "Hi, Cassie," the doctor said. "How are you feeling?"

"I'm feeling really well, Doctor George." Then Cassie told him that if all was well with her medically, she had made plans to go to Seattle for the summer.

"That's wonderful Cassie. As I suspected all your tests came back normal, but you are not out of the woods yet. You'll end up right back in here if you don't keep your stress levels down. Do you want me with you when you tell Jim your decision, Cassie?"

"I plan to call Sylvia this weekend and set up all the details. I appreciate your offer of help but I think I will be fine. Knowing I'll be going away and that you will help if I need it, is all the reassurance I need," Cassie replied with such a satisfied smile even the doctor felt joy.

Shortly after the doctor left, Jim called her. After she told him the tests turned out well he presented such an "I told you so" attitude regarding her tests that Cassie found herself making up an excuse to say goodbye. Both of her children also called a little later and Kit agreed to be at the hospital at 10:00 a.m. the next day to pick Cassie up and take her home.

Cassie never said anything to her family about Seattle. She decided she would have all her arrangements in place before she sat them down and told them about her summer plans. In that way, Cassie knew they could not easily talk her out of going when she had everything set up.

Cassie went home from the hospital on Tuesday morning. For some reason Jim left her alone that day and she enjoyed a long nap before fixing dinner for the two of them. Kit called her school Tuesday morning to let them know she was taking a sick day but would return bright and early on Wednesday.

Cassie's colleagues and her students were concerned about her since she was very rarely sick. But they did sense something different about her when she returned to school. She seemed much happier and there was a new tranquility about her demeanor. Cassie assured everyone she was fine, and everything got quickly back to normal as the week sped by.

Cassie called Sylvia the following Saturday morning. From their conversation she liked Sylvia immediately and felt she was getting the better end of the deal taking care of the condo after she heard Sylvia's description of her home.

Cassie told Sylvia she would drive to Seattle the weekend after Memorial Day. Her teaching duties would be finished by noon the Wednesday after that holiday which would allow her a couple of days to finish packing and organizing for her trip out to Seattle.

Only Jane knew about Cassie's decision and it stayed that way until Mother's Day. Jim, as usual, was too preoccupied with his own feelings to sense anything had changed. Kit,

Paul, Gray and Karen arrived with presents expecting she would be making dinner for everyone. Instead she announced she planned to go out to eat.

After her family's protests, Cassie lost the calm she had been feeling the last few days and with clenched teeth said, "Today is Mother's Day and you kids bring me presents and as usual no gesture from your father. However, you and your father expect me to work making everyone dinner. I am beginning to feel my only purpose in this family is to cater to all of your needs. So, I have decided to take a break from all of you!"

Before they recovered from the shock of Cassie speaking out, she told her family of her summer plans. She sensed they did not really believe she would do it, but deep in her heart she knew it would happen.

Without saying a word, both of her children upset with Cassie stormed out the door with their spouses.

"Now, look what you've done! We were supposed to have a nice family gathering today and instead you have upset everyone. I don't know what has gotten into you lately, Cassie. You might as well get any ideas of going to Seattle or anywhere else out of your head right now. Your job is to be my wife and take care of me. Quit acting so crazy and call your children and apologize."

Furiously, Cassie replied, "Jim I'm not acting crazy! For the first time in a long time I feel like I am doing something for myself. Why don't I deserve equal feelings in this family? And who made the rule that I was suppose to cook a big dinner on Mother's Day? I am so sick of your selfishness and refusal to even be kind to me. You just want everyone to feel sorry for you and cater to you because of your medical problems. I refuse to do that anymore. I am going to Seattle this summer and when I get back after we have both had time to think about our marriage we'll see what the next step will be."

Without replying, Jim angrily turned his wheel chair back towards his den, slammed the door and turned the TV up as loud as it would go.

*Well that went well,* Cassie thought to herself. She did not know whether to laugh or cry. She could not believe how relieved she was after telling her family about her plans. She had been dreading the confrontation but now that it was over she finally felt free.

Driving to the KFC, she bought Jim dinner. When she took the food back to the house Jim was still locked in the den and she knew from past behavior he would stay there all day. She left him a note on the kitchen counter that his dinner was in the refrigerator and that she was going out. If she had any sense she would have let him fend for himself for dinner but at this point she did not want to do anything to upset things any further which could prevent her from leaving.

She took a bottle of wine from the liquor cabinet and drove over to Jane's house. They had a wonderful afternoon and evening savoring the wine and when Cassie got home the empty box of chicken was sitting on the counter.

Normally, it would have upset her that he hadn't even thrown the empty box in the garbage but the fact that it was less than a month before she would leave is what she focused on instead. Cassie found Jim in bed facing the wall. She had no idea whether he was awake or not and after her fun day with Jane she really did not care what her husband was feeling. "Happy Mother's Day to me", she said softly to herself as she slipped quietly into bed.

Jim was still asleep the next morning when Cassie left for school and she decided that was just as well. Doctor George said Jim might react with extreme anger but it still surprised Cassie when it happened. He had not even tried to convince her not to go. That probably hurt the most. Cassie felt as if he could care less whether she was there or not except in her role as a maid. Because of that, Cassie knew nothing would change her decision to leave.

# Chapter Six

Cassie could not believe how fast the rest of May seemed to fly. She was a little sad to be leaving her school after so many years teaching but she was heartened when the teachers and some of her students held small celebrations for her.

Jim did not speak to Cassie for three days after the announcement of her decision to go to Seattle alone for the summer. It was almost as if he was trying to chastise her but Cassie did not even get upset. She felt that if they started to talk about her plans they might both say something to each other they might later regret.

The nicest thing that happened to her was Gray calling the day after Mother's Day. Cassie realized his wife, Karen, had probably been a big contributing factor to the call but it had pleased her no matter how it had occurred. Gray had apologized for his actions the previous day and told her he would help her however he could. He knew he would miss her at home for the summer but he wanted her to be happy and healthy and if Seattle was the answer, then he was all for it. Cassie thanked him for calling and felt tenderness for her son that had been missing for awhile.

Since the time for leaving was getting closer, she now awoke each day worried something would happen to prevent her from going west. She could hardly contain her excitement over her impending move. Each afternoon as she walked, she made mental notes of what she needed to do before leaving. Finally, at dinner one night Jim broke his silence to reiterate how upset he was with her.

"Are you willing to go to counseling to save our marriage, Jim?"

"There's nothing wrong with our marriage. The only problem is with you leaving me when you know how much I need you."

"What about my needs, Jim? When did our marriage quit being a 50/50 proposition?"

"You didn't lose a leg, Cassie," Jim answered angrily.

"You lost your leg because of your cigarette smoking and bad eating habits, Jim. Are you willing to give up cigarettes?" Cassie yelled back.

"Cigarettes have nothing to do with my health problems, Cassie. I don't know why you keep harping on that subject. I get so sick and tired of listening to you go on and on about my smoking."

"Well, the good news is you won't have to listen to me go on about that subject for four months, Jim."

"Maybe it should just be forever," Jim said back in an angry voice.

"Don't say something you might regret later, Jim. I think it's obvious that we need a break from each other. I refuse to spend the next few years either arguing with you or getting the silent treatment like you've given me the past few days. Maybe after I come back we'll both have a better perspective."

Kit and Gray came over to the house the Sunday after Cassie's announcement to them about her summer plans. They began quarreling with their mother almost immediately about her leaving with Gray in support of his mother's journey.

"Stop this right now, the two of you! Your mom's leaving is between the two of us and has nothing to do with you two. I want you kids to stay out of our discussion in this matter."

Looking at their father in disbelief they both left quickly, continuing to argue as they walked to their cars.

The next day when Cassie came out of school for her walk, she saw Kit waiting for her. "Mom, can I talk to you while you walk," Kit asked quietly?

"Cassie simply nodded her head as her daughter fell into step beside her."

"I want you to know I'm sorry for all the mean things I said to you and not helping you when you needed it. Lately, I've watched how Dad treats you and I've seen how unreasonable he has become. It's almost like he refuses to be happy. I've also overheard you several times ask him to go to counseling. I started thinking about what you were going through last evening and I tried to put myself in your place. I now realize if it was me I would have left a long time ago. I guess I just wanted to hang on to the image of a happy family but now I know if Dad won't change, it's never going to be like it used to be."

Cassie looked at her daughter as tears ran down both cheeks. "Thank you for understanding, Kit. You'll never know how much it means to me."

Kit threw her arms around Cassie. "I love you, Mom. Karen and Gray met me and Paul for dinner yesterday and they helped me realize how important it is for you to go to Seattle. We're all sad you're leaving but we don't want you to jeopardize your welfare."

"I love you, too Kit. And I have to tell you I've hired a woman to come in for a few hours every day during the week to cook, clean and grocery shop for your dad. I know you and Gray have busy lives and I don't want to leave you with that kind of a burden. If the two of you could visit your dad on weekends, Doctor George said he will be as happy as it is possible for him to be considering everything."

"We'll both do anything we can to help him and to help you. We want you to be healthy and happy. I really hope you have a lot of fun in Seattle. You deserve the best, Mom," Kit said as her arms tightened around Cassie in a hug. "I was just so afraid of losing you, Mom. I didn't want you to go anywhere. But I realize that isn't fair to you."

Cassie returned the hug, feeling relieved and happy for the first time in days as she walked Kit back to her car.

However, her husband was a different story. It appeared Jim was deliberately ignoring Cassie, rarely talking to her over the next couple of weeks. Cassie went back for a last check up with Doctor George just before the Memorial holiday weekend. The doctor pronounced her fit and told her how glad he was she was separating from Jim for a few months.

"Jim is also my patient and I am concerned about him. But it's obvious he is not going to take my advice and I don't want your health to suffer because he is making bad choices. Go and have a fun summer. Who knows what you might find out there. I wish you happiness, Cassie."

Cassie thought that was a pretty strange statement for the doctor to make to a married woman. She had no idea how prophetic the doctor's words would become.

Kit had a barbecue at her home on the Saturday of Memorial Day weekend. Cassie was thankful she did not have the stress of putting on a family picnic in the midst of her packing. Plus, it gave Cassie and Jim a place to be so they would not be constantly trying to avoid each other in their own home.

On Monday Jane came over to Cassie's and helped her get organized with her final packing. Cassie had decided to ship several boxes of clothes to Seattle. She was probably taking more than she needed but she knew the weather would be cooler there and she would be gone nearly four months.

Also, Cassie did not want to leave anything visible inside her car. She wanted to be able to see out her rear view mirror as she was driving and did not want to worry about someone breaking in to her car.

Finally, the weekend had arrived. Cassie was now officially retired from teaching and that Saturday morning the whole family, including Jim, went out to breakfast together before she began her long drive west. Cassie had wanted to get an early start but she knew her children wanted a little time with her before she left.

Cassie had left several meals for Jim in the freezer so he would have plenty to eat before the housekeeper started coming in on the following Monday. She had a retired teacher friend, Marge Anderson, who had agreed to come in and take care of Jim, as needed, for four to five hours every week day while Cassie was away.

This had been her biggest relief knowing Jim would have someone cook and clean the house for him and Marge had quoted a very reasonable price. Cassie suspected Marge was happy to be a little busy as well as earning some extra money. Plus, her children would not be faced with the extra chore of taking care of their dad. *We might well put Jim's "vacation money" to good use*, she thought.

It was 9:30 a.m. when Cassie was finally able to start her journey. She gave everyone hugs and she could not help smiling to herself as she felt her heart soar when she finally drove away from the restaurant. She knew she was on an adventure and could not wait for it to start. She also could not help but wonder what the summer held in store for her in Seattle.

# Chapter Seven

It was three long days by car to Seattle. Cassie, driving on I-94, made it almost all the way through North Dakota the first night. When she arrived in Billings, Montana on Sunday, I-94 ended and she merged onto I-90. This interstate would end in Seattle. She drove through the mountains in Montana and Idaho, marveling at their beauty before staying overnight in Spokane, Washington.

Staying at a hotel overlooking the river in downtown Spokane, it was about 9:30 p.m. when she heard a loud noise outside. As she looked out her window she saw fireworks in the sky.

Cassie had no clue why there were fireworks but she almost felt as if the state of Washington was welcoming her. The next day she asked the waitress at breakfast if she knew why there had been a fireworks display. The waitress told Cassie it was for the high school graduation going on that evening. Cassie decided she liked her explanation better.

Cassie still had three hundred miles to Seattle from Spokane and she was full of anticipation. She had no idea that the most beautiful part of the drive was ahead of her. At first the terrain was high desert but she finally spied the Cascade Mountains and as she got closer the landscape began to change. As she began climbing vertically the lush vegetation of the extremely tall evergreen and cedar trees began appearing. The rest of the drive through the Cascades was so beautiful Cassie almost wanted to turn around and drive it again. Naturally, she did not turn back and it was about 3:00 p.m. on Monday when Cassie finally pulled into the underground parking at Sylvia's condo. Sylvia had given Cassie the entrance code and informed management that Cassie and her car would be "in residence" until October. Cassie was welcomed with a big hug by Sylvia, a petite blond woman, when she arrived at the apartment door.

Sylvia was flying to France the next morning and planned on having dinner with friends and staying overnight at a hotel near the airport, since she had an early flight. The two women liked each other immediately and Sylvia was reassured her condo would be in good hands.

When Cassie walked into the condo she saw an L-shaped area. Sylvia had a sunken living room with a fireplace and glass patio windows that opened out to a balcony that overlooked Elliot Bay and the Olympic Mountains beyond.

The dining room and kitchen faced the south and completed the L. There was another balcony off the dining room and Cassie could see Mount Rainier in the distance. The view was so incredible it took Cassie's breath away which pleased Sylvia to no end.

As they went down the hall, Sylvia showed Cassie the master bedroom that also had a view of Mount Rainier. Cassie could just picture herself propped up with pillows while sitting in bed reading and glancing up every once in awhile to look at that sight.

The master bedroom's full bath blew Cassie away. There was a separate shower and a deep tub which was also a hot tub and she sighed as she walked out of the bathroom. Sylvia heard her sigh and smiled.

In addition, on the other side of the hallway there was a smaller bedroom with a queen bed and a third room that was an office/den with a sofa hide-a-bed where Cassie could keep her computer. Between the bedroom and office was another full bathroom. The kitchen was almost as large as Cassie's in Minnesota and just beyond the kitchen was a pantry and a separate laundry room with a washer and dryer stacked on top of each other.

Cassie was astounded at how wonderful the apartment was and could not believe how lucky she was to be able to stay there. Both Sylvia and Jane had described the condo to her but there was no way to envision the difference the views made.

Cassie only had to pay utilities and her underground parking fee which was more than reasonable. Sylvia's housekeeper was scheduled once a week but Cassie told her she would be happy to keep the place up, saving Sylvia that money while she was gone. She felt it was the least she could do since she was not paying rent.

"A trip to Europe just came up this spring and I really wanted to spend a summer over there Cassie, just like you wanted to come here. But, I didn't know what to do with my plants. I have been nurturing some of these plants for many years. I worried if someone was only coming in a couple of times a week and something happened to delay them my flowers might suffer. I know it sounds silly but it really means a lot to me to know someone is taking proper care of them. Many of these plants were given to me as gifts for special occasions in my life so there is also a lot of sentiment attached to some of them."

Sylvia showed Cassie how to tend to her many plants even going so far as to give her a list with a watering and fertilizing schedule. Finally, she went over a few other things she wanted Cassie to know about her condo. It wasn't long before Sylvia said goodbye, leaving Cassie with the keys and several emergency numbers.

Checking to see what kind of food was in the refrigerator, Cassie discovered Sylvia had left a bottle of wine chilling for her along with a welcoming note. As she opened the bottle, Cassie called Kit to let her know she had arrived all right.

Gray was taking Jim to a Twins game that evening and because of the time change they had already left so Kit told her mother she would let the two of them know she had arrived safely.

Next, she called Jane. Jane had visited Sylvia the previous year and knew how beautiful her condo was. Jane understood exactly what Cassie was feeling in that wonderful home and they chatted awhile before hanging up.

Cassie took a glass of wine out to the living room balcony. She had some cheese and crackers left over from her journey to Seattle and took those out with her drink. She sat outside until after the sunset still a little in shock at how lucky she had been to be able to come live here. With a sigh, Cassie finally left the balcony when the reds, pinks and purples had faded from the distant sky.

Cassie knew she had not even unpacked but she felt such a sense of freedom being on her own with no one to answer to. She decided to soak in the tub before going to bed. Her overnight bag had everything she needed until she could get settled and unpacked the next day.

Cassie had gone through a time zone change both of the last two days and she could feel a sluggishness catching up with her. Getting organized could wait until the next morning when she would feel refreshed. For the present, the hot tub called to her.

As Cassie climbed into bed she could not stop smiling. She could not believe she was really there in Seattle, ready for any adventures that came her way. She sensed this journey had beckoned. The fact she did not know anyone in that city did not diminish the feeling of pure joy pouring over her. Cassie fell asleep quickly with the smile still on her face.

# Chapter Eight

The next morning Cassie awoke early. There was morning fog that obscured her view of the surrounding mountains. Actually, she welcomed the fog enveloping the city; without it she might have gone to sit on the balcony half the morning when she needed to tackle her boxes and get everything unpacked.

Looking at her watch, Cassie realized that Sylvia's plane had already left. She hoped Sylvia had as good a time on her journey that Cassie expected she would have in Seattle.

By 1:00 p.m. Cassie had everything organized and her computer hooked up. She felt like she had accomplished a great deal and now it was time to go exploring. Cassie had noticed a hotel about three blocks from the condo and that was her first destination.

Entering the hotel, she immediately went to the display rack that offered brochures about the city. Cassie gathered maps of the area, a ferry schedule, and some other pamphlets about tourist places that looked interesting.

Before leaving home, Cassie had researched the city on her computer. She had read all about Pike Place Market and was anxious to experience that area. As Cassie headed for the market she watched with amazement all the different people and sights around her.

There was a good view of the market area from her balcony and she wanted to stop somewhere for lunch as well as find some fresh flowers for decoration and some food for dinner. As she walked through the area, she found a small cafe down Post Alley that served seafood, salads and soups.

The restaurant had seating inside and outside with a small fence around the outside. There were four different soups to choose from the menu. Cassie knew she would have to come back until she had sampled all the soups.

From her seat at one of the outside tables, Cassie noticed other people eating while their dogs lay snoring under their tables. Animals were not allowed in outside restaurants back in Minnesota but no one seemed to pay any attention to them in Seattle.

As Cassie ate her soup, she studied the Seattle map. The north/south Interstate 5 did not run right through the downtown but was a few blocks away. The exits and entrances were on different streets and Cassie thought whoever had designed an interstate without clover leafs must have been drunk or sick. It was very complicated to get to the interstate and was compounded by all the one way streets downtown.

It seemed to be a very confusing system. Cassie knew it would be a little bit of a challenge finding her way around but was looking forward to the exploration. She also needed to find a large grocery store to go to on occasion to load up her supplies since there weren't any stores right downtown.

The map was very easy to read and she noted that there were two malls downtown and yet she had walked right by one and did not realize it was there. She supposed many restaurants and stores were inside larger buildings so people would not have to walk outside too much when the winter's rainy season hit.

Cassie knew she would be busy for many days just getting her bearings. It would definitely be easier to walk than take her car and she also discovered there was a free bus zone in the downtown area so if she got tired or had too many things to carry she could just hop on a bus to get home.

The next few days Cassie spent exploring all over the downtown area but she did take her car to find a grocery store. She found a chain grocery store about two miles away in the Queen Anne district. It was a little too far to walk, especially when it came to getting the groceries home.

The store was out of the free bus zone so it would definitely be easier to drive her car there. She also discovered the area around the grocery store had many unique businesses and restaurants with people strolling around and decided she should spend time exploring the Queen Anne area after she learned about downtown.

Cassie could not believe the fun she was having just watching the people, visiting the different stores and sitting on her balcony gazing at the distant mountains. Watching the water with the various boats, including the ferries, as well as the sunsets over the mountains never ceased to amaze her. Some days Cassie wished she could just stay there forever but she was grateful for even the few months that had been allotted to her.

One weekend, Cassie went to an annual festival on Ballard Street which was about five miles from her condo. She had read about it in the paper and thought it sounded interesting. Was she ever in for a surprise. She had not realized how quirky Seattle could be until she arrived at the festival.

Getting out of her car she saw about fifty men on bikes ride past. To her amazement they were naked. Cassie could not believe what she was seeing. She started laughing after the bike parade went by. Maybe these men were expressing themselves but she thought that had to be a pretty painful way of doing it.

As she walked to the main square in the center of town, she saw a thirty foot statue of the Russian, Lenin, supposedly a friend to the working man. She had read about the statue but was shocked when she saw it. In the middle of the night some pranksters had dressed Lenin in drag with lots of rouge, eyelashes and an outlandish outfit made from balloons. She took a picture of the statue to prove what she had seen.

As she photographed the statue, a couple passing her asked if she was new to the area. When Cassie nodded they directed her to a street under the highway bridge about four blocks away. When she arrived there she found a giant cement troll squashing an old VW.

Seattle was home to a troll under the bridge. Cassie took more pictures of both Lenin and the troll. She knew no one back home would believe her otherwise. Sadly, she realized Jim would not care and would probably make some remark about not wasting his time going to see something so stupid.

Before her trip out west, Cassie had bought a cell phone at her family's insistence since she was traveling alone. Her plan included free minutes on weekends so Cassie could call her family every weekend to let them know how she was doing and catch up on their news.

Cassie called Jim and her children that Sunday as soon as she got back to the condo. They had just returned from taking Jim to dinner and both of her children told her things were going well. However, when she talked to Jim he kept making little digs about Cassie not being there to help him with his problems. Cassie just sighed and was so relieved she was not at home where she would have to listen to Jim's negativism every day. She decided not to mention anything she had seen at the festival that afternoon, knowing he would not care, anyway.

The less she told Jim of her adventures, the better off she would be. He could easily manipulate her into feeling guilty whenever she was having fun and she did not want Jim to spoil her day. She knew he would be upset with her for being so happy when he was so miserable.

Cassie did not want him angry at her for enjoying herself. That would definitely put a damper on her happiness and she realized how free she felt being away from him.

Eventually, she and Jim would have to come to terms with their differences or their marriage would be over. It pained Cassie to think about not growing old with Jim, after spending so many years together, but for the present she just wanted to enjoy her time in Seattle and not have to think about her husband and their troubles.

Cassie did not talk long to Jim. He did not seem interested in anything she had to say about Seattle and it seemed like they had less and less to say to each other ever since she got sick.

One Sunday morning Cassie found Sacred Heart Church which was closer to her condo than the one she had been going to since she first arrived. She had no idea how this new place of worship would change her life. The church was only a few blocks away from the condo next to the Seattle Center and Space Needle Park.

Cassie arrived about five minutes before Mass began. A couple of minutes later a man walked in and sat in the pew in front of Cassie. She noticed he had khaki pants, a white shirt, and navy blue V-neck sweater on. He was a little less than six feet tall and had a mix of platinum and white hair.

When the service began everyone turned and welcomed each other and Cassie noticed his handshake was firm as they smiled and greeted one another. He looked like a slimmer version of Phil Donahue and she also noticed he had the bluest eyes she had ever seen.

After church Cassie stopped and had breakfast at a nearby restaurant. The same man from church was eating alone a few tables away from her. As she ate her food, Cassie spent the time going over her maps and brochures since she was planning her first overnight trip the next morning.

The next day Cassie was up early. She took the ferry to Bainbridge Island and from there drove over to the Olympic Peninsula. Her first stop would be the rain forest at the end of the peninsula to the west. After that she would turn south following the Pacific coast. She wanted to drive the entire coast of Washington.

When she arrived at the rain forest there was an entrance fee to get into the park. After paying the money she drove down a narrow road. Cassie loved the rain forest. However, there was not a cloud in the sky and she wondered what it looked like when it was raining. Little did Cassie know she would soon be visiting another rain forest area and would have an intense dislike for the constant drizzle. But today was beautiful. The sun was shining and the tall cedar and Douglas fir trees towered a couple of hundred feet above her making a canopy of trees overhead.

On her way out of the park, Cassie noticed cars parked along the side of the road. As she pulled over, she looked to the left across the road and saw a whole herd of elk in a meadow. Marveling at being so close to wildlife, she realized they were almost close enough to pet.

Cassie found a cute little motel on the Pacific Ocean and had dinner at a small seafood restaurant adjacent to her lodging. The ling cod she ordered for dinner tasted very fresh and she realized, given her location, it probably had been caught that day.

When she got back to her room she turned on the gas fireplace and bundled under the covers with her window opened a little. Listening to the surf crashing on the shore lulled Cassie to sleep almost as soon as she lay down.

The next morning she awoke as the sun was rising. The only trouble with falling asleep before dark the night before was awakening so early. After a long walk on the beach, she ate the continental breakfast the hotel provided in the lobby and then drove back on the highway she had come from the previous day.

Cassie's next destination was Neah Bay and Cape Flattery. This area was at the western end of the peninsula just before the road had turned south to follow the coast. The morning went quickly and Cassie was soon diverting off the main highway. Neah Bay was a small Native American fishing village.

Two miles after leaving town, the street became a dirt road. She knew she still had five more miles to go on the road that was rapidly rising up. She wasn't sure if she should be on this dirt track in her car but she wanted to drive until the road ran out.

Cassie finally made it to the end of the road and the turn around. There was another car there with a couple from the Seattle area. Off in the distance, Cassie could see Tatoosh Island. She knew she had reached her destination. She was in the most northernest spot in the contiguous United States where the waters of the Pacific Ocean met the Strait of Juan de Fuca.

Cassie had such a sense of accomplishment finding this area on her own. She asked the couple if they would take her picture with the island in the background. After making her way back down the dirt path filled with potholes, Cassie stopped for a bowl of fresh clam chowder that had just been prepared in a little restaurant owned by a Native American woman.

It was a little chilly being by the water and the hot soup hit the spot. However, Cassie had discovered a seafood restaurant on the waterfront in Seattle that made the best clam chowder soup she had ever tasted. She knew every time in the future she had clam chowder she would always compare that soup to any others she tried. Although this soup was good it was not as thick and could not measure up to her favorite.

Cassie's first month in Seattle developed a rhythm. She went to Mount St. Helens, Mount Rainier, and Whidbey Island. She even went overnight for two nights and followed the Cascade Loop staying at Lake Chelan and the cute little Bavarian town of Leavenworth nestled in the mountains. When she was in Seattle she walked all over the city and people watched.

Cassie kept a journal of her adventures so she would be able to remember everything when she went back to Minnesota. And, of course, every Sunday she went to Mass and the man she had seen her first time at Sacred Heart was also there each week. They always smiled at each other, now in greeting and since he was always alone Cassie wondered if he had friends or relatives in the area.

One Sunday Cassie drove to church so she could go to the grocery store afterwards. There was a big festival going on at the Seattle Center next to the church. As Cassie walked out of the building she did not realize the man was a few steps behind her. "Oh, no!" Cassie exclaimed as she stopped abruptly. She stopped so fast that the man crashed right into her.

"What's the matter?" He seemed annoyed as he bumped into her.

"Look at my car," Cassie cried.

As the man looked in the direction Cassie was pointing he noticed her front window on the passenger side had been broken as if a large rock had been thrown into it.

"I usually walk to church but today I drove so I could go to the grocery store." As Cassie turned towards him he noticed tears in her eyes.

"Let's go check the damage. Oh, by the way my name is Ryan."

"Mine is Cassie."

They walked over to the car and looked a little closer at the window. "I'm afraid some trouble makers from the festival did this Cassie. We could call the police but there's not much they'll be able to do. Usually, the cost of the window is less than your deductible. I think you'll need to chalk this up to a bad experience and simply get it fixed.

I know a glass place close by that won't rip you off. Do you live near here?"

Cassie nodded.

"Tell me your address and I'll meet you tomorrow morning. I'll call the repair shop and make an appointment and we can take it in and have breakfast while we are waiting to have it fixed. I've noticed you often eat breakfast where I do."

"I really appreciate the help, Ryan, but I don't want to inconvenience you."

"It's no problem, Cassie. My schedule is pretty flexible. I'd be happy to help."

The next morning Ryan was waiting outside the condo as Cassie drove out of her garage. They dropped the car off at the glass business and then rode in Ryan's car to the same restaurant they had eaten alone at on Sundays after church.

"I always noticed you eating in here, too, Ryan. But I didn't want to disturb you since I didn't know you."

"Well, Cassie, you were always so busy reading maps and brochures and I wondered what you were doing. I almost asked you one day."

Cassie laughed and told Ryan she was spending the summer in Seattle and being new to the area would go either on a day trip or overnight every week on some adventure. Usually, Sunday was spent organizing for her weekly jaunts.

As they ate, Ryan told Cassie about himself. He and his wife had owned several radio stations but had sold all of them but one. They did not really need the income but they had kept one station because Ryan wanted a purpose and liked the challenges of running a radio station. At the same time he was not totally tied down. He could be as busy as he wanted to be.

Cassie was intrigued with the fact that he had a wife since she had never seen them together at church. When she tactfully asked Ryan about her, he said his wife was partially paralyzed and never went outside their home.

After Ryan had confided about his wife's condition, he asked Cassie about her life. For some reason, she felt comfortable with Ryan and trusted him. She did not know why she felt that way. Maybe it was seeing him in church each week. Every time he had turned and shook her hand in greeting, she saw an extremely sad expression in his eyes.

Cassie found herself telling Ryan about her life in Minnesota, her husband and children and how she had ended up in Seattle. Ryan seemed surprised by her story.

"We appear to have a lot in common, Cassie."

All too soon they finished eating and Cassie knew her car would be ready. For some reason, she felt she could sit and talk to Ryan all day and she felt sad to be leaving him. As Ryan dropped Cassie off at the glass shop, she thanked him for all his help and told him she would see him the following Sunday in church.

Before Cassie knew it, Sunday had arrived. This time as she waited for the service to start, Ryan came in and sat next to her. When the service was over Ryan asked her if she would like to join him for breakfast. Cassie had mixed feelings. She knew she was married but she enjoyed talking to Ryan. Besides, it seemed silly that they should go to the same restaurant and sit at separate tables now that they knew each other. She decided to say "yes".

As Ryan began to tell Cassie even more about his life, she felt as if she was making her first real friend in Seattle. Later that Sunday afternoon when Cassie made her weekly calls to her family she told them about her broken car window and that she had needed to get it replaced. But, although she had nothing to hide, she did not mention Ryan to any of them.

Cassie's second month in Seattle went by as quickly as the first. But now, she and Ryan not only went to breakfast on Sundays but also met for breakfast on Tuesdays and dinner on Friday nights. Cassie continued to take her side trips, usually on Wednesdays and Thursdays.

Ryan was squiring Cassie all over downtown to restaurants she probably never would have gone to on her own. They never seemed to run out of conversation. He told Cassie about the many things that happened at the radio station that week and she began to feel she was getting to know his staff even though she had never visited the station. And then Cassie would tell Ryan about her travels that week.

Gradually, Ryan began to talk more about his wife, Joyce. After they had been married for fifteen years, Ryan and Joyce had a big argument one night. Ryan wanted to have children and he felt if it did not happen soon it would never happen. Joyce was still resisting. She said she was having too much fun to have children.

Joyce was an only child whose mother had died when she was five. Her father owned two profitable radio stations when Ryan married her. A year after their marriage Joyce's father was killed in a small plane crash. Joyce was devastated and began to party and especially to drink more than she should have. Ryan took over the day-to-day operations of the stations and had done so well that he had bought three more stations. Joyce continued to drink and play. Many times she would get angry with Ryan saying he wasn't fun any more. She felt all he wanted to do was work.

One night two years after her father's death, Ryan had again begged Joyce to get help for her drinking and consider having children. Joyce had laughed at him as she dressed and gone out without him. She was meeting an old classmate named Gene. The two of them both had drinking problems and often partied together. At midnight Ryan received the call. Joyce was in the hospital in surgery and Gene, who had been driving drunk, had been killed instantly when they hit a tree head-on. After subsequent surgeries, Joyce's doctors realized they could do no more for her.

At the time of the accident, Joyce was thirty-eight and Ryan was forty years old. Joyce was now paralyzed for life and any chance for children was lost forever. Ryan became resigned to the state of his marriage but Joyce never had. She became very bitter as the years went by.

Ryan, feeling responsible for his wife's well being since she had no one else, stayed with her. He buried himself in his work and had his close circle of friends for emotional support. He knew Joyce was not grateful for his sacrifice but there was no one else he wanted to be with. He had a boat he spent summers on and the radio station work kept him fulfilled.

As he told Cassie about his life, Ryan was surprised to realize it had been fifteen years since the accident. He found it hard to believe time had passed by so quickly. In his own way he found peace in his life.

# Chapter Nine

One Tuesday morning in late July, Cassie and Ryan were at their favorite restaurant having breakfast together.

"Where are you going this week on your journey, Cassie?"

"I'm not going overnight, Ryan. Even though I enjoy exploring, day trips are also nice because I miss Seattle when I go overnight. I like sitting on my balcony watching the boats and the distant mountains, especially at sunset, when I'm here. Thursday, though, I thought I would take a ride over to those mountains," as she pointed towards the west.

Ryan knew she was referring to the Olympic Mountains over on the Olympic peninsula. It was the same area she had driven by to get to the rain forest on her first overnight adventure.

"So where are you planning to visit?"

"I was thinking of going back over to Crescent Lake and then just past the lake to Marymere Falls. The last time I drove over there I stopped briefly at the park but the sign said the falls were a one and a half mile walk and since I was headed to the coast I didn't have time to do the trail then."

"You know that sounds like fun and I could use a break. Would you mind if I came along with you?"

"Not at all, Ryan. It would be fun to have your company."

Before they knew it, Thursday morning had arrived and Cassie picked Ryan up in front of his condo. Cassie was happy to see Ryan waiting for her. She was not sure if he would be ready on time and she wanted to catch the 8:30

a.m. ferry over to Bainbridge Island. When they arrived at the ferry docking area down by the waterfront there were only two lines of cars waiting for the boat. Cassie knew they would not have a long wait.

One of the things Cassie had learned early on her explorations was not to try and catch a ferry during commute times or weekends. The wait was so long during those hours that it was not worth trying to get on. But it was early morning and they were going the opposite direction of the commute. So not only would the lines be short, but the ferries were running more often due to the commuters trying to get to work from the island.

After the ferry ride, they continued across Bainbridge Island until they reached the Hood Canal Bridge. This bridge was the longest floating bridge in the state of Washington and would take them over to the Olympic peninsula. Cassie loved looking out over the water as they crossed the bridge. The evergreen trees on the hills always looked such a vibrant green when reflected against the blue of the water. However, today the fog had settled in and they could hardly see anything in front of them as she drove very slowly across the two lane bridge while watching for oncoming traffic.

They finally reached Highway 101 and gradually the heat of the day caused the fog to dissipate. When they reached Port Angeles they decided to take a quick break. It was only a few more miles to the lake but once they left Port Angeles civilization would practically disappear. As they came out of a fast-food restaurant, Cassie gasped and Ryan immediately turned towards her.

"What's wrong, Cassie?"

"Oh Ryan, the sun is shining. And look at those mountains in the distance. It's almost too beautiful for words. And in a short while we'll be right in the middle of that area."

"Cassie, I've never known anyone to take so much pleasure out of a simple scene of nature."

"Ryan, how can anyone not marvel at this scenery?"

"I guess a lot of us just take it for granted."

"I loved looking at all the lakes in Minnesota but the scenery here is so much more spectacular. It's hard to believe you take it for granted."

Ryan just smiled at her. There was something about the joy she had over simple things that touched his heart. He had forgotten how good it felt just being with someone enjoying the beauty around them.

"Cassie, I'm so glad I came with you today. I really needed a day off like this just to slow down a little."

Cassie smiled at him. "Ryan you can come with me on my trips any time you want." She felt so lucky to have found a friend like him. Cassie knew Jim would have hated this adventure.

After driving about a half-hour, they spotted the lake. They stopped at one of the pull-outs so Cassie could take pictures.

"Oh Ryan, I just don't know how this lake can be so beautiful."

"Cassie, do you want a scientific explanation?"

"Science was never my strong suit so explain away."

"Well, Crescent Lake is a glacial lake. Notice the steep rocks around the lake?"

"Yes."

"Imagine a glacier as an immense tongue of ice coming through this area. As it receded from this area it left this lake which is about six hundred feet deep."

"You make it sound so simple. But why are glacial lakes such a beautiful blue-green color Ryan? I noticed that color in the water up by Mount Rainier and the Cascade Loop."

"That's also pretty simple, Cassie. As glaciers recede they wear down the mountains and the grinding of rock against rock produces what is called rock flour which becomes suspended in the water. The reflection of light off the particles produces those colors."

"Thank you, Ryan. I'm glad you told me about glaciers."

"Well, I certainly didn't mean to lecture to you, Cassie," Ryan said, looking a little embarrassed.

"Ryan, I don't know whether I'll ever come back to Seattle after this summer but something draws me to this part of our country. It's almost as if I can't learn enough about the Pacific Northwest. I love the ferries and the mountains and the water. Next, I want to start exploring the islands in the San Juan chain."

Even though they were only friends, Ryan felt a sadness penetrate his heart at the idea of Cassie's leaving Seattle. He had not been interested in women in such a long time that he had a hard time understanding why he felt that way. As they were getting ready to leave, another couple in a car arrived at the pull-out.

"Let's ask them to take our picture by the lake, Cassie. Then you'll have a memory of today when you go home."

Cassie agreed immediately. Only afterwards did she wonder what Jim would think if he saw a picture of her with Ryan standing by the lake.

They sat on a log at the end of the parking area with the lake as their backdrop. Ryan casually put his arm around Cassie as the photo was being taken. Cassie felt a shiver at Ryan's touch and was extremely surprised by her reaction.

After having their picture taken they continued traveling the shore line of the lake for a few more miles. Before they knew it, they were at their destination, Marymere Falls.

Driving into the parking lot they saw two other cars in the lot. Cassie knew there were several trails in this area but seeing the sign for the Marymere Falls trail she pointed the direction out to Ryan. The trail was one and a half miles and some of it was uphill. Before they started out Ryan glanced across the street of the parking lot.

"Look Cassie. There are two sticks. Let's go get them. They will be handy when we start climbing."

Crossing the street, Cassie and Ryan picked up two sticks that had been carved from large thick branches that someone had apparently just tossed on the ground.

"I can't believe someone just left these here. They are perfect. Even though they are homemade, people would pay good money to have walking sticks like these."

"They are perfect, Cassie. I guess we were meant to take this hike today."

As they walked towards the trees, Cassie was once again in awe of the scenery. A large field of green grass dotted with hundreds of daisies stretched before them and beyond the field was water and mountains of evergreen trees beyond the lake. As they continued on the trail, they passed a small log cabin which served as an information center.

"Ryan, let's see if someone will take our picture in that field of daisies. I wonder if the picture will do it justice. It's almost too beautiful for words."

A hiker who was on his way to his car took their picture and then they continued on their way to Marymere Falls. At first the area was flat and opened so that sunlight surrounded them. But before they knew it, they were in the middle of a forest.

A narrow path was marked so they knew they were on the right trail. Cassie marveled at the Western Red Cedars, that were well over one hundred feet tall, surrounding them. Crossing a little bridge that was made out of a large log over a stream, the path began to rise.

"Shall we take the longer path that goes to the base of the falls or the shorter, steeper one that will take us past the half way point of the trail?"

"Definitely, the steeper one, Ryan."

The narrow path continued its steep ascent and Cassie realized she would never have made it without her walking stick. A couple of times her knee almost touched the ground and she wondered why she had told Ryan she wanted to take that path. About the time she was ready to give up they rounded some bushes and the falls were in front of them.

The falls were not very wide, but they were steep, as Cassie could attest to from the walk up. The two of them stood a little over half way up the gorge and as Cassie looked down, the sun hit the water at just the right angle so she could see a rainbow across the water.

"Oh, Ryan, that rainbow was definitely worth the walk up here."

Ryan just smiled and shook his head.

The way down was easier, although the walking sticks definitely made the difference, preventing them from going too fast and stumbling. They stopped at the bottom of the falls to take more pictures before continuing on. On the walk back they stopped on the little bridge and listened to the stream underneath and the quiet of the forest that encircled them before continuing back to the parking lot.

As they reached the car Cassie asked, "Ryan, why don't we leave these sticks here like the other people did? I couldn't have made it up that hill without them and maybe someone else will appreciate having them."

Ryan nodded in agreement as he placed the two walking sticks by the curb for someone else to use. Saying very little to each other, they once again retraced their drive along the shore line of Crescent Lake and back to Highway 101 towards Seattle.

"Cassie, the ferry runs every hour during commute time so we won't have to wait long. A friend works for me and lives on Bainbridge Island. He took me to a great restaurant on the water overlooking the Seattle skyline. With such a clear day the mountain will be out today. Shall we have dinner there?"

"That sounds great, Ryan."

As they reached the restaurant, Cassie saw Ryan was right about the mountain, as locals referred to it. There was Mount

Rainier looming up across the water and Cassie realized the awesome sight was an appropriate end to a wonderful day.

# Chapter Ten

August arrived and Ryan was ready for a longer break from work. He asked Cassie if she wanted to take a trip with him to Vancouver Island. Neither of them had any realization what was about to take place, but it was time for Cassie and Ryan to begin the next phase of their journey together.

Cassie had not yet visited Vancouver Island in British Columbia, including Victoria, and Ryan was eager to show her that beautiful island.

Since the two of them had established their boundaries as friends and planned to get separate rooms wherever they went, they both felt it would be fun to have each other as traveling companions. Neither of them realized how naïve this assumption was on their parts.

Cassie was waiting down in the lobby with her luggage when Ryan arrived at 8:00 a.m. on the following Tuesday. From Seattle they took the ferry over to Bainbridge Island as they had done on their journey to Marymere Falls. They continued from the island to the town of Port Angeles on the Olympic Peninsula. At 12:30 p.m. they embarked on a ninety-minute ferry ride that would take them to Victoria in Canada.

After going through customs, they drove to a hotel on the waterfront by the inner harbor. They walked to the ivy-covered Empress Hotel, which covered a whole block downtown, for afternoon tea.

After tea they walked to Thunderbird Park, a block away from the Empress. Cassie was fascinated by all the totem poles carved by the ancient Indian cultures that had inhabited the area long before white men had arrived on the island.

Ryan and Cassie decided to act like real tourists as long as they were there. They hopped on a double-decker bus to get a feel for the city that was decorated with hanging flower baskets and gardens everywhere. The bus trip ended back downtown at the stone-walled-inner harbor and they watched all the pleasure boats bobbing in the water as they walked along the sidewalk that was at the water's edge.

Lots of people strolled along the waterfront and everyone stopped from time to time to watch the "street people" who were putting on magic shows and other displays.

Because they were not very hungry after their high tea, they ended up at a restaurant down on the waterfront ordering a seafood salad for dinner. Then they climbed into a horse-drawn carriage for the ride back to their hotel.

Their horse and carriage clip-clopped along the inner harbor just as the sun began to set. As it darkened, Christmas-like strings of more than three thousand lights outlined the Parliament building and together with the lights on the Empress Hotel a glow was cast on the water. It was the ideal end to a perfect day.

Cassie sighed as she and Ryan rode along the waterfront in the carriage. She felt as if they were in another world that afternoon. As they climbed down from the carriage, Cassie gave Ryan a hug and thanked him for such a magically wonderful day. As she turned to go into the hotel, Cassie did not notice the longing in Ryan's eyes as she walked in front of him.

Ryan was very surprised by his feelings and was glad Cassie did not know what he was thinking. It had been a long time since he had a woman wrap her arms around him but it had never bothered him until now.

Being with Cassie on these excursions brought a feeling of joy that made him ache deep down inside. He had not felt that way in many years and was very surprised how he was feeling when he was around her.

It seemed his heart knew something his conscious mind had not yet realized. He felt faint stirrings when they had spent their day hiking at the falls but he had convinced himself he had imagined feeling anything towards Cassie except friendship.

Ryan knew that Cassie's friendship was all he could hope for but it did not diminish the strong feelings towards her that were beginning to grow deep inside of him. Ryan was afraid Cassie would be horrified to know what he was thinking so he decided to try to get past the feelings and just have a good time being with her. The problem was she was making him feel again, which was something he had avoided for a long time.

The next morning they were up early. They followed the Canadian Highway Number One up the east coast of Vancouver Island. They stopped briefly in Duncan to take pictures of the totem poles downtown by the railroad station for which that city was famous. Colorful flowers were planted all around the station, and it was a dazzling sight.

The next stop was Chemainus. This town was called the city of murals with over thirty murals painted on the buildings depicting the city's early lumbering history. After driving by the many murals and strolling through Old Town, they drove on to the town of Parksville.

Even though one could easily see from their vantage point on the island east over the water to the mountains of Canada's mainland, all the signs referred to the water as the sea. The water was called the Strait of Georgia and it seemed strange to Cassie to be standing on one side while looking at the shoreline of the other side and still refer to the water in between as a sea.

At Parksville they turned west on Highway Four towards the Pacific Ocean. They planned to stop in the little fishing village of Ucluelet for lunch before driving north along the

Pacific Ocean through the Pacific Rim National Park to their night's lodging.

Tofino was their destination that day and the town was also where the road going anywhere north on the western side of Vancouver Island ended. However, before they reached the Pacific Coast they drove ninety miles of mostly two-lane roads over mountains, around lakes and through a rain forest. Cassie saw two eagles in the trees but although there were road signs warning of bears and other wildlife, they saw no other animals.

About half-way to their destination Cassie and Ryan ran into rain. They had to slow down in the downpour but the many small waterfalls coming down the rocks of the mountain next to their car were an incredible sight. After driving straight through the village of Ucluelet, since the weather was so dreary and misty, they skipped lunch there and continued to Tofino.

Tofino was a touristy town. The city proper had been built on a bay to protect the inhabitants from the constant onslaught of wind and waves from the ocean. From the downtown many small islands dotted the landscape filled with Douglas fur and Western Red cedar. Signs everywhere advertised whale watching trips as well as bear and other wildlife boat rides. Cassie and Ryan soon discovered all the hotels on the Pacific Ocean side of town cost two to three hundred dollars a night.

Cassie could not believe the prices for such a remote area; especially considering it was during the week. She had read that many people came here in the winter to watch the storms come in but for some reason Tofino did not do much for her.

They decided to stay in a small motel with views overlooking the bay side of the town for one hundred twenty five each a night. The price seemed a little high for such a small plain room. But then Cassie thought maybe she would like the place better if it would stop raining. However, that was something that was not going to happen during their visit.

They ate lunch at a small seafood place downtown by the waterfront. Because it was chilly, they could not eat outside at the tables on the deck. Instead, as they were eating, they watched out the large picture window from inside the restaurant as the boats and seaplanes came into the dock in front of them through the misty fog that began to encircle the town.

The food was good. They both had shrimp Caesar salad wraps but their sandwiches were over ten dollars each and Cassie thought the price was a bit inflated considering they were in a seaside town where seafood was plentiful. And then, when the waiter converted their bill to American dollars, Cassie knew he had not deducted enough.

Ryan tried to joke with her and told Cassie he would buy lunch, but that was not the point. She knew he could afford it and she also knew that when you traveled things cost more than they did at home. She was more than willing to pay her fair share. It was simply the feeling this town was trying to gouge the visiting tourists that upset her more than the money.

Ryan knew Cassie did not like Tofino, and was trying to make the best of a bad situation. She did not want him to know that as wonderful as yesterday had been, she now felt the exact opposite. It seemed like the drizzle in this little village never stopped but she was wrong for sometimes the drizzle turned to sheets of pouring rain.

Cassie thought it would be fun to go whale watching but Ryan said it would be a pretty rough trip with the blowing winds and bad weather. Considering the present weather conditions Ryan figured any whale watching excursions had probably been cancelled for the day, anyway. Ryan told Cassie they could look for whales another time, perhaps on a trip through some of the San Juan Islands. There were several pods of Orcas that lived in that area year round.

After lunch they drove to the ocean side of the town but the waves were crashing onto the beach since the wind was blowing so hard and it was raining much too hard to get out of the car for any period of time. Besides, the sea fog was rolling in and there wasn't much to see. A walk on the beach was definitely out of the question.

Ryan was relieved not to go whale watching. It would have been miserable on that boat if they had gone out and they would never have spotted any whales with so much fog swirling around. He was also glad they were staying on the protected bay side of the town. Even if they had ocean front rooms the water was not visible and he worried the howling winds might have kept them awake most of the night.

They gave up on the idea of walking the beach and went back to their motel. They had taken adjoining rooms on the second floor which shared a balcony. There were white plastic chairs outside their doors with a roof overhang protecting them from the constant rain. Since they had brought heavy jackets and hats they sat in their chairs and read the rest of the afternoon while watching the boats circle around the different islands in the mist of the bay.

Since there was no fireplace or hot tub, Cassie finally got so chilled she told Ryan she wanted to take a hot bath and retire for the night. "You don't want to go to dinner with me?" Ryan asked.

"No, I'm not very hungry, Ryan. Do you mind too much if I just go soak in my bathtub and go to bed early? I really wouldn't mind leaving Tofino early tomorrow if you agree since the weather is still supposed to be rainy and foggy." Ryan nodded in agreement and Cassie went into her room.

For dinner Ryan went downtown for a fish sandwich but it did not taste very good. He was concerned Cassie's depression was rubbing off on him. He knew she had tried hard to feel upbeat all day but the incessant rain was even getting on his nerves.

Ryan called after dinner to check on accommodations for the next evening and then he also went to bed early. He had a hard time sleeping and kept waking up from the sound of the rain pounding on the roof all night. Cassie, on the other hand, went to sleep immediately. For some reason she felt relaxed knowing they would be leaving that area soon.

The next morning they were both awake early. Given the continued gloominess and a steady misting, Cassie was anxious to go and Ryan felt the same way. They fixed coffee in their rooms and were on their way by 8:00 a.m.

Port Alberni was a town about half way between Tofino and Parksville. Cassie and Ryan decided that would be a good place to stop for breakfast and they could also look around the shops there. It took them an hour and a half to drive the forty-five miles to Port Alberni back through the rain forest they had entered the previous day.

The fog was extremely heavy on their journey. If they had not seen the mountains and lakes the day before, they would not have imagined they were even there. Just before they arrived at their destination the weather began to clear and the day began to brighten.

Originally, Ryan had talked about spending two nights in Tofino because he knew how much Cassie liked the ocean. But, for the first time in her life Cassie was happy to be leaving a body of water and her spirits rose as she saw the sun breaking through the fog.

After Port Alberni, they still had almost fifty miles of two lane roads. They traveled through a redwood grove as shafts of the sun filtered down through the tall trees. As they drove further away from the coast, the sun began to shine even more brilliantly.

Cassie kept glancing back at the coast at the clouds still hanging over the mountains they had just come from. She knew it had been the right decision leaving that coastal rain forest area.

# Chapter Eleven

Cassie was wondering where Ryan would take her next. He told her he had found a perfect B&B that they could stay at for a couple of days and make it their home base. From there they could make day trips to a variety of places since they were in a central location but still have time to walk the beach in the morning or late afternoon.

There was a summer festival going on but the B&B had a cancellation at the last minute and was able to take them a day earlier than planned. They soon arrived in a little village by the sea called Lantzville. Ryan had not stayed in this area before but he had friends who had raved about the place.

As they drove through the little downtown, Cassie spied a pub. "That might be an interesting place to have dinner, Ryan. Look, they are advertising a halibut sandwich with caesar salad as their special. That sounds good to me."

"It looks like a fun place, doesn't it? And the fish sandwich for dinner does sound like it would hit the spot," Ryan answered as he looked at the large banner hanging from the second floor advertising the special.

As they drove out of the little town, Cassie was able to look at the water on her right. According to her map, it was the Georgia Strait, part of Nanaimo Bay.

The water was a deep blue and Cassie watched the fishing boats trolling over the whitecaps created by the blowing wind. There were several rocky islands with evergreen trees and Cassie could almost hear the sea lions that she was sure lived on those outcrops.

The coastal mountains from both the island and the Canadian mainland could be seen in the distance. It was almost too beautiful to look at and Cassie let out a deep sigh as they continued along. This was how she had hoped Tofino would look. Ryan hearing her, smiled in satisfaction that they had decided to leave the coast that morning.

As they drove along the highway, Ryan slowed and Cassie saw a small sign on the side of the road that said Graycliff Cottage Bed and Breakfast. Under those words was another smaller sign that said "no vacancy."

There were so many trees and bushes that the house could not be seen from the road. They made a right turn into the property and drove about a half a block down a winding blacktopped road. As the trees thinned, Cassie saw a tall Western red cedar tree on the left and in front of her a home with hanging pots of flowers with an overgrown garden on both sides of the house.

This was definitely Cassie's definition of a charming little cottage and looking at the house she knew the name was very appropriate for the property since it was built on a bluff and was painted gray. There was a separate garage and the property was surrounded by various types of evergreens at least eighty feet tall.

Cassie and Ryan parked by the back door. They could see the water on the front side of the house and the same tree-lined rocky islands that Cassie had spotted from the little village. The clouds partially obscured the mountains in the distance and she felt a serenity that was hard to describe.

Cassie and Ryan went up to introduce themselves to Nina, the owner. They asked her if it was too early to check into their rooms since it was only 1:00 p.m.

"There must be some mistake," Nina said to them. "I thought since there were only two of you that just one room was needed."

Cassie and Ryan looked at each other. Ryan spoke first. "I talked to your husband on the phone and he said there was a cancellation and there were two rooms available for us."

"I'm truly sorry," Nina said, "but my husband gave me the wrong message. I rented the other room yesterday. There is only one room available for the two of you. I call it my Ocean Suite. I had some other travelers stop by this morning looking for a room and I called all around but with the festival going on I know for a fact that there isn't a single room to be found for many miles around."

Cassie could not believe it. How could a trip that had started off so wonderful deteriorate so quickly? This place was like a refuge, a little bit of heaven and she hated to leave it. As she looked at Ryan she could tell he was thinking the same thing.

"Here, let me show you the room," Nina continued. "You have a separate door with a little porch on the side of the house. There are some chairs and a table on the porch if you want to sit outside and have some privacy. There's a four-poster king-sized bed which should give you plenty of room."

Nina walked them around the right side of the house and up a little porch that had two chairs and a table on it. The view was incredible and Cassie did not want to leave. As they walked in the door, they saw a loveseat and overstuffed chair along with the four-poster bed. There was also an armoire with a little TV inside and a small refrigerator.

The bathroom pushed Cassie over the edge. It held a large bathtub that two people could easily get into. She could feel herself soaking away in that deep tub after a day of walking the sandy beaches in the area.

The room was decorated in dark pink, maroon, and green and Cassie could tell that she would sink right down as she climbed into the bed with the lacey patterned beige down comforter. There was even a small coffee pot to make coffee or water for hot chocolate or tea. Cassie knew there was no way she and Ryan could stay together in that room and felt an incredible sadness that they would have to leave the place.

As Cassie looked out the picture window she saw a seal jump out of the water. She heard Nina tell Ryan they would have to go back to Victoria if they hoped to find two rooms anywhere. As much as she had enjoyed Victoria, Cassie knew they would not be able to explore this area if they went all the way back to Victoria. And this was the type of setting she had been looking forward to with long walks along the beach.

Nina insisted on showing them the front of her property. There was a large hot tub on the front lawn, "perfect for relaxing with a glass of wine in the evening," she told them.

There was also a Canadian flag on the flagpole and just a mere two hundred and twelve steps down to the water and beach. Since the tide was in there was not much beach at that time of day but Nina assured them that when the tide was out they would find sand dollars and all sorts of things while they were walking.

Ryan asked Nina if the two of them could go back and take another look at the room. "Just come in to the main house and let me know your decision when you are ready."

Cassie could not believe Ryan was even considering staying but followed him back to the bedroom. Once inside, Cassie stared out the picture window in the direction of the water.

"Look, Cassie, this is your decision to make. We can either stay here and make the best of it or we can go back to Victoria. Look at that bed. It is huge. We can put those pillows between us and still have plenty of room to sleep. It would almost seem like we're in separate beds. I know it's asking a lot for you to stay in the same room as me but I want you to know if you decide that we'll stay here, I'll respect your privacy."

Ryan was uncomfortable bringing the whole subject up and was upset that the other bedroom had been given to another person. He was also tired from not getting a lot of sleep the night before and was not looking forward to the drive back to Victoria. Even though he said nothing to Cassie, he also felt drawn to this place.

There was a feeling Ryan could not shake that they were meant to stay here at Graycliff. Nina told them how lucky it had been to even have a cancellation; that very rarely happened and she wasn't worried. If they did not want the room she would have it rented before dinner.

Nina knew the other guests would not bother them and that their privacy would be guaranteed with no questions asked. She mentioned that the man who had rented their other room was a bird watcher and wasn't around much. They would see him at 9:00 a.m. each morning for breakfast but he kept to his room in the evening.

There was also a much older couple from Germany in the last bedroom but they spoke very little English and they left each morning after breakfast for the day and retired early every night.

Finally, Nina told them that she knew their reservation was for three nights but due to her cancellation, the room was available for four nights and she would give them the fourth night for half-price since her husband had messed up their reservation.

The two of them took one last look around the room. As Cassie turned and looked at the bed, she heard Ryan say, "I really wish we could stay here but it's probably better that we leave for Victoria."

Cassie did not even know she was saying anything but as she turned and looked once again out the picture window at the water, she heard her voice say, "I want to stay here, too, Ryan."

Ryan's heart leapt with joy when he heard Cassie say those words. "Let's go tell Nina we'll stay. We can wait a day or two before committing to the last day. Since she'll give us a deal on the room for the last night, if we decide not to stay she shouldn't have a problem renting it out if we tell her a day in advance that we'll be leaving."

"After we get unpacked, do you want to try out those two hundred and twelve steps, Ryan?"

"Sounds like a perfect plan to me."

Cassie knew she was a little embarrassed about staying in the same room as Ryan but he had never even hinted at anything improper and she knew he would respect her wishes. The problem was being in such close proximity with him the last couple of days had made her realize that she liked Ryan more than she should. There was no way there could be anything between them and she did not want to lead him on in any way.

Cassie also realized the bed was so big that with the pillows down the middle it would feel like they were sleeping in separate beds. She just felt deep down inside they were meant to stay in that place. She had not felt anything so strongly since she realized she needed to leave Jim for the summer.

Cassie had tried not to think about her life with Jim. She was just thankful for every day she had been able to spend in the Pacific Northwest. Soon enough, she would have to face the reality of her home situation.

However, for now, she was happy to just enjoy the simple pleasures of each day and the companionship she had with Ryan. Cassie realized things would have to change when she went back to Minnesota but felt that somehow everything would work out when she faced her old life again.

After telling Nina their decision, Ryan decided to go back into town while Cassie was unpacking and get some wine at the liquor store. By the time he got back, Cassie was unpacked and was waiting wearing her walking shoes. As he put the wine in the small refrigerator, Ryan told Cassie he only needed a few minutes to unpack and change his shoes.

Cassie went out and sat in one of the chairs on their porch while waiting for Ryan. To her surprise, as she looked up in the tall evergreen tree to her left, a pair of eagles seemed to be looking back at her. At that instant she knew she had made the right decision about staying.

As they began their descent to the water, Cassie reflected on their location. Nina's husband, Carl was a carpenter by trade and Cassie could tell he had put a lot of work into converting the cottage into a B&B. He had also put a lot of time and money into building the staircase down the rocky mountainside to the water.

About every thirty stairs, the staircase would turn another direction. Also, half-way down, he had built a little deck which Cassie suspected was for the climbers to rest on the way back up. There was even a little built-in bench to sit on and watch the water through the trees.

As they descended the stairs, the only problem they encountered was the last ten feet. Cassie suspected the staircase had ended before the bottom so when the tide came in, it would not undermine the bottom of the staircase. Because of that it was a little steep and slippery getting to where the beach began. Ryan held on to some branches to get to the bottom and turned to give Cassie his hand.

As Ryan touched her hand to help her down, Cassie felt a shock go through her body. She pretended nothing had happened and chided herself for even thinking about Ryan that way. Cassie knew Ryan would be disturbed if he knew he was affecting her in any way other than as friends and she knew she had to change the direction of her thoughts.

When Cassie made it to the bottom she looked around. The tide was still in, so there wasn't too much of a beach, but there was enough to walk along the shore without getting wet. Large logs that had washed ashore lay strewn all over the beach. Some of them had been floating in the water quite awhile since they were totally stripped of bark.

On the land side, stood a tall rocky cliff they had just climbed down with evergreen and maple trees seeming to come out of the rocks. They were both glad they had decided to take the staircase down to the beach.

They walked quietly beside each other for almost an hour. Looking out at the water they could see fishing boats and an occasional seal jumping out of the water. Although they did not talk during their walk, it seemed comfortable just being with each other.

Cassie's concentration was broken when she heard Ryan say, "I think it's time we turn back. By the time we tackle those stairs, I have a feeling we'll be worn out going to dinner."

"Now, I know why they have the hot tub in the front yard, Ryan. Do you suppose we should get in the tub with a glass of wine before dinner as Nina suggested?"

"That sounds like an excellent plan. Let's go back now since the idea of a glass of wine while sitting in that tub makes me want to get there sooner."

Cassie was right. She was not sure if it was the long walk or all those stairs but they definitely needed to stop and rest at the halfway point going back up the staircase. They were both extremely happy when the flag came into view and they knew they were almost at the top.

When they got back to their room, Ryan opened the bottle of wine and got out the plastic glasses Nina had supplied while Cassie went in the bathroom and put on her swimsuit. Nina had even furnished white robes like you found in better class hotels. Cassie put her robe on over her swimsuit. She imagined it might feel a little chilly when they climbed out of the hot tub.

Cassie then took the wine and the glasses out to the hot tub while Ryan put his suit on. By the time he came outside, Cassie was already in the tub. She could not believe how good the swirling jets felt around her legs after their long walk and especially after the climb up and down all those stairs.

Thinking to herself, Cassie decided that a day that had started out so unpleasantly had turned into an extraordinary beautiful day. "Do we really have to get out of the tub and go to dinner Ryan? It's been such a wonderful afternoon I hate to leave this place."

"You weren't thinking of staying in the water all night?"

"I imagine we would shrivel up like raisins if we stayed in here. Right, Ryan?"

Cassie purposely kept her eyes closed or focused out to the sea as they sat in the hot tub. She knew she could not hide her developing feelings from Ryan if she looked at him with no shirt on. Because she never looked in his direction, Cassie missed the raw desire in Ryan's eyes as he looked at her in her bathing suit.

"I'm going back to the room and get ready for dinner, Cassie. I only need about ten minutes and then the bathroom will be yours."

"I guess you're telling me it's time to leave this wonderful hot tub. Oh well, there's always tomorrow," Cassie said looking at Ryan's back when he climbed out of the tub. This time a shiver went through her spine as she watched him put his robe on and walk back towards the room. Cassie knew she had to get control of herself but wasn't sure how that would happen spending the evening alone with him in their bedroom.

As it turned out, the evening took a very pleasant twist. Cassie and Ryan went to dinner at the pub and began speaking to a couple at their next table. The couple listened to Ryan's radio station all the time. They were excited to meet the owner of the station and the woman whose name was Emma discovered that she and Ryan had grown up in the same city near Seattle.

Ryan and Emma had a lot to talk about reminiscing about the way life had been while growing up. And both Cassie and the woman's friend, Jerry, enjoyed listening to Ryan and Emma talk of their past.

Before they realized how quickly time had slipped away, it was past ten o'clock. Emma and Jerry were staying at another B&B in the area but it was not on the water. They had been to the festival and this was their last evening in the area. Tomorrow they would be heading back to Seattle. After getting some advice on places to visit the next day, Cassie and Ryan said goodnight to the couple and drove back to their room.

"Do you want to use the bathroom first, Cassie?" Ryan was thinking how glad he was that he had packed some pajamas. He seldom wore pajamas and did not know what had possessed him to bring them but now he gave a little sigh of thanks.

"That would be fine, Ryan."

Ryan sat on the little porch listening to the noises in the night, as Cassie got ready for bed. She called to him as she climbed into their bed.

As Ryan walked in he saw Cassie in bed with the covers pulled up to her chin. Cassie had left the window opened and there was a chill in the room but he knew she was nice and warm with the comforter over her. He also smiled to himself when he saw the two pillows marking the mid-line of the bed.

Although Ryan wished they could be more than friends, he knew that was not right since they were married to others. He had enjoyed their day together and did not want to cut short their time in this area because of the sleeping arrangements. Maybe staying in the same bed as Cassie would work out okay as long as they kept to their own sides.

It was not long before Cassie felt Ryan get into bed and pull the covers up over himself. She wondered if she would be able to sleep with Ryan so close to her. She started thinking about their plans for tomorrow but the warmth of the comforter soon lulled her to sleep. Her last thought before closing her eyes was wondering what the new day would bring.

Ryan, having had a bad night the evening before, also fell right to sleep. Although they stayed on their own sides of the bed, somehow in the middle of the night the pillows between them wound up at the bottom of the bed and they both would wonder about that when they awoke the next morning.

# Chapter Twelve

Cassie had forgotten to close the curtains before going to bed and the next morning the sun streaming in woke her about 7:30 a.m. At first she could not remember where she was but then she sensed Ryan's presence and the memories of yesterday came flooding back. She also realized the pillows were no longer between them but scrunched up at the bottom of the bed by their feet. She wondered how that had happened.

Even though the room seemed cool she felt nice and warm under the comforter. They were both lying on their backs on their own side of the bed but when Cassie turned her head, her eyes met Ryan's. Looking at him, she had to keep herself from moaning. Cassie knew she had to say something to Ryan before he realized the direction of her thoughts.

"I'm not exactly sure what happened to those pillows last night."

"I'm not either but I guess we really don't need them. Nina was right. This bed is plenty big for both of us with room to spare."

"I know I told you I didn't want to get out of the hot tub yesterday afternoon, but that's how I feel about this bed right now. It's so toasty warm. Maybe we should stay in it all day," Cassie teased.

"What, and miss that wonderful breakfast Nina will be making for us this morning," Ryan answered while thinking he would like nothing better than staying in bed all day with

Cassie. He knew he had to change the direction of his thoughts or they would both be in trouble.

"I think I'll get up and make you coffee this morning. Then you can make the coffee tomorrow, Cassie."

Cassie could smell the coffee brewing as she heard Ryan in the shower. At least they were compatible roommates she thought to herself. He showered in the morning and she liked to bathe at night. She also did not like the TV on unless she was catching the weather or a news report and Ryan had told her he felt the same way.

Jim always turned the TV on every night when he went to bed and before they had moved to separate rooms it had been difficult for Cassie to get to sleep with the TV blasting. She appreciated all the more the fact that Ryan did not need it on constantly.

Ryan came out of the bathroom with a cup of coffee for her in his hand. "I can't remember if anyone ever brought me coffee in bed before, Ryan."

As Ryan looked at her, he heard Cassie sigh loudly. "Oh look, Ryan! That pair of eagles is back in that tree. I saw them there yesterday before our walk."

"Do you think that means it's time for another walk?"

"Definitely not before breakfast, Ryan. Are you trying to wear me out before the day even starts?"

"Definitely not before breakfast," Ryan told her with a twinkle in his eye.

At 9:00 a.m. they were seated in Nina's dining room at a table set for five in front of a big picture window overlooking the water. Nina explained how she arranged breakfast.

There were two taller tables along the walls. One table had a large bowl of cheesy scrambled eggs and a plate of ham. The other table had two kinds of cereal, glasses of orange juice and freshly-baked croissants still warm from the oven. On the dining room table was a large platter of freshly cut fruit and breakfast breads as well as homemade jam for the croissants.

Cassie could not remember when she had such a wonderful breakfast. As she and Ryan looked at each other, they both knew their morning walk was going to be needed after that breakfast. Nina introduced everyone and told her guests to get acquainted with each other since they would all be staying there the next few days.

Nina was right about the German couple. They barely spoke to anyone at breakfast and would only answer any questions put to them with a grunt. Tim, the bird watcher, on the other hand, never quit talking.

Tim told Cassie and Ryan that the other couple had not said a word to him the day before. He was beginning to wonder if they spoke any English at all. After that, he started talking about all the birds he had seen in the area and where and when he went to find them. Cassie was thinking she was learning more about birds than she wanted to when she glanced at Ryan.

Cassie felt a shock go through her body as Ryan looked back at her. She knew exactly what Ryan was thinking and it startled her. She had never felt a connection like that before with Jim and she was astonished. She instantly wondered if they would be able to read each other's minds even more so if they ever became intimate. Even though they were saying less to each other, she knew they were communicating more through their thoughts.

Cassie had a momentary fear that they should leave before it was too late. And then she wondered "too late for what?" They weren't school-age kids. They were both married to spouses who hadn't been physical with them for several years. Being in their fifties, Cassie knew they were not going to live forever. Would it be so wrong to have a little happiness at their ages? Who exactly would they hurt? Maybe it would make their home lives more tolerable if they could be with each other from time to time.

Cassie jumped as she felt Ryan touch her hand. "Earth to Cassie." She looked at him with a dazed look in her eyes. "Cassie, where are you?"

"I'm right here eating breakfast," she snapped back at him. All of a sudden Cassie came back to reality. "I'm sorry, Ryan, I guess my mind wandered for a minute. I didn't mean to snap at you." Cassie noticed both Tim and the German couple looking at her very strangely.

"Did you need something, Ryan?"

"No. I just thought you'd like to watch Carl feeding the eagles."

As Cassie looked out the picture window in the dining room she saw a platform on the lawn. Nina entered the room at that moment and explained that Carl had been feeding the same pair of eagles for many years. She told them their eagles had eighteen babies in the years they had been taking care of them.

Cassie wondered what could possibly be more special than having a pair of eagles living in your front yard. As she mentioned that to Ryan, she saw him looking at her with a funny look. She certainly hoped he did not know what she had been thinking before he touched her hand. Little did she know that while having coffee in their room, Ryan had been having the same thoughts about her.

Nina realized that Tim had been monopolizing the conversation with his birds and turned to Cassie and Ryan to ask what they planned for the day. Ryan told her about meeting Emma and Jerry at the pub the night before. It was suggested they follow the eastern coast and stop at the towns along the way and look at the different arts and craft shows going on as part of the summer festival.

They heard about an outdoor play going on in Nanaimo that evening and were thinking of attending. "You should probably wait and go to the play tomorrow night. The forecast is calling for rain later this afternoon and since the play is outdoors it might be rather uncomfortable if it gets too wet."

Nina explained that the festival only ran for a few days each summer so the performance went on rain or shine. Unless you want to sit outside with umbrellas watching the play, I think you may want to see it tomorrow night when the weather is supposed to be better."

"Do you think there will be time for our afternoon walk down on the beach before the rain hits, Nina?"

"Cassie, it's never for sure around here with that large body of water out there, but I would guess you would have time for a walk before the rain starts."

"I think Nina is right," Ryan said. "We should probably wait and go to the play tomorrow night. If we have a big lunch later in the day, we could pick up some snacks, and take our walk. Then if the weather gets miserable we won't have to go out at all tonight."

Cassie looked at him with a strange look on her face. "I was thinking the same thing, Ryan."

As they continued to look at each other, neither of them had any idea that not only would there be no play tomorrow night but they would not be leaving their room at all the next day. Nina, not saying a word, looked at the two of them and wondered if she would need to fix breakfast for them in the morning.

# Chapter Thirteen

As they drove north up the coast, stopping at the little towns along the way, the sun was shining brightly. Cassie glanced over to the west and saw the huge clouds hanging over the mountain.

"Ryan, I wonder if it ever stops raining over in Tofino?"

Ryan glanced to the west and replied, "Leaving there was probably the best thing we ever did."

"I know it was."

Cassie had always been a superstitious person and felt that things happened because they were meant to. "For some reason we were meant to find Graycliff and stay these extra days here Ryan."

Ryan was not a superstitious person and did not think things necessarily happened for a reason, but he was beginning to come to the same conclusion as Cassie. He had not been with a woman for years. Between running his radio station and seeing to Joyce's needs, he had felt complete with the friends in his life. He never imagined he would feel anything for a woman again. Now, he felt a growing emptiness compounded with a longing for this woman sitting next to him. Ryan felt shaken by this discovery.

It was almost as if every breath Cassie took and move she made seemed alluring and fascinating. Ryan realized he had barely scratched the surface as far as knowing her but he realized she made his heart smile. Her smile could make a dark day seem bright as had happened in Tofino.

Ryan thought he probably started falling a little in love with Cassie when she tried so hard to stay upbeat in Tofino, when he sensed how much she did not like that town. Just sitting at that little motel in their chairs reading that afternoon had certainly made that dismal day much brighter for him.

Ryan had gone to dinner with a heavy heart knowing he would not be with Cassie the rest of that evening. Every time he saw her twinkling eyes, he realized there was a radiance about her that was hard to describe. Even with the deplorable situation of her marriage she still found so much joy in the little things she encountered each day.

Joyce, Ryan's wife, was a lot like Cassie's husband, Jim. They both tended to be very negative people blaming the world for what had happened to them instead of trying to find something positive in their lives. Ryan understood Joyce was now beyond any hope of being happy and was thankful that he had such wonderful friends and his radio station that had given him a fulfilling life.

Ryan realized a long time ago that the happiest people did not necessarily have the best of everything; they just made the most of whatever came their way. He never harbored any illusions that his life would be happy after Joyce's accident. He did not even feel any guilt for the way he and Joyce had argued on that fateful day. He did, however, know he might not have owned all those radio stations if it was not for Joyce and he felt he owed her some companionship in return for what she had brought into their marriage.

Celibacy was not a deliberate choice. The first few years after the accident he had affairs with women in his social circle, but he had never felt an affinity with any of those women. It had merely been a sexual release for both parties. Finally, he had become so busy with his work and having never really met anyone who had changed his mind, Ryan felt it was his fate to live without love.

If happiness was in his destiny, it would find him and because of that thinking Ryan had never really looked very hard. After fifteen years he had decided it just wasn't going to happen and had become resigned to his lifestyle.

Ryan understood he was making his life's journey alone but he had a lot of help from his friends who supported his decision to stay with Joyce. And, after awhile he had found a kind of peace and contentment and did not feel he was missing anything.

Now, Cassie made him wonder if he had made the right decision so many years ago. He knew that if anything developed between the two of them, it was not going to be a solution for either of them. They were both married and had no plans to change that part of their lives.

It dawned on him that morning when their eyes had met when they were lying in bed that he desperately wanted Cassie. Ryan realized he needed to quit thinking about the developing situation. He knew he had to let his feelings go and get beyond the desire that was growing so intense inside of him.

The morning passed very quickly as they visited the coastal towns and checked out the different arts and crafts on display. Ryan bought a painting for his office that he liked at one of the outdoor art booths where they stopped. And Cassie found some craft items for her children and their spouses that she thought would make nice Christmas stocking stuffers. It turned into a fun relaxed day for the two of them and they were glad Emma and Jerry had suggested that particular outing.

It was 4:00 p.m. when they found themselves back in Parksville. They were only a few miles from the B&B and they decided to stop and have lunch. They spotted a cute little place down a side street and smiled at each other when they read the name of the restaurant. It was called Barnacle Barney's Fish and Chips.

"Oh, my gosh, Ryan! I don't know if the food is any good, but with a name like that, we have to try the place."

Ryan looked at her strangely. "Sometimes it's scary how you read my mind." Cassie turned to look at the restaurant but felt a chill go through her body at what Ryan had just said.

Cassie was thinking about what a nice day they had driving along the coast but she also sensed a charged atmosphere developing between them. She knew she wanted to eat and go for their walk along the beach. Being in such a close environment with Ryan was definitely starting to bother her.

Cassie had not even thought about that evening when she and Ryan would be spending the night in their little room together. Cassie was concentrating so hard on trying to keep her feelings under control in the present that she wasn't capable of thinking very far ahead.

The restaurant's food turned out to be as good as the name. They both ordered lightly-breaded salmon burgers and Caesar salads. The bun the salmon came on tasted bakery-fresh and the price was so reasonable, Cassie felt a momentary irritation about the restaurant they had lunched at in Tofino.

Although the sandwich had an excellent flavor, for some reason Cassie almost had to choke her food down. She was really upset with herself. She had never once been attracted to anyone in the last few years since Jim had gotten sick and she felt like she was acting like a teenager with a crush on the boy next door.

Cassie even avoided looking directly at Ryan when they were talking for fear he would be able to tell from her eyes what she was thinking. She kept telling herself to get past her feelings before they ruined the vacation.

After lunch they bought some snacks at a little store next to the restaurant to take back to their room and by the time they got back out to the car, Cassie was in control again. She almost convinced herself that she had imagined what she knew deep down she was really feeling. Ryan suggested taking the other direction on their walk along the beach and Cassie nodded as she looked out the car window towards the water.

As they drove back to the B&B neither of them saw the storm clouds gathering in the distance. They had no idea the developing storm was about to be a pivotal point in their relationship.

# Chapter Fourteen

The temperature felt a little cooler when they got back to the B&B. Cassie and Ryan changed into walking shoes and donned sweatshirts over their long-sleeved shirts. The two of them were looking forward to their walk. They could feel mist as they began their descent down the staircase so they walked slowly holding on to the railing.

When they reached the bottom, Ryan once again went first. He turned at the bottom and automatically reached his hand out to Cassie. As she stepped onto the ground her foot slipped on the wet earth. She totally lost her balance and felt herself slide against Ryan.

Cassie's arms automatically went around his neck while Ryan's encircled her waist to keep her from falling down. Cassie felt herself pressing against Ryan's body as she lost her momentum. Gravity continued to crush her against him and she felt her face turn red with embarrassment.

"I'm sorry, Ryan, I slipped," Cassie said stating the obvious. Ryan murmured something but she could not hear what he said. Cassie quickly moved away as she felt his need of her. She was surprised Ryan apparently wanted her as much as she wanted him. This became even more noticeable when she realized they were walking the beach in the opposite direction Ryan had originally suggested.

Cassie could hardly think straight. For the first time she understood Ryan was feeling as desperate about her as she was about him. They walked about ten minutes keeping their thoughts to themselves but Cassie had an ache in her stomach that would not go away. She had no idea that Ryan had the same ache in his stomach.

Cassie was shocked that another man, beside her husband, would desire her. Actually, since Jim had not wanted her in such a long time, she had never dreamed someone else might. Cassie had come to the conclusion a long time ago she was too old to be yearning for sex.

The two of them had been thinking about each other so intensely they were totally unaware of their surroundings. All of a sudden the sky opened up. Within seconds they were drenched, and since they had layered their clothes, they could feel their wet sweatshirts weighing them down. Turning around, they walked as quickly as they could back to the staircase.

"Be careful, Cassie," Ryan said. He climbed up the slight embankment slipping as he held on to some branches for support. Ryan could not believe how hard the rain was coming down. When he got to the first step he turned and held his hand out. This time Cassie managed to get to the step only wobbling a little bit. She knew that without Ryan's help she would have fallen down.

"We need to go up these stairs slowly so we don't slip."

"I'll be careful, Ryan."

As they moved upward, they did not stop at the halfway point but just kept slowly making their way to the top. The rain stung Cassie's face and at times it was hard to see. She had to keep wiping her eyes to remove the water dripping down from her hair. Cassie did not think the two hundred and twelve steps were ever going to end.

The two of them were never so happy to see a flag in their lives. The rain continued to pour down and by the time they reached their door Cassie was shivering from the cold and the crushing weight of her wet clothes.

As soon as they entered their room Ryan immediately went into the bathroom and took off his clothes and put on his robe. As he came out, Cassie, still shivering was struggling to take her wet sweatshirt off.

"Here, come into the bathroom, Cassie."

As she walked into the bathroom Cassie noticed Ryan had tossed all his wet clothes into the bathtub. "Put your arms up."

Cassie could not believe how heavy a wet sweatshirt could feel. Before she knew it, Ryan had taken off her sweatshirt, long-sleeved shirt, and jeans and thrown them in the tub on top of his clothes.

"Here, take off your underwear and put this robe on," she heard Ryan say and he quickly left the bathroom after handing her the other robe. Cassie, still shivering, did as she was told and also dried her hair with a towel before combing it. When she entered the bedroom, Ryan's back was to her and she could smell the hot chocolate he had made for them.

"Ryan, I'm still freezing."

As Ryan turned he saw Cassie shaking uncontrollably. "Cassie, come lie in bed with me."

Forgetting the hot chocolate, they lay down in bed together. Ryan put his arms around her and she snuggled up against him. He put the comforter over them as she put her arm around his waist and her leg pressed against his. Continuing to shiver, Cassie could feel the heat emanating from Ryan's body as she continued to press against him.

She was finally getting control over her chill but as her face pressed against Ryan's neck, Cassie felt a warmth spread throughout her body as she became aware they only had robes on. The tie on Ryan's robe had come loose and her arm was on his bare skin. As she lay almost on top of him, Ryan's need became apparent to her.

Cassie felt an intense desire she had not felt for a long time. As she looked up at Ryan, their eyes met and she realized Ryan was experiencing the same emotions she was feeling. There was no way they could prevent what was going to happen next. As she felt his lips crush against hers, she moaned with such intensity Ryan knew he was going to have her.

Jane had once told Cassie if she ever had a sexual relationship to make sure she had condoms. Since she had never planned to have anyone besides Jim in her life, she had laughed at Jane's suggestion then. Now, remembering the talk she realized she had been naïve because nothing was going to stop the desire now overtaking the two of them. Since neither of them had had any intimate relations in such a long time and had physicals every year, Cassie figured that was one problem she need not worry about with Ryan.

Because it had been so many years since Cassie and Jim had been together, she wondered if the feelings assaulting her body were more intense than she remembered. She felt chills, and not from being cold, ravage her body as Ryan kissed her. As they explored each other's bodies, Cassie realized Ryan was doing things to her that Jim had never done. At the same time, she sensed a power she seemed to have over him that she had never felt with her husband.

As the waves of ecstasy rolled over them, Cassie and Ryan exploded with a oneness they had never experienced before. Neither of them had ever felt anything so intense. Maybe it was because they had liked each other and became friends before lovers. Whatever the reason, they both knew something special had happened.

As they stared at each other in awe, they sensed at the same instant how they felt and at that moment they fell totally in love. They both knew their love was like a drug that would be hard to give up, but despite knowing how hopeless their situation was, they gave their hearts completely to the other.

# Chapter Fifteen

"I'd like to tell you I'm sorry, Cassie, but I'm not," Ryan said as he kissed her forehead when it was over.

"I can't believe what we did, Ryan. If someone told me this would happen, I would never have believed it. Even though Jim and I have not been together for years, I have never even been attracted to anyone else. I thought my life was over that way. But, Ryan, I want you to know I'm not sorry either. And, I hope it happens again."

"That is definitely one wish you are going to get. It's kind of ironic. I thought my life was full and I was happy. Don't get me wrong, Cassie. There were a lot of women in my social circle and some I even slept with after Joyce's accident. But, I never planned to leave Joyce and as the years went by after a while it seemed like too much trouble to get involved with anyone."

"I can't and won't leave Jim either, Ryan. He would be devastated and I wouldn't do that to him. But is it wrong to share a little happiness with each other? It's not like we're kids anymore and we are certainly not going to hurt our spouses by having an affair. Actually, they are the ones who have hurt us."

Cassie, rubbing her hand on Ryan's chest continued, "I know for some reason our paths were meant to intersect at this time in our lives. I won't resist it when we have to go our separate ways and I hope you won't either. Even though our journey is crossing now, we have to respect the fact that we both may need to go in another direction in the very near future."

"You're absolutely right, Cassie, and I think we need to talk about that more a little later. Right now I want to snuggle with you."

As they lay under the covers wrapped in each other's arms, the warmth of the comforter and Ryan's body relaxed Cassie so much she could feel her eyes beginning to close. By the time they would remember the hot chocolate it would be beyond saving.

And that was all Cassie remembered as she and Ryan both fell asleep. Night had descended when they awoke and Ryan's lips hungrily descended on hers again. As their kiss ended Cassie looked at Ryan with a twinkle in her eyes.

"I think the water has pretty much drained out of our clothes, Ryan. Since the two of us will probably fit into that bathtub quite nicely, don't you think we should get those clothes out of the tub and start running the water? Do you mind some bubbles in your bath water," Cassie asked rather wickedly?

"I'm always ready for new experiences. I think a bubble bath might be fun!"

Cassie had been looking forward to soaking in a bubble bath in that large tub ever since they had arrived at Graycliff. However, the thought of Ryan in the tub with her sent chills down her spine. She and Jim had taken showers together before but never a bath. This was a new experience and she could hardly wait. She was hoping Ryan would enjoy it as much as she intended him to.

Since the spigots were in the middle of the tub they both climbed into an end and faced each other with Cassie's legs on top of Ryan's. Then, they laid back and rested their heads against the back of their side of the bathtub. It seemed like they were in the tub forever. Ryan had even poured two glasses of wine and that reminded them of when they were in the hot tub with swimming suits on. They felt like they had come a long way in just twenty-four hours.

Cassie was having a great time in the tub. She was teasing Ryan's body with her toes but when she started laughing he suddenly looked at her with such a longing in his eyes it made her tremble. He pulled her leg up out of the water and began kissing down the length of it. When he got to her knee, Cassie lost it. Before she knew it she was laying on top of him. She never even heard or saw Ryan's plastic wine glass hit the floor.

# Chapter Sixteen

After their bath, Cassie and Ryan cuddled up next to each other in their bed. They were not tired after their nap and they began talking. It was several hours later before they finally fell asleep. Cassie woke up a couple of hours after that with a terrible ache in her stomach. At first she could not remember where she was but then all the memories of what she and Ryan had shared came flooding back. She realized she had an intense longing to have Ryan again.

Cassie knew the emotional comfort she was feeling with Ryan was creating a romantic atmosphere. She thought about her life with Jim and realized that taking care of others was noble work, but not if you never received any emotional support in return, resentment was sure to follow.

Cassie remembered something Doctor George had said and it seemed to have more meaning to her as she was reflecting. The doctor had told her, "Cassie, if you have no life, you will have nothing to give."

At the time it seemed a rather odd thing for the doctor to say but after being with Ryan these last few days she realized just how empty her life had been. Ryan's embraces were becoming like a drug to her especially since she had not known anything so intense for so long.

Cassie knew she was becoming lost in the magic of Ryan's kisses. She knew there was a line between fascination and love but she and Ryan had spent the last few weeks getting to know and respecting each other before starting on their romantic journey. She knew what she and

Ryan shared was a hopeless situation but she also knew she could not stop loving him.

The rain finally stopped and the full moon came out from behind the parted clouds. Once again, they kept the curtains opened and the light from the moon shimmered on the water while also providing some light into the room. As Cassie was reflecting on her life, she glanced at Ryan. Thinking he was asleep Cassie gasped. She realized Ryan had been watching her as she was contemplating her life.

"Don't think those thoughts Cassie," Ryan said. "Can't we just enjoy what we have with each other for this brief time and keep reality at bay?"

"I was thinking if you don't kiss me pretty soon, I'm never going to get rid of this ache in my stomach," Cassie told him.

"Then I guess that's where my duty lies," Ryan said as his lips descended on hers.

It was almost dawn before they finally fell asleep again and it was noon before they woke up. The rain was once again pouring down but this time neither of them minded it.

"I think we missed breakfast, Ryan," Cassie said with a mischievous look in her eye. Cassie felt her heart flutter when Ryan looked back at her. As Ryan began to kiss her, Cassie's only thought was how she could have been so lucky to have found him.

As the kiss ended, Ryan, with laughter in his eyes, suggested a shower together. "I don't trust you in a bathtub right now, Cassie. What do you want to do today, sweetheart?"

"I'm not real excited about going out in the rain. We have some snacks here and I'm hungry since we never had anything to eat last night. Maybe we should stay in our room and read a little. Hopefully, the rain will end later and we can go out and get something to eat. But right now, I want to stay in bed with you. There's something I have to do." With that, Cassie got out of bed and made them coffee.

"Remember you told me it was my turn today," she told Ryan as she handed him his cup of coffee in bed.

After their shower, Cassie had just finished drying her hair when Ryan reentered the bathroom. "We've solved the food problem."

"How did you do that, Ryan?"

"While you were in here drying your hair there was a knock on the inside door of the house that connects to our room. When I opened the door there was a big tray filled with food and a note from Nina. She said she had a feeling we didn't want to go out in the rain and since we missed breakfast she knew we'd be hungry."

Nina had filled the tray with some of her freshly-baked croissants, deli meat, slices of cheese, potato salad and fruit salad. There was also a pitcher of lemonade. Cassie and Ryan could not believe how good everything tasted.

When they finished eating, Ryan put the leftovers in their little fridge for later. Neither of them had much of a desire to go outside. All they wanted to do for the day was stay in bed together. They wrote a note of thanks to Nina and put the tray outside the door that went into the inside of the house. Then they propped up their pillows and climbed into bed to read. They had been reading for about an hour when Cassie looked at Ryan.

As Ryan looked back at her Cassie said, "I can't believe the way you read my mind."

"You must have read mine since you put your book down and looked at me," Ryan answered as once again his lips found hers.

"Ryan, I can't believe I want you as much now as I did the first time."

This time Ryan felt chills run down his spine at Cassie's words. And neither of them was aware of when the rain stopped. They were too wrapped up in each other to know what was happening in the outside world.

# Chapter Seventeen

Cassie had never had so much fun staying with someone in a room alone as she had with Ryan.

The next morning when they awoke the sun was shining brightly. Cassie and Ryan took a shower together and this time they were up in time to go to breakfast.

When they sat down at the dining room table, they thanked Nina once more for the wonderful food the day before.

"I know how hard it is to get out of bed when it's raining like that," Nina told them with a gleam in her eye.

Tim, the bird watcher, immediately jumped into the conversation. "It wasn't hard for me to get up yesterday. Birds love the rain and with the sun not shining it's easier to spot them in the bushes."

Nina rolled her eyes at Cassie as Tim continued with a dissertation of what he had seen the day before.

"Oh, look," Cassie interrupted him. "It's time for the eagles to be fed."

As they continued with their breakfast, they all watched in silence as Carl fed the eagles.

"What are your plans for today?" Nina asked Ryan.

"We plan to stick close to the house today if you don't mind Nina. Cassie and I wanted to walk along the beach and see if we can find any sand dollars or whatever else we might encounter. We want to make use of your hot tub again and then we'll probably go to the pub for an early dinner. Since we only have two more days here we thought we'd just enjoy your home. We still want to do the play but we'll probably go tomorrow night. And we also plan to do a little reading this afternoon." Ryan's eyes had a twinkle as he looked at Cassie with a playful glance while speaking to Nina.

"Reading is always a fun thing," Nina replied with a knowing smile.

Once again Tim started in on his birds and his plans for the day and Cassie just kept nodding at him as Ryan's hand felt for hers under the table causing her to shiver. Since the German couple was not saying anything and Cassie was having a hard time keeping control of her emotions in front of all of them, she decided it was time for a serious conversation with Tim about birds.

As they descended the stairs for their morning walk on the beach, Cassie and Ryan looked at each other as Cassie came off the staircase. Neither of them could believe how far they had come in such a short period of time.

The day passed all too swiftly and Cassie realized at times like this she wished there was a way to stop time. She knew the memories she and Ryan would have of their stay here at Graycliff would be a part of them forever but she also selfishly did not want their time here to end.

Actually, there was time to do a little reading later in the afternoon. While Cassie read, Ryan sat at the little table in front of their picture window writing something.

When Cassie asked him what he was doing he told her he had some notes he needed to jot down for his work and so she dismissed his actions and went back to her book. In a little while Ryan told Cassie he wanted to run into town and get another bottle of wine. She told him they could wait and get some when they went to the pub but he insisted on going in case they wanted to get into the hot tub before dinner.

It was forty-five minutes before Ryan returned. Cassie could not understand what had taken him so long but Ryan was whistling when he came back and seemed so happy she never questioned his disappearance. They ended up sitting in the chairs on their little porch having a glass of wine before heading for the pub.

Later that night after darkness descended they made their way to the hot tub. There were no other lights on in the house except in their room so they figured everyone was asleep. This time they weren't wearing any swimming suits. They turned on the jets and removed their robes. Since there was a chill in the air they quickly sank down into the warm waters. Moving close to him, Cassie trembled as Ryan reached for her.

# Chapter Eighteen

The next morning dawned all too quickly. Cassie and Ryan were both sad their vacation was coming to a close. After breakfast they once again took a long walk along the shore. Cassie looked at Ryan as they descended the staircase and knew exactly what he was thinking. The stairs actually did seem to be getting easier.

Cassie could not believe how she could read his mind. There was a connection between them she had never felt with her husband. They were even beginning to start their conversations in the middle of a sentence and knew exactly what they were saying to each other.

Cassie thought of her relationship with Ryan as a gift. She knew it would end but she had never dreamed she would have these few weeks of happiness with him. Instead of worrying about when they would part, she savored every moment with him. Cassie knew the memories of their time together would be a part of her forever. But for the present, just being together, doing simple things, held great joy for her.

Later, in the afternoon, they drove over to Nanaimo Bay. The play was starting at 7:00 p.m. and they wanted to browse the shops and have dinner before the performance started. One of the stores they were perusing had a display of jewelry made by the Native Indians in the area. Ryan pointed at the counter where he was standing.

"Look, Cassie, at that ring. The color is the same green color as your eyes. I want to buy it for you."

"You don't need to buy me anything, Ryan. And that is a very expensive ring."

"I know I don't, Cassie. But, I want you to have that ring. It will remind you of our time here together."

Ryan bought the ring and their eyes met as he slipped it on her right hand. Neither of them said anything to the other. Ryan knew it could not be right now but he wished it could have been an engagement ring for Cassie. It felt so right being together, he could not believe they were going to have to part soon.

After they left the jewelry store, they strolled to the waterfront where the play would take place. The performance was being held in an open area down by the water. Bleachers had been set up for the occasion. Nina was right. Those bleachers would have been miserable to be sitting in during a rainstorm. Since there was a small stage with an overhead cover, the actors would not have gotten wet but the audience would have.

They sat, holding hands, while they watched the play. By the time intermission came they knew they needed to go back to their room. Cassie hardly made it inside the door before Ryan started taking her clothes off.

As Ryan kissed her, she reached down to pull his sweater off. They barely made it to the bed, tossing their clothes along the way. For some reason they had a hunger that could not be sated and neither of them knew what they were going to do when Cassie went back to Minnesota.

For now, they had each other and they were thankful for their moments together. They did not get a lot of sleep that night. It was as if they were afraid to lose any precious time together. After they made love they talked to each other about their hopes and dreams. When they did fall asleep Ryan held Cassie in his arms as if he was afraid to let her go. They both tried very hard not to think about what was going to happen when summer ended.

For now, they had each other and Ryan decided he would take some time off from his work at the radio station. He wanted to go with Cassie on her little trips as she continued to explore the area. Ryan wanted to spend as much time with her as possible before she had to leave. When Ryan asked Cassie if he could go with her on her weekly adventures she looked at him and answered him with a deepening kiss.

# Chapter Nineteen

Ryan was just coming back in the door from outside as Cassie came out of the bathroom. "You went outside, Ryan?"

"Yes, Cassie. I was talking to Carl."

The two of them entered the dining room at 9:00 a.m. for breakfast for the last time at Graycliff. Both Tim and the German couple were still staying a few more days since they had booked the B&B for a week. Tim told Cassie how much he would miss their talks about birds and Cassie told him she would miss his little talks, also, as she smiled at him.

Ryan noticed before how kind Cassie was when she met people and it was something he loved about her. After Joyce's negativism about everything and everybody in her life, it was refreshing to see someone take such joy in people and their feelings as Cassie did.

They left the B&B at 11:00 a.m. after they had hugged Nina and Carl goodbye. Cassie was a little puzzled when Ryan told Nina they would be back and thanked Carl for all his help.

"What did Carl help you with?" Cassie asked him.

"I needed his advice on a project," Ryan told her rather mysteriously.

"I would love to come back here again. However, I don't know if we'll have time before I go back to Minnesota."

"Cassie, you know how you always believe things happen because they are meant to be?"

"Yes."

"Well I believe we will be together again at Graycliff and I think it will happen someday."

Cassie just smiled at Ryan and said a little prayer that what he believed would really happen in the future.

After getting in their car, they headed back for Nanaimo Bay. Just outside of town was a ferry landing and if they caught that particular ferry they would end up just south of Vancouver, BC. Then they would have about a two-and-a-half hour drive back to Seattle. That would save them a couple of hours rather than taking the ferry at Victoria and going east on the Olympic Peninsula as they had at the beginning of their vacation.

Cassie could not believe it. It seemed like they had just had breakfast and before she knew it, Ryan was depositing her at her condo complex. The B&B was now a distant memory.

"I'm really going to miss sleeping with you tonight, Ryan."

"Do you think I could move in with you while you are living here, Cassie? All I do is look in on Joyce each evening. We sleep in separate rooms and Joyce won't even eat dinner with me anymore. Sometimes I think she gets upset just seeing me because I have my health."

"I can't believe how similar our circumstances are, Ryan. I would love it if you would move in with me. There's plenty of space and I have a computer and fax machine you could use if necessary." Cassie was excited at the prospect of Ryan moving into the condo with her.

"Tomorrow is Saturday and I need to go into the office and also do some things around my apartment. I'll get everything organized. Let's go to dinner tomorrow night and then we'll go to church on Sunday and after breakfast I'll get my things and move in."

As much as Cassie had enjoyed her time alone in the condo, the prospect of not being with Ryan at night was painful to her. She wanted to spend as much time with him as possible before she left in the fall. She also knew that Ryan felt the same way about being with her now.

As Cassie entered the apartment she heard the phone ringing and ran for it. When she picked it up she realized Jane was on the line. Jane had been trying to call her for several days and wondered what had happened to her. Cassie also had her cell but she had not had service in Canada so there was no way for anyone to reach her.

Jane was taking a cruise to Alaska in a couple of weeks and wanted to spend a couple of days with Cassie before the cruise. When Cassie hesitated with her answer, Jane immediately knew something was up.

"What's going on, Cassie?"

"Jane, promise me you won't say anything to anyone?"

"You know I won't." Jane was becoming worried something bad had happened to Cassie.

Jane could not believe Cassie had found a friend, as well as a lover. Cassie told her the whole story of how she and Ryan had met and how they had just come back from a few days in Canada together. Cassie also told her about Ryan's wife and how neither of them planned to leave their spouses, although Ryan planned to move in with her.

Jane, too, was surprised by how similar Cassie and Ryan's circumstances were. She also wondered since the two of them had gone without love for so long and if they were as compatible as Cassie said, would they really be able to give each other up in the fall. Cassie told Jane she would love to have her visit and meet Ryan. Since Ryan only lived a few blocks from her, she was sure he would not mind going back to his place while Jane was there. Jane gave her the date she was coming and told her she'd get a limo at the airport to take her to Sylvia's condo.

After they hung up, the phone rang again. This time it was Ryan. Cassie told him about Jane's call. He thought it was nice that her friend was coming for a visit.

"Cassie, I was wondering. The day after Jane arrives I have an important cocktail party. It's a yearly tradition for station employees and sponsors that I need to attend. Do you think you and Jane could go with me?"

"We'd be happy to go with you. I have some cocktail clothes and since Jane is going on the cruise I know she'll have dressy clothes. Although knowing Jane, she'll probably say she has nothing to wear and will want to drag me to the 'Bon' shopping before the party. But, Ryan, won't your friends think it's funny that you are bringing us to your party?"

"No, there are quite a few sponsors and sometimes I escort some of them so no one will think a thing about it if I show up with the two of you. Cassie, I miss you so much. I don't know if I can wait until Sunday to sleep with you again."

"Even though you are not moving in until Sunday, couldn't you stay over tomorrow night, Ryan? Then after church and breakfast you can go get whatever you need from your apartment. I think I'll fix dinner so we don't have to go out Sunday night."

"That sounds perfect, Cassie. Goodnight love and I'll see you tomorrow."

Cassie smiled at Ryan's words as she hung up the phone.

It was 5:00 p.m. the next evening when Ryan rang the buzzer to Cassie's apartment. She buzzed him in and opened the door as Ryan came out of the elevator. He had a small suitcase and a large bouquet of flowers in his hands that he had stopped at the Market and bought for her.

"Oh, Ryan, the flowers are so beautiful! Thank you." Cassie found a vase, filled it with water and put the bouquet in it. As she turned around Ryan came up behind her. She wrapped her arms tightly around him and kissed him. Cassie could have sworn she heard Ryan say something about "there goes dinner" but she was so busy taking off his clothes and dragging him to the couch she could not be sure.

It was much later when they walked down Second Street in the Belltown area. Since it was Saturday night, the restaurants were still open and they had a candlelit dinner before going back to the apartment.

Sunday dawned and as soon as church and breakfast were over Ryan went back to his home. He told Joyce's nurse, Nancy, he would be spending his nights at an apartment near by and gave her the phone number to call in case of an emergency. He informed Nancy he would continue to look in on Joyce each evening after work unless he was out of town. Ryan also told the nurse he would prefer Joyce not know he was not living there.

Nancy reassured Ryan that Joyce retired very early each evening, right after his visit and since she had several numbers to call him if the need arose, there would be no reason for Joyce to know he wasn't living there.

Nancy had been with them for twelve years and she had watched as Ryan had tried to stay devoted to his wife even as Joyce sank more and more into a depressed state. Nancy was surprised Ryan had lived such a lonely life for so long and was glad he had found someone to be happy with.

And so, after knowing each other for a little over a month, Ryan moved in with Cassie. They knew they had less than two months together and were determined to savor every moment they were given.

# Chapter Twenty

Cassie could not believe how compatible she and Ryan were. They respected each other's space but at the same time she was so comfortable with Ryan around, it was like they had lived together for many years.

Ryan also noticed how easy it was to live with Cassie. He would help her around the apartment whenever he could and they both took turns preparing dinner or going out. They continued taking little side trips in the middle of the week whenever Cassie wanted to go. Ryan did not care where they went, as long as he was with her.

On the Tuesday after Ryan moved in with Cassie, he was sitting at his desk at the radio station smiling when his accountant and friend Jeremy walked in. Ryan was thinking how he had probably done more touristy things the last few weeks with Cassie than he had his whole life living in Seattle.

"You seem awfully happy today, Ryan. In fact, lately you seem happier than I've seen you in years. I have to believe a woman has come into your life."

"Yes, there is a woman, Jeremy but it's not that simple."

"It never is Ryan."

For some reason Ryan felt the need to confide in someone and he told Jeremy all about Cassie, her marriage, and how she happened to be in Seattle for the summer.

"That's very ironic Ryan, how the two of you are living such similar lives and then meeting as you did."

"I haven't felt this much satisfaction being with someone in years, Jeremy. Cassie makes me forget all my past heartaches with Joyce. Being with her makes me want to live again. I never imagined I could feel so much happiness, especially at my age."

"She's got to be a real special person to have affected you like that, Ryan. When do I get to meet her?"

"Actually, she has a friend coming to visit her in a few days and I asked both of them to the annual cocktail party we are putting on for our sponsors."

"Good, I'll look forward to that. What's her friend like, Ryan?"

"I have no idea, Jeremy." Ryan's friend had lost his wife to cancer six years earlier. He was Ryan's age and was always looking for new women to date but only on a casual basis. He had loved his wife dearly and did not think he would ever again find someone to love that much. He also knew he could not take the pain of losing someone he cared so deeply for ever again.

"All I know is she's been divorced for years. I guess her husband cheated on her more than once and she doesn't trust men anymore."

"She sounds like my kind of woman," Jeremy told his friend with a gleam in his eye.

When Ryan went home that night he told Cassie about Jeremy and what he had said about Jane. "Wouldn't it be interesting if they fell for each other when they aren't looking like we did Ryan? I don't suppose lightening can strike twice."

Little did Cassie realize how prophetic her words would be.

# Chapter Twenty-One

Jane flew into Seattle on a Thursday morning. Her cruise was leaving on Saturday afternoon. After awaking that morning, Ryan packed an overnight bag to take back to his place since he and Cassie would be sleeping apart on Thursday and Friday night.

Cassie knew she would be busy with Jane but she also knew how much she would miss Ryan. The two of them had decided to take Jane out to dinner that night and Ryan had invited Jeremy. Ryan wanted his friend to meet Cassie before Friday night because he knew they would not have much time to socialize during the party since they needed to mingle with their sponsors.

Jeremy was curious about the woman who was making Ryan so happy. He knew there were many women over the years who would have loved to have become involved with Ryan but he had been oblivious to their advances. Jeremy also thought it would be fun to meet Jane. Unlike Ryan, Jeremy was always looking for new conquests, the more casual the better.

The four of them went to dinner at a fancy downtown hotel that had a dance floor. Jeremy could see right away why Ryan loved Cassie. She was quick-witted and at the same time very down-to-earth. The two of them spent most of the evening looking at each other and touching each other in little ways when they thought no one was looking.

Ryan and Jeremy told Cassie and Jane all about their annual cocktail party. They described some of the people they would be meeting and Jeremy was surprised how many of the people Cassie already seemed to know. He realized Ryan had been telling her a lot about his station.

When Jane heard how important the party was she immediately turned to Cassie and told her friend she had nothing to wear. Jane told Cassie they needed to go shopping at "the Bon" the next day so she could try and find a suitable outfit for the party.

"Surely you brought some dressy clothes for your cruise," Cassie said to Jane as she rolled her eyes at Ryan with a smile.

"I'm sure I don't have the right dress, Cassie."

After dinner the band began playing. Jane and Jeremy had taken trips to some of the same areas and discovered they had a couple of friends in common. It was a good thing they had something to talk about because when the music started Cassie and Ryan went out to the dance floor and never left until the band took a break.

"They can't seem to keep their hands off each other," Jeremy observed. "Jane, will you tell me about Cassie's husband?"

Jane told Jeremy about Jim and the way he had treated Cassie the last few years.

"That's amazing, Jane. I know Ryan said they had a lot in common but I can't believe how similar the relationships with their individual spouses are."

"From what Cassie tells me, you had a wife you truly loved, Jeremy. I thought I was in love and would be married forever. I guess it's kind of odd how things sometimes work out. My former husband is now married for the fourth time and from what I hear he isn't being faithful to her either. I guess I was lucky to get out when I did."

"Don't you miss having someone in your life, Jane?"

"No. Do you?"

"No. I have my work and I like to travel whenever I can and I keep myself very busy."

"I travel a lot, also, Jeremy and I have many friends who keep me busy when I'm back in Minneapolis, which isn't too often lately."

"Would you like to dance with me, Jane?" Jeremy asked when a new song started.

"Yes, that would be nice."

When they went out to the dance floor they said something to Ryan and Cassie. However, the two of them were so intent on each other they never even noticed Jane and Jeremy dancing next to them.

"I almost feel like I'm keeping them apart by staying with Cassie."

"Ryan told me Cassie goes back to Minnesota the first part of October and they want to be together every moment they are able. But, I also know Cassie was looking forward to your visit."

Jeremy had taken the cruise that Jane was going on a couple of months previously and as they danced he told her what she should do in the different ports and what shore excursions she should take. They ended up having a very enjoyable evening together and discovered they had a lot in common.

Neither of them thought anything would come of their being with each other but both realized they were having a lot of fun and were looking forward to talking again, the following evening, at the cocktail party. Besides, Jeremy and Jane realized if they kept each other occupied, their friends would not feel bad about leaving them alone together.

Cassie & Ryan did not leave the hotel until the band quit playing. Jane was tired from her day of traveling and Jeremy offered to drive her back to the condo. They knew Ryan and Cassie wanted to be together as long as possible, especially since they were not sleeping together that night.

Jane told Jeremy how much she enjoyed meeting him and would see him the next night at the party. Jeremy gave Jane a quick hug as he left her at the condo door.

It was quite late and Jane had been asleep for a while when Cassie finally arrived home.

Cassie felt a little bad she had left Jane to fend for herself with Jeremy but figured Jane would not have gone home with him if she did not want to. Cassie had told Jane to let her know if she got tired because of the time change. Cassie would have been happy to take Jane back to the condo earlier if she had wanted to go.

Cassie liked Jeremy a lot. She could see why he was Ryan's friend and she was happy Ryan had someone like that to lean on emotionally. She did not see anything happening between Jeremy and Jane but realized they were very alike. Cassie felt they might become friends since they had a lot in common and seemed to have a good time together.

# Chapter Twenty-Two

The next morning Jane and Cassie woke up early. Jane's body was still on central time and so it was two hours later to her than actual Seattle time.

They took their coffee out to the balcony by the dining room which overlooked Mount Rainier. Jane commented on how surreal that mountain looked when it was out and Cassie told her she thought the same thing. Cassie was thinking how much she would miss morning coffee on the balcony when she left the city.

"I'm getting so I love Seattle more and more, Jane. The water and evergreen trees remind me of northern Minnesota where I grew up."

"I can also see why you love Ryan. He seems to be so thoughtful and caring. How are you going to be able to go back to Jim?"

"I just don't think about it. I want to savor and cherish every moment I've been given with Ryan. I can't expect more than that. You know if it hadn't been for you, Jane, I would never have had this summer. I can't thank you enough for what you did for me."

"Cassie, you've always had the burden of having to do everything for everyone else and have never asked for anything in return. Unfortunately, I think your family takes advantage of you for that reason. This should be a wake-up call for them. It's not fair that you don't have a chance to have some happy times yourself. Personally, I hope things work out between you and Ryan. I believe you were meant for each other."

"Don't even think that, Jane. I have to go back to Jim. He needs me. Plus, Ryan will never leave Joyce. We can only have this summer with each other but at least we will have lasting memories of our time together."

Then Cassie told Jane about all her excursions in the Seattle area. Jane laughed when Cassie described how Ryan was dragging along playing tourist with her.

"Cassie, you have found something so special with Ryan. Sometimes people never find what you have with him in their entire lifetime. You mark my words. I really believe you two were meant to be together."

Cassie had a very sad look on her face when Jane said that. "No, it just can't be, Jane."

"C'mon, Cassie," Jane said, trying to lighten the mood. "It's almost 10:00. We need to get to the 'Bon' as soon as possible. My charge card is burning a hole in my pocket."

Cassie laughed but Jane was serious about the shopping expedition. Jane found several outfits she just had to have and Cassie found an emerald green dress that Jane insisted she buy.

"It matches your eyes and your ring, Cassie. Ryan will have a hard time keeping his eyes off you, as if that would ever be a problem for him, even without that dress."

Since the party began at 6:00 p.m., Ryan knocked on their door at 5:00 p.m. He could not believe how beautiful Cassie looked in her new dress. He bought her a white corsage and the flowers contrasted beautifully with the color of her dress. He knew people were going to be curious about Cassie but he pretended that wasn't the case because he did not want her to be nervous.

When Ryan entered the room where the party was being held, several of the people from the radio station were already there attending to last-minute details. Ryan walked in with Cassie on one arm and Jane on the other.

Everyone turned to look at them. Jeremy was watching from the back of the room and he watched as all eyes focused on Ryan and Cassie even though Jane was right beside them. Everyone took for granted that Ryan and Cassie belonged together and Jeremy thought how strange that was since Ryan had not dated in years. He immediately went over and gave Cassie a hug and corralled Jane.

"I believe they will be together someday," Jeremy told Jane as he moved her to the back of the room with him. "And I think people need to get use to seeing them together. That's why I decided to shanghai you."

"Jeremy, you're sweet. And that is very thoughtful of you to feel that way about Ryan and Cassie. I told her the same thing this morning but unfortunately she wouldn't believe me."

Jeremy looked at Jane with a smile. "You know, Jane, you're okay."

Jane smiled back at Jeremy. "I think you're okay, too."

Before they knew it, the party was in full swing. Many of the station employees came up to Cassie. They were curious about her but were too polite to ask any questions about her relationship with Ryan. However, they knew Ryan had to mingle with his guests and they did not want Cassie to feel left out or alone since Jane was off meeting some of Jeremy's friends.

Cassie enjoyed her introduction to the many people from the radio station. She was finally able to put faces to names. Ryan's employees had no idea how much he had told Cassie about them but she seemed to pull the life stories out of anyone who spoke to her. Everyone who met Cassie, liked her, and knowing how lonely their boss' marriage to Joyce was they all hoped Cassie would be in his life for a long time to come.

Ryan and Cassie were apart most of the evening since Ryan kept mingling with his guests but it was very noticeable to the station personnel how their eyes constantly met across the room. They could feel the electricity flowing between the two of them.

"I can't believe how they can carry on conversations with other people while silently communicating like that," Jeremy told Jane. "I loved my wife dearly and we were very compatible but we never had that level of communication that they seem to have and they haven't even known each other very long."

"Jeremy, do you want to take me out after the party? I feel guilty for keeping them apart. I can tell Cassie you want me to meet some of your friends and that I won't get home until later. That way they can be alone for a while tonight. I hate to ask you but I know how precious these last few weeks they'll have together will be and I don't want to interfere."

"Jane, that's an excellent idea. I still have a few more things I want to tell you about what to do on your cruise and I planned to have a late dinner with some friends. I would love it if you went out with me after the party. And that'll give Ryan and Cassie some time alone tonight."

Jane and Jeremy did not realize that the bond they were forming because of Cassie and Ryan's relationship would create a deeper understanding and friendship between the two of them. They only knew they needed to give Ryan and Cassie time together since summer was slowly drawing to a close.

# Chapter Twenty-Three

The party ended about 9:00 p.m. and Cassie and Ryan were surprised when Jane told them she was going out with Jeremy.

"Do you think there's an attraction there Ryan?"

"Don't get your hopes up, Cassie. Jeremy is a womanizer and he knows Jane is a free spirit. I think they just plan to enjoy each other while they are together."

"I know Jane won't do anything she doesn't want to do and Jeremy seems nice enough. I just feel a little bad she came to visit me and she seems to be spending a lot of her time with Jeremy. I want to be with you every moment I can, Ryan, but not at the exclusion of my friend. If it wasn't for Jane, I would never have come to Seattle in the first place."

"Don't worry, Cassie. I'll definitely back away if Jane needs time with you."

Cassie looked at Ryan and wondered how anyone could be so compassionate and loving. It seemed like he always thought of everyone else before himself. With the way her family had been acting, Cassie was not used to that kind of behavior.

Since they had snacked all evening, neither of them was hungry and they decided to go back to Cassie's condo. Ryan poured both of them a glass of wine and they went out on the balcony since the evening breeze was so pleasant. They rehashed the happenings of the party and what Cassie had thought about some of the people she had met. Cassie made some observations to Ryan about both his employees and sponsors. Ryan could not believe the insight she showed after just meeting those people for the first time. She had even found out some problems a couple of his employees were having that he had no idea about.

"Cassie, what am I going to do when you leave me? I'm going to lose my best friend."

"Ryan, we can't think about it. If we start thinking that way we'll just get sad and we won't enjoy our time together."

"I know you're right, Cassie." But deep down in his heart Ryan knew that did not make any difference. He ached for her even when she was with him because he could not help thinking about what would happen when their time together was over.

"As much as I love your dress, Cassie, I keep thinking about the body inside it. How about we go into the bedroom and I check to make sure your zipper works."

Cassie could not help laughing at Ryan. "You know, Ryan, I had the feeling you were thinking that all night."

"I think you're beginning to know me too well," Ryan said with real sadness in his eyes.

"What if Jane comes back while we're together, Ryan?"

"Cassie, I tossed and turned all last night without you. Please let me sleep with you tonight. I'll set the alarm for 5:00 and be out of here before Jane wakes up. She'll never know I stayed the night."

There was no way Cassie could refuse Ryan's request. She wanted him just as much as he wanted her. She, too, had spent a miserable night the evening before. She kept waking up and reaching for him but he wasn't there. It seemed strange since she had been sleeping in a separate room from Jim for quite a few years and found it hard to believe how quickly she had adapted to having Ryan in bed with her.

After Ryan unzipped her dress, Cassie turned and looked at him. They both had been waiting for this moment all evening. Cassie and Ryan had meant to hang up their clothes but all they were able to do was throw them over a chair.

They both started giggling when Cassie stumbled on the shoes she had taken off and landed on top of Ryan as he tumbled on the bed.

After they made love, the two of them fell asleep almost immediately wrapped in each other's arms. They were both tired from not getting much sleep the night before so they never heard Jane and Jeremy come into the condo.

Jeremy noticed Ryan's car parked out front and had pointed it out to Jane. Neither of them was surprised to find the apartment dark and quiet. They had no idea they were doing exactly what Ryan and Cassie had done as Jane poured wine for the two of them. They made their way to the balcony for party rehashing which they had not had time to do since they had the late supper with Jeremy's friends.

Jane and Jeremy spent a couple of hours on the balcony watching the nightlights of the city and talking. For some reason Jeremy found Jane very interesting and for the first time in a long time he did not try to make a move on a woman he was with.

Jane also liked being with him and felt very comfortable. Since they had their friends in common, they never considered that they were on a date. Instead, they were just two people talking about the evening they had just shared.

They were enjoying their time with each other and they did not give much thought to their developing relationship. They knew they were being thrown together because they had Ryan and Cassie in common. They were there because of their friends or at least that is what they told each other. It really made for a relaxed atmosphere between the two of them.

At one point, Jane even mentioned to Jeremy that perhaps they were meant to be confidants. She imagined both Ryan and Cassie would take their break up quite hard and at least they would have someone to talk to who knew about their love.

Jeremy told Jane he was sorry she was not spending any time in Seattle after her cruise. For some reason, he wanted to hear her reaction to the places she was going and the activities she planned to participate in since he had done the cruise a few weeks earlier.

"I really don't want to intrude on Cassie and Ryan's time together."

"Ryan told me they are going away for a few days that week when you come back. Can't you stay in the apartment here for a couple of days while they're gone? That way we can catch up on what's happening between them and you can tell me about your cruise."

That idea was very appealing to Jane. "Sylvia gave me a key to her place and told me her guest room was always available. I know Cassie wouldn't mind since she's not using the room. I don't want to intrude on your life, Jeremy but it would be fun to spend a few days together. It sure would be wonderful if we could come up with some plan to keep those two from parting. Although, I really don't see that happening, do you, Jeremy?"

"No, I don't either," he said while thinking how much he wished that for his friend.

It was almost 3:00 a.m. when Jeremy left. Jane was leaving at noon for the cruise ship terminal and was suppose to be going out for breakfast with Cassie at 9:00 a.m. Neither of them could believe the time had gone by so quickly that evening.

Jane told herself they only had their friends in common but when Jeremy kissed her on the cheek when he left she began to wonder. She was used to men coming on strong to her and liked it that Jeremy was not acting that way.

# Chapter Twenty-Four

Ryan, true to his word, left just after 5:00 a.m. He had awakened a little before the alarm was set to go off. He wanted to leave without disturbing Cassie but she instantly woke up when he got out of bed.

Dressing quickly, Ryan took Cassie in his arms for one last kiss. Since it was Saturday, Ryan was going home to sleep a little more since he had only had about six hours of sleep. Cassie was planning to go to breakfast with Jane and then drop her at the terminal for her cruise around noon.

There was a festival going on downtown on Pike Street that afternoon and Cassie and Ryan had decided they would walk around and see what was going on at that street party. They wanted to have dinner out somewhere and then come home early. Ryan told her he would be back about 2:00 p.m.

And that was exactly what Ryan was thinking about when he entered his condo at 5:30 a.m. However, Nancy, Joyce's nurse, still in her night gown, greeted him with a worried look as he came in the door.

"Ryan, Joyce had a very bad night last night. She's having trouble breathing and I'm worried she might have developed pneumonia. I was getting ready to call you. I really think we should take her to the hospital. She's also developed a fever."

Ryan immediately went into his wife's bedroom and heard her tortured breathing. When he put his hand on her forehead he could feel the heat emanating from her body.

"Nancy, let's call for an ambulance. I think it will be better for Joyce to be transported to the hospital that way."

The nurse nodded at Ryan as she went to the phone and dialed 911 for an ambulance. By the time the paramedics came to the condo, assessed Joyce's condition, and took her to the hospital, it was close to 7:00 a.m.

Nancy rode in the ambulance and Ryan followed in his car. He knew he and Nancy would need transportation to and from the hospital since it was obvious Joyce would be there for a few days.

As the doctors examined Joyce, Ryan thought about calling Cassie but realized she was sleeping and since there was not any thing he could tell her about Joyce's condition, he decided to wait. Then, by the time the doctors had admitted Joyce and had gotten her up to her room, Ryan knew Cassie was having breakfast with Jane. So he put off calling her.

Nancy was right. Joyce did indeed have pneumonia, and the doctor began treatment immediately including giving her oxygen. Joyce awoke a couple of times and seeing Ryan sitting beside her seemed to calm her labored breathing.

The doctor, who came in to check on Joyce later that morning, noted the soothing effect Ryan had on his wife. When the doctor told him how his being there was helping her, Ryan knew he would have to spend the day at the hospital.

After his wife was settled in, Ryan went down to the cafeteria and had breakfast while Nancy sat with Joyce. Ryan called Jeremy to inform him of Joyce's condition. Naturally, he woke Jeremy up since it had been after 4:00 a.m. before he had gotten home.

Jeremy lived on Bainbridge Island and had to take the ferry to his house. He was shocked Joyce was so sick and told Ryan so. Jeremy asked Ryan if he had talked to Cassie but Ryan told him no. Jeremy then told Ryan to call him and keep him informed and let him know if there was anything he could do to help him.

Ryan told Jeremy how much it meant to him to know he would be there if he needed him. Ryan counted himself lucky to have such a friend.

When he got back to Joyce's room he told Nancy to take his car and go back to the condo. When the nurse protested, Ryan insisted she go back and rest since she had been up most of the night with Joyce.

Nancy told Ryan she was coming back that evening so he could go to dinner and have a little break from being in Joyce's room all day. Ryan told her it wasn't necessary but Nancy cared about Joyce after being with her for so many years. When she told Ryan she was coming back he told her he would see her at dinner time. Ryan also asked Nancy to bring him some toiletries and fresh clothes since it looked like he would be at the hospital overnight. It was 1:00 p.m. when Ryan finally talked to Cassie. She was shocked to hear of Joyce's condition.

"Ryan, I wish I could come and sit with you but I know I can't do that."

"Cassie, Nancy is coming back here to relieve me for awhile at dinner time. I really would like to see you. I could be tied up at the hospital for a couple of days. Do you think you could come here and have dinner with me tonight?"

Ryan gave Cassie directions to the hospital and Cassie told him she would meet him in the cafeteria at 6:00 p.m. Since Joyce was in a double room and the other bed was empty Ryan had asked the doctor if he could use the spare bed.

The doctor told him they would try and keep the bed empty if possible so he could use it. Ryan told him he would gladly pay for the bed if necessary but the doctor told him not to worry about it unless for some reason they needed the bed.

When Joyce woke up, Ryan told her he was staying at the hospital with her and he could tell she became calmer when he told her that. Then Ryan told her he was going to take a nap and pointed out where the other bed was located. His wife nodded and went back to sleep when Ryan lay down on the other bed to rest.

Ryan could not believe how tired he was. It seemed like days since the cocktail party even though it was not even twenty-four hours.

Ryan awoke when Nancy came back at 5:30 p.m. Nancy looked rested and Ryan knew she had needed the break. He also felt much better after his nap. Nancy had packed a small bag for Ryan with a few necessities he had asked for since he was definitely spending the night with his wife.

Going into the bathroom, Ryan freshened up before going to meet Cassie for dinner. Nancy told Ryan she wanted to stay for awhile and that he should take his time. He then told the nurse he would be down in the cafeteria if she needed him for any reason. Nancy smiled at Ryan and told him to enjoy his dinner. She then went and sat down next to Joyce and held her hand.

Cassie was so happy to see Ryan come through the cafeteria doors that she gave him a long hard hug not caring who might see them.

"Oh, Ryan, I'm so sorry Joyce is sick." Ryan knew Cassie meant what she said and it made him love her all the more.

"Cassie, I know you know there is no love between Joyce and me anymore but I do care about her. I just hate to see her suffer like this. After the doctor pointed out the soothing effect I seem to have on her, I knew I had to stay with her."

"Ryan, that's exactly why I love you so much. You are so compassionate towards Joyce. We both know as much as we love each other we have responsibilities to other people and we don't let our love take away from those responsibilities. The hardest thing will be for me to leave you in October but

I know I have to go back to Jim. I can't leave him anymore than you can leave Joyce."

Ryan could see love as well as despair in Cassie's eyes as she told him how she felt and he had an unbearable ache in his heart. He did not know what he was going to do when Cassie left him and the only thing that made it more bearable was the fact he knew Cassie felt the same way about him. He realized, however, that even though they both felt as they did, it would not make it any easier when their time came to separate.

Two hours sped by and Cassie knew Ryan had to go back to Joyce. Once again she hugged him hard as they left the cafeteria. Cassie told Ryan she would be back at 8:00 a.m. for breakfast. When he protested, she gave him an astonished look and he felt his heart melt.

"Have a good night, love," Ryan told Cassie as he kissed her good-bye.

"Ryan, I know this sounds terrible with Joyce upstairs in the condition she's in but I sure wish I could sneak into that bed with you."

"It will be a lot easier for me to sleep in that bed imagining you there with me. I'll see you at breakfast, Cassie."

Ryan went back upstairs to Joyce and sent Nancy back to the condo. He told the nurse she could stay overnight tomorrow night as long as Joyce was doing better. Ryan had no idea when he was talking to the nurse that he would not be leaving the hospital the next evening.

# Chapter Twenty-Five

Joyce's pneumonia worsened during the night. Ryan could hardly stand listening to her tortured breathing and the coughing she could not seem to control. He spent most of the night sitting in a chair next to Joyce holding her hand. The physician on duty tried some new medication after consulting with her doctor. He hoped it would better relieve Joyce's condition since the other medications had not seemed to do much for her.

By morning Joyce was totally unaware of her surroundings. Joyce's physician brought other doctors in for more opinions on methods of treatment. Ryan was exhausted but he was too worried about Joyce to sleep.

Nancy called about 7:00 a.m. and was shocked to learn that Joyce's pneumonia had worsened. Ryan asked her to bring him some fresh clothes and more toiletries. He was afraid to leave Joyce's side.

Ryan also called Cassie and told her what was happening. He told her he wanted to eat with her sometime that day but he would call her and let her know when to come to the hospital. At the moment he did not want to leave Joyce. He thought it was important that Joyce know he was there if she woke up.

After Nancy arrived with a fresh change of clothes for Ryan, he went into the bathroom and took a shower and changed clothes. Nancy sat next to Joyce and stroked her hand as she had the night before. Since Joyce's condition remained unchanged, Ryan lay down in the other bed. He found he could not keep his eyes open any longer. Within two minutes on the bed, Ryan was fast asleep.

It was noon when Ryan awoke. Nancy was still sitting next to Joyce and Ryan could tell nothing had changed. He told Nancy to go down and get lunch. When she started to protest he told her he had nothing to eat since dinner the night before and he wanted her to bring him a sandwich when she finished eating.

As Ryan held Joyce's hand, he called Jeremy and told him what was happening. After the call to Jeremy, the doctor came back in to check on Joyce. He was encouraged that her condition had not worsened in the last few hours. She was a long way from being out of the woods but the doctor was hopeful she would get better.

It was not long before Nancy was back. Ryan told her what the doctor had said and took his sandwich out in the hallway so he could call Cassie while he ate. Ryan told Cassie if things stayed the same he would meet her again in the cafeteria for dinner like the night before.

Nothing changed that afternoon. Ryan lay down on the bed but found he could not sleep so decided to start reading a book Nancy had brought along. The nurse sat in the chair next to Joyce's bed and also spent most of the afternoon reading.

At 5:00 p.m. Cassie met Ryan once again for dinner. He wanted to go a little earlier than the night before because not only was he hungry but he also wanted Nancy to get home at a reasonable hour since she had been sitting in the hospital all day.

"This is starting to become a habit," Ryan joked to Cassie as they hugged each other.

"Oh, Ryan, you look so tired. I wish there was something I could do to help."

"Trust me, Cassie, just seeing you and being with you for a little while, means so much to me."

After dinner they went outside and sat on a bench under one of the large shade trees that surrounded the hospital grounds. They held hands, not saying a lot to each other. Just being together seemed to help both of them.

When Ryan got up to re-enter the hospital, Cassie hugged him a little longer and harder before she left him to return home. She missed him but she was comforted knowing he would be sitting with her if she were the one who was sick. Cassie wondered if Joyce appreciated how wonderful Ryan was to her. She felt a terrible ache inside knowing there was not much she could do to assist Ryan.

Nancy left right after Ryan got back. She was ready for dinner since it was close to 7:00 p.m. and the strain of the last two days was taking a toll on her, also. Ryan told her not to come until 8:00 a.m. the next morning. He told her if Joyce did not get any worse that night, he wanted to go home and clean up and he had some calls to make to the station.

Joyce's uneven breathing continued but her condition remained unchanged that night and Ryan was able to sleep through the night for the first time in days. Just as Nancy arrived, the doctor also came in.

"You're here early," Ryan told the doctor.

"I had an early morning surgery so I thought I would look in on Joyce. I think it's a very good sign that Joyce's condition has remained constant. With her health issues she could have easily gotten much worse. I think you'll start to see a dramatic improvement in her condition as she wakes up."

Ryan breathed a sigh of relief and gave Nancy a big smile. He was much happier as he left the hospital for the first time in three days. He called Cassie and asked her to meet him for breakfast in an hour and a half.

After cleaning up and making his calls, Ryan met Cassie at their favorite breakfast restaurant, the same place they had breakfast after church on Sundays. Cassie's heart soared when she saw how relieved Ryan looked.

"Ryan, you are the most amazing, wonderful man in the whole world," Cassie said as she pressed tightly against him on the street in front of the restaurant.

"What brought that on, Cassie?"

"Oh, just because," Cassie answered as she kissed him tenderly before going in to have breakfast.

It was not long before it was time for Ryan to go. "Joyce still isn't awake so I'll be spending tonight at the hospital again, Cassie. Can you come about 5:00 and have dinner with me?"

"I hate to admit it but I think I'm beginning to like that cafeteria food," Cassie said as she smiled at him.

Ryan kissed Cassie a little longer and hugged her a little harder. She could feel the relief coursing through his body that his wife seemed to be on the mend.

It was after lunch when Joyce opened her eyes for the first time since Saturday. She saw Nancy sitting beside her and Ryan on the other bed with a book in hand. Joyce did not say anything but she had a frown when she looked at Ryan. It was not long before she went back to sleep but this time her breathing was much easier.

"Nancy, I don't understand why Joyce looked at me like that."

"Ryan, it's probably a natural reaction on her part. She knows you've spent the last few days at her side while she has been so sick. I know she was scared because she told me so when she first came into the hospital. Now, she feels guilty that you were so kind to her when she is never very kind to you. The way she copes with her illness is to try and drive you away. It upsets her when you are there to support her when she's so ill, even though she wants you to be with her. It's a shame she can't appreciate what you do for her."

Nancy asked Ryan to go out in the hallway with her for a moment. "I don't mean to overstep my bounds with you, Ryan. I wouldn't say anything except you asked my input first. No one could be kinder to a wife than you have been these last few years. You know as well as I do Joyce feels guilty for the way she treats you but she can't change the way she is. Joyce is very resentful of the fact that you have remained her husband after the way she acted towards you before as well as after her accident. She will never soften her attitude no matter what you do for her. Joyce needs to hate someone so she can live with herself. Don't ever feel guilty for any happiness you have found. You deserve all the good that comes to you."

Ryan felt a little choked up by what Nancy had said to him and as he hugged the nurse, all he could say was, "Thank you, Nancy for all you do for Joyce and me. You'll never know how much I appreciate you."

"We better go back and check on Joyce," Nancy said as she felt a tear come to her eye. Nancy had always admired Ryan and she was glad she had finally been given a chance to let him know what a wonderful man she felt he was. Nancy had been a nurse for almost forty years and she had never met a nicer person than Ryan. She really hoped he could find lasting happiness with the woman he was living with. She had no idea Cassie was also married and had a similar situation to Ryan's. Nancy would have been pained to know how star crossed-Cassie and Ryan were.

At 5:00 p.m. Ryan went to the cafeteria to meet Cassie for the third night in a row. Not caring if anyone was looking, they kissed passionately and hugged each other tight when they met by the door. After going through the cafeteria line they found a table near a window.

"Sometimes you forget what the world looks like when you are in a hospital room all day, Cassie."

"At least you've had a chance to catch up on your reading, Ryan."

"Something happened this afternoon, Cassie."

"Is Joyce alright?"

"Yes, but the way she looked at me when she woke up gave me the feeling she hated me." Ryan then told Cassie what the nurse said about Joyce's feelings toward him.

"Nancy is right, Ryan. Sometimes Jim says mean things to me or gives me a look like he almost hates me. I finally realized it was because he was jealous I had my health and he didn't. I knew I had to ignore his feelings but sometimes it is difficult to take care of someone when you feel they just expect it while not really appreciating what you are doing for them. Jim's demeanor is almost a 'serve me or I'll emotionally abuse you' attitude."

"Even though we've spent it in this hospital, I am so glad we have this time to be together, Cassie. There are no words I can say to tell you how much I love you."

Once again they went outside and sat on the bench and held hands. Cassie, wanting to get Ryan's mind off of Joyce's condition, began telling him about some new places she had been researching for their next little trips. Ryan smiled as he listened to her and all too soon it was time for him to go back to his wife.

"I hate to leave you, Cassie but Nancy needs to go home and have dinner. "I worry what a strain this has been on her, too. I know we'll all be happy when this hospital stay is behind us."

Once again they kissed passionately and then Cassie watched as Ryan went back into the hospital. Turning to go to the car, a couple passing by her noted the sadness they saw reflected in her face as she walked slowly back to the parking lot.

# Chapter Twenty-Six

After Nancy left, Ryan went right to sleep. Today had been Monday and he had a feeling that even though he would be spending a couple more days at the hospital, this would be the last night he would be sleeping there. He could hardly wait to tell Cassie he would be with her tomorrow night.

The next three days seemed to fly by. Ryan was able to go back to Cassie's Tuesday night as he had hoped. Their days settled into a routine.

After breakfast, Ryan went into the office for about an hour and then arrived at the hospital around 11:00 a.m. just in time for the doctor's rounds. He would then stay with Joyce until about 5:00 p.m. Joyce got upset with him on Tuesday afternoon, but after what Nancy had told him Ryan decided he did not want to listen anymore to Joyce's griping and wanted to nip her anger in the bud.

"Look, Joyce, I know you're irritated that I sit here all afternoon but be reasonable. Nancy is here at 8:00 until 11:00 when I come to give her a break. When I leave at 5:00 she comes back and sits with you until 9:00. Personally, I don't care what you think about me but you should have some compassion for Nancy. She cares about you and I don't want her to get sick from taking care of you."

After Ryan's talk with Joyce they settled in to a limited peace. She sat and watched TV and Ryan read. He discovered if he did not try to make conversation with her, things stayed on a more even keel.

The doctor was pleased with Joyce's recovery and felt she could go home on Friday. Ryan was thrilled. Not only could he hardly wait to get back to his life with Cassie but the strain of sitting with Joyce every day while they pretended they liked each other was getting to him. At least with Joyce back to her fighting self, Ryan felt more secure that she was well on the way to recovery.

Jane was going to be back from her cruise on Saturday and Ryan and Cassie had asked Jeremy if the four of them could go to dinner together Saturday night. Ryan assumed Jane would go back to Minneapolis on Sunday.

"You know," Jeremy told the two of them. "I like Jane. Oh, it's nothing serious but we sort of talked about spending a few days together when she comes back from her cruise. She planned to stay in your guestroom, Cassie because originally Ryan told me that you two were going away for a few days. I suppose because of Joyce's condition you've decided to cancel your trip?"

Ryan looked at Cassie. "Joyce is much better and I think you wanted to go someplace just a few hours away, right Cassie?"

"Yes, I didn't plan to go too far, Ryan."

"I don't see any need to cancel our trip. It might do us some good to get away for three or four days after all the stress we've been through this last week."

"I know the perfect trip, Ryan. The Victoria Clipper is running a special to San Juan Island including whale watching. I really wanted to stay there a couple of nights. If Joyce is okay we could leave on Sunday."

Jane returned on Saturday and was shocked to discover what had happened the week she was gone. She did give Jeremy a happy look when he told her about Cassie and Ryan's vacation plan. She had been thinking all week about Jeremy and was looking forward to spending a few days with him when Cassie and Ryan left on their trip.

Jane told herself it was only because she wanted to talk with Jeremy about Ryan and Cassie's future but she was beginning to wonder if she was being honest with herself. She was curious why Jeremy had only kissed her cheek the night of the cocktail party, especially since Cassie had told her about all the women who came in and out of his life. She decided she wanted to get to know Jeremy a little better.

Jane also knew she needed to be a little stand-offish with Jeremy. They would talk about her trip and Cassie and Ryan but she decided she would cool it as far as getting too close to him too quickly. Jane was wondering if having a long-term affair with Jeremy, even in a long distance setting, might not be a lot of fun.

Because of her decision, Jane had Jeremy take her back to the apartment shortly after Cassie and Ryan had gone home after dinner on Saturday night. She told Jeremy she was a little tired from her cruise. Jeremy was disappointed she did not ask him in but they made plans to meet for brunch the next day. Jane told him she was looking forward to brunch as she gave him a quick kiss on the cheek at Cassie's apartment door as he had done on their previous two encounters.

When Jane mentioned the kiss on the cheek after the party to the two of them, Ryan wondered what had come over his friend. He did not believe Jeremy had ever given just a quick kiss on the cheek since he had started dating. The situation developing between Jane and Jeremy was beginning to intrigue him.

# Chapter Twenty-Seven

As Sunday dawned, Cassie and Ryan walked down the hill from Cassie's condo to the waterfront. They went into the ferry office at Pier 69 and stood in line for tickets on the Victoria Clipper for their three-hour journey to San Juan Island.

As they walked down the gangway to board the vessel, they entered the bottom level and saw booths and tables around large windows. The Clipper was a catamaran that rode on top of the water. Most of the ship rode above the waterline, which made it much easier to handle and produced a faster and smoother ride. There was a small snack bar on the lower level offering food and drinks including free coffee, tea and water.

The upper deck had tables and booths along the windows and theater like seating amidship. At the bow of this deck the master, mate, and chief engineer could be seen at work on the bridge. Finally, one more level up was an open-air sundeck.

Cassie and Ryan headed to the sundeck and sat at the stern of the boat. From this vantage point, they could see the wake left by the jet engines as they gazed at the Seattle skyline receding as the boat cruised farther from the shore. They watched Mount Rainier disappeared as they traveled north up Puget Sound past many small islands. There were over seven hundred islands in the San Juan chain although only four of them had year round residents.

Because San Juan Island was just south of Vancouver Island, the United States and Britain had both laid claim to the island with Germany finally settling the dispute by awarding possession to the United States in 1872. Cassie and Ryan's first stop on San Juan Island would be Friday Harbor for a two-hour lunch and shopping visit. This was the largest town in the island group and the most often visited by tourists.

When they left Friday Harbor, which was on the eastern side of the island, they would go whale watching before heading to Roche Harbor on the western side of the island. They planned to spend two nights at the Hotel de Haro in that small village where almost four hundred yachts anchored during the summer months.

Speeding by several mostly uninhabited islands on their way to Friday Harbor, they saw sea lions, eagles and cormorants. Cassie enjoyed watching the cormorants sitting on the buoys with their wings stretched out. They were black birds that looked like geese and Ryan explained that they could not fly with wet wings so after diving for food they would stretch out their wings to dry them before flying.

At Friday Harbor, they strolled casually through the streets window-shopping before having a salmon lunch special at one of the seafood restaurants overlooking the waterfront. It was all too soon before their time was up and they heard the whistle signaling their return to the boat.

As they circled the south side of San Juan Island and turned north again, they entered the Strait of Georgia. To their left they could see the Olympic Peninsula with the snow-capped Olympic Mountains as a backdrop. In the distance across the strait to their right was Vancouver Island including the city of Victoria they had visited on their first journey together.

They headed toward a number of other boats arranged in a large circle. The orcas lived all year in this area and the pods were even named. The captain commented that the boats had to stay one hundred yards away from the whales so as not to stress them.

Cassie and Ryan both had binoculars and they could see the waterspouts and an occasional whale jumping out of the water. The captain explained that whales jumped up hitting their tales in the water as they came back down. That was called breaching and it was an incredible sight watching the whale jumping into the air. Everyone oohed and aahed whenever that occurred.

As the boats continued to circle around the Orcas, the sun dancing on the ocean gave the water the appearance of thousands of sparkling diamonds. The whales continued to swim in lazy circles but all of a sudden one of the Orcas broke from the pod and made a beeline straight for their boat.

Just before getting to the boat the Orca turned quickly in a direction parallel to the boat. Cassie and Ryan looked at each other as an Orca about twenty-five feet long swam along side them briefly. It was a sight that took their breath away. Cassie knew it was an experience she would never forget.

Ryan put his arm around Cassie and she rested her head on his shoulder as the boat headed for Roche Harbor. Cassie began thinking of her time with Ryan. Minnesota seemed to be in another world, a world of unreality. Being with Ryan was reality for her, now.

Cassie would often remember this wonderful afternoon that was now so deeply a part of her. She could not even conceive of her life without Ryan. Days like this made her feel their time together was timeless but she knew that was not true. Soon they would have to leave each other forever. Cassie remembered a saying "We do not remember days…we remember moments." She knew this moment in time would be a part of her for as long as she lived.

# Chapter Twenty-Eight

Cassie and Ryan watched as the Clipper came alongside the wharf and moored. As they walked a maze of piers to the shore and over to their hotel, they rolled their suitcases past all the yachts that were berthed in the harbor.

As they exited the boat on the last pier, to their right they saw a café, laundromat and grocery store. To the left about a half a block away was an older building that housed a restaurant and bar with patio seating overlooking the water. Beyond the restaurant were a church, an outdoor pool and several cabins.

Directly in front of them were the beautiful formal Victorian gardens where many weddings took place and beyond the gardens the hotel. All of the buildings on the property were painted white with dark green trim. Cassie knew both the hotel and restaurant would have breathtaking views of the sunset.

Two brothers who discovered lime quarries in the area bought Roche Harbor in 1881 and the little village had thrived with that industry. The hotel was built in 1886 and had twenty-two rooms. It was on the National Register of Historic Places and Cassie fell in love with the place as soon as they walked into the lobby. Theodore Roosevelt had stayed in the hotel and a page containing his signature in the original guest book was framed on a wall near the hotel desk.

To the left as they entered was a door that went into a gift shop. To the right of the desk was a large fireplace with two easy chairs. Just past the fireplace around the corner was a narrow staircase. The hotel had three floors but no elevator.

The second and third floors contained the guestrooms. Balconies ran the entire length of the hotel on the second and third floors overlooking the side that faced the water. Cassie and Ryan carried their suitcases up to the third floor. Their room was at the end of the corridor overlooking the water.

The walls in the hallway were totally covered in old fashion looking wallpaper. The thin carpet runner had an 'old-time' look to it and Cassie could feel the bumps in the floor from the wood settling over the years. The middle rooms had sinks but guests had to go across the hall to the bathrooms.

Cassie and Ryan had chosen an end room with a bathroom. As they opened their door, Cassie sighed with pleasure. There was a queen-sized four-poster bed and two stuffed chairs next to a small fireplace. There was a door that led out to the balcony with chairs so they could sit outside and watch the sunsets.

The walls and doors were completely covered in wallpaper although a different pattern than the hallway. Hanging on hooks attached to the outside of the closet door were two white terry cloth bathrobes with the hotel logo imprinted on them. Cassie also noted the absence of a television set.

The bathroom, in a separate area, held a huge old bathtub with feet. Cassie wondered why the Pacific Northwest offered such large bathtubs. She was not going to complain, though. It was the same size and look like the one at Gray-cliff and Cassie knew she and Ryan would enjoy their time soaking in the tub.

Cassie turned to Ryan and said, "This hotel is absolutely perfect! How do we luck out and find these places? After seeing the Orcas this afternoon I didn't think we could top that experience but I have a sense of belonging here, Ryan, like I had at the B&B."

"I never knew this little village was here. If it wasn't for the special promotion the Clipper was running we might never have found this place. I have that same sense of belonging here too, Cassie.

It's amazing I have lived in Seattle my entire life and this summer I've discovered so many places I never knew about until I met you and we started exploring. While you are unpacking I'll walk over to the grocery store and buy a bottle of wine. It's too early for dinner but we can sit on the balcony and have a drink while we watch the Clipper leave."

Cassie watched through the hotel window as Ryan walked to the little grocery store. Her heart ached as she saw him walking away from her. Cassie knew she had to let go of her feeling of potential loss and just enjoy Ryan while she was with him. It seemed like such a bittersweet time for her. Their time together seemed so precious.

Ryan was so thoughtful and Cassie knew she would miss that about him, too. Even during their good days, Jim would never have gone out to buy a bottle of wine. That was an errand he would have sent Cassie on.

Returning with the wine in hand, Cassie opened the door as Ryan came down the hallway.

"Are you waiting for me, sweetheart?"

Cassie did not respond. She simply circled her arms around his neck as he entered the room. As she kissed him, she kicked the door closed with her foot and began moving slowly towards the bed. Ryan barely had a chance to set the wine bottle down on the nightstand as Cassie pulled him down on top of her.

"Ryan, let's watch the Clipper leave tomorrow," Cassie said as they fell together onto the bed.

Cassie shivered as she saw the longing in Ryan's eyes as he descended on her. After spending the nights in the hospital watching over Joyce, Ryan felt he could not be with Cassie enough. Her embrace was like a drug to him. Cassie was so open with her affection towards him and he had lived in such an empty void for so long he marveled at her need of him.

Ryan felt an emotion he never dreamed he could experience again. He could not help but worry about the emptiness that would grow inside him when Cassie left. Everything about her was alluring and fascinating. And he knew, even though his life would be agony without Cassie, he would be a better man for having loved her.

After Cassie and Ryan had their fill of each other, they sat on the balcony and watched the sun set as they drank their wine. Since it was during the week, they discovered a couple of the second floor rooms had been rented out but they were the only guests on the third floor. Consequently, they had the entire balcony to themselves.

After the sun set, they walked hand in hand through the gardens to the more casual restaurant attached to the bar area. Since they had such a big lunch, they each ordered the crab bisque soup and a salad. The soup was outstanding and Cassie told Ryan they had to get past the fat grams she was certain the cream based soup contained. Ryan just laughed at her when she told him that.

As they walked back to the hotel after dinner, they noticed how much cooler the temperature was with the sun down.

"Cassie, I think we should try out that tub to warm up."

"Ryan, I swear you are getting addicted to bathtubs," Cassie said laughing at him.

"I have to tell you Cassie, I don't remember ever taking a bath in my life although I probably did as a young child. But there's a lot to be said for a nice hot bath. Especially, when the tubs are as deep as the ones we have encountered."

"Let's go break in that tub, Ryan."

After their bath, Ryan started a fire and they climbed into bed. And that was how Cassie and Ryan spent their first night at Roche Harbor, entwined in each other's arms, wondering how they had been so lucky to have found each other.

# Chapter Twenty-Nine

As Cassie awoke she saw Ryan looking at her. "You look radiant this morning, Cassie."

Cassie leaned over and kissed Ryan. His words literally stirred her soul with passion. "Ryan, do you know you make me believe in the possibility of happiness for us? I don't know when but I believe someday we will be together when the time is right. I think I need to believe that or I might not be able to go on without you."

"We will definitely be together someday, Cassie. I believe that with all my heart, too. What are we going to do today, love?" Ryan gave Cassie a leering look.

"Ryan, you're incorrigible. After breakfast we are going for a walk. I read about an interesting mausoleum not too far away, a memorial to the island's founder. It's supposed to look like something out of a Greek myth. There's also an outside sculpture park we can wander around. And naturally, there are trails all over this side of the island we can explore."

"I wasn't thinking about the walking tour you had planned for us, Cassie."

"Really? I guess you wanted something else from me?" Cassie murmured to Ryan as she covered her head with the blanket and began kissing her way down Ryan's chest.

Ryan moaned as Cassie continued kissing him. This was definitely a moment that took his breath away. Ryan decided he would lay back and let Cassie have her way with him. He knew later in the afternoon it would be his turn to have his way with her.

Ryan smiled to himself as he thought what Cassie would say if she knew what he was thinking. Cassie would say he was a very wicked man and he laughed with pleasure thinking about her reaction to his thoughts. Cassie raised her head from under the covers at his laugh.

"I'm afraid to ask what you're thinking," she said smiling before she returned her attention back to what she was doing to Ryan.

When they were finished, Ryan went downstairs and brought back coffee from the pot that was always filled in the lobby.

"I suppose this means it's my turn tomorrow."

"No, I think I want to bring you coffee in bed every morning. I like doing things for you, even if it's something simple like bringing you coffee." Cassie felt a tear in her eye at his words.

After dressing, the two of them went over to the cafe that was attached to the grocery store. They both decided on the huckleberry pancakes. There was a definite chill in the air but there was a potbelly stove with a fire going in the cafe that warmed the room. Both of them wanted a bigger breakfast to fortify themselves for the long walk they planned to take.

After breakfast they went into the grocery store and bought bottles of water, fruit and some power bars for later in the morning. Next, they stopped in the lobby and picked up a brochure on the hiking trails around the area before setting off on their day's journey.

First, Cassie and Ryan wandered through the outside sculpture garden that contained over one hundred sculptures by local artists. From there they tramped across a small airfield and through some woods to the mausoleum.

After reading the local history and how the Pig War between the Americans and British set the stage for United

States occupation of the island, they wandered to the British camp to look around. While at the British camp they ate their power bars and fruit as they sat on an overlook of Haro Straight. After a twenty minute rest they started back. It was close to 3:00 p.m. by the time they returned to the hotel.

"Cassie, why don't we go sit on the patio by the bar and have a glass of wine?"

"That sounds like a good idea and after we've rested we can walk out on the docks and look at some of the yachts moored there."

As they got close to the patio Cassie heard Ryan exclaim, "Wow! Jack, what are you doing here and how are you?"

Cassie watched as Ryan went and hugged a tall man with very bright red hair. Even though he was an older man, his freckles made him look much younger than he really was.

"Cassie, this is my brother-in-law, Jack. He was married to my sister, Anne, but Jack moved to Florida after she died five years ago."

Cassie said hello to Jack and he took her hand and shook it with such warmth that Cassie liked him immediately.

"Ryan, I decided to come back to Seattle for a little while. I've never really gotten used to those Florida summers. I had dinner with Jeremy last week and he caught me up on your life and about Cassie here." As Jack turned to look again at Cassie, he said, "You know everyone is so glad Ryan has found you, Cassie."

Jack did not miss the momentary flash of pain he saw cross Cassie's eyes as she thanked him.

"Ryan, I tried calling you on Sunday. I wanted to wait until everything with Joyce had settled down. You know there was never any love lost between Joyce and me. Nancy gave me Cassie's number but then told me you were out of town for a few days. I asked Nancy if you were on your boat but she said you sold it right after I left. So, I decided to take a little trip until I knew you would be back. I can't believe we ran into each other like this."

Cassie turned to Ryan and said, "You used to own a boat?"

"Yes, I had a boat. I kept it a few years after Joyce's accident but I became so busy with Joyce's medical problems and the work at the radio stations that there wasn't a lot of time to use it. Besides it wasn't much fun going out alone so I finally sold it."

"Did you ever come up here to Roche Harbor, Ryan?"

"No, Jack, this harbor was redesigned for all these boats after I sold mine. Since I haven't been boating in awhile, I had no idea this place even existed."

"How long are you planning on staying at the hotel, Ryan?"

"This is our last night. We leave tomorrow afternoon on the Victoria Clipper back to Seattle."

"I have a great idea. Do you and Cassie need to be back tomorrow night, Ryan?"

"No, not really."

"Why don't you two come with me tomorrow instead of going on the Clipper? I plan to slip over to Orcas Island tomorrow afternoon and sail back in to Seattle on Wednesday afternoon. That would give me a chance to get to know Cassie a little better."

"You know, Ryan, if we go with Jack that would give Jeremy and Jane an extra day together."

"Who's Jane?"

Cassie smiling at him said, "Jack, let me catch you up on Jeremy and Jane."

Ryan started to laugh. He had always liked Jack. Jack had been devoted to his sister, Anne, and even more so when she had been diagnosed with ovarian cancer. The two of them had gone through a lot in the year before Anne died. Ryan had been very sad when Jack moved to Florida but knew he needed to escape the painful memories of losing a wife he loved dearly.

"Listen, why don't you come over to my boat about 7:00 for cocktails? Then if I'm not intruding on you two, I'll treat you to dinner in the restaurant."

"That sounds like an excellent plan as long as you let me treat you to dinner tomorrow night."

Cassie wrote down the slip number and directions to Jack's boat, Sail Away, as she and Ryan said good-bye to him.

When they got back to their room Cassie told Ryan she thought a nap might fit into their schedule quite nicely.

"Oh, no you don't. You walked me all over this island today and I have the aching muscles to prove it. Since I don't like to bathe alone and was looking forward to a long soak in our tub, I need you to reschedule your nap plans."

Cassie felt an intoxicated stirring pass through her at the idea of another bath with Ryan. "I can't believe after all this time we've been together I still get excited at the prospect of getting into a bathtub with you."

"Well, I've been thinking about it for the last two hours and I can't take it anymore," Ryan told her as he propelled Cassie towards the bathroom.

By the time they climbed out of the bathtub they really did not have time for a nap. Ryan held Cassie in his arms as they lay in their bed. He told Cassie all about his sister Anne and also about Jack. Soon, it was time to go to Jack's boat for cocktails, and Cassie felt like she knew Jack extremely well after her talk with Ryan.

Spending the evening together turned out to be quite pleasant. Jack served drinks while they watched the sunset from the upper deck of the yacht. At dusk they walked over to the restaurant for dinner. Cassie and Ryan looked at the menu and then looked at each other and laughed.

"What's up with you two?"

Ryan explained they had no lunch and it was getting late. He and Cassie realized they were so hungry they could not decide what to order. Even though she could not eat all the food, Ryan knew Cassie would order one of everything if she did not get something in her stomach soon.

Jack looked at them. "You know Anne and I used to read each other's minds like that."

Cassie looked at Ryan and trembled. Jack saw the sadness reflected in both of their eyes and realized how much they loved each other. He was sorry they could not be together forever. He knew that neither of them would ever be happy again unless they found a way back to each other.

Jack decided he was meant to yacht back to Seattle for the summer. He might need to stay a little longer than he had planned. He realized Ryan was going to need a lot of support when Cassie went back to Minnesota. The sadness was forgotten as soon as their waiter served the appetizers Ryan had ordered.

"Let's dig in," Cassie said as she took the first helping.

Jack laughed at her and pretty soon he was telling the two of them stories of his life in Florida. It seemed as if the night flew by even quicker than possible.

Before they knew it, dinner was over. It had been an enjoyable evening and Cassie and Ryan both looked forward to spending the next two days with Jack.

"What time are we leaving tomorrow, Jack?" Ryan asked as they left the restaurant.

"Why don't you plan to come aboard after 11:00? I usually stay up late reading and that way I know I'll be awake and ready to go."

Cassie and Ryan said goodnight to Jack and they headed back to the hotel as Jack ambled down the pier to his boat.

# Chapter Thirty

For some strange reason Cassie did not hear Ryan leave the room the next morning but she smelled the coffee as he put the cup down on the bedside table next to her. Cassie put her arms around Ryan as she drew him back under the covers.

"Ryan, I can't tell you how lucky I am that you came into my life. It's hard to believe I can feel such happiness simply being with you. You will always be special to me even when we go our separate ways. And I'll never stop thinking about you until the day I die."

Cassie could feel the tears in her eyes as Ryan kissed her passionately. Like the hot chocolate at the B&B, the coffee was quickly forgotten and would be very cold before she was able to give it another thought.

The morning passed very quickly and soon it was time to check out of the hotel. Cassie turned and looked back at the building as they wheeled their suitcases down the pier towards Jack's boat.

"Ryan, I'll never come back to this place without thinking about our time here with each other."

"I know exactly how you feel, Cassie. After you leave I think it will be too painful for me to return to any of the places we have visited together this summer for a long time."

Cassie thought she saw tears in Ryan's eyes as he put his sunglasses on and she had to look away from him as she felt herself choke up.

The mood lightened considerably when they reached Jack's boat. He was up on the deck to greet them and showed them to his guest bedroom.

"This sure is a nice boat, Jack."

"Thanks, Cassie. It's given me a few years of pleasure. Anne and I always talked about having a yacht and going south in the winter and coming back here to the Seattle area in the summer. I'm sorry we never had the chance to do that."

"You've never found anyone else you wanted to be with, Jack?"

"No, Ryan. I had such a special relationship with your sister and I find I compare every woman I meet to her. No one seems to measure up. However, I have many friends and we have lots of good times together. I think sometimes you're meant to journey alone."

Ryan smiled to himself thinking how he once thought the same thing. Maybe Jack would not spend the rest of his life alone. Ryan knew from experience that someone could come along when you least expected it.

As they sailed back around San Juan Island they saw all the boats circled around the Orcas again. Jack pulled his boat into the circle and they watched the whales playing in the water before heading between Lopez and Shaw Islands to their evening destination, Orcas Island. There was a yacht basin that Jack was headed for and it was not long before the boat was moored.

The evening was like the previous one although this time they had company. Jack invited some of the people from the boats docked next to them to come over for drinks. Cassie met a lot of interesting people as they sipped cocktails. The party broke up after the sun set and the three of them made their way to the restaurant on shore. This time Ryan paid for dinner.

Cassie could understand why Ryan liked Jack so much. The more she got to know Jack the fonder she became of him. She was sure Anne's last year of life had been a lot easier with someone as thoughtful as Jack taking care of her. However, it was probably also hard on Anne knowing she would soon be taken from this wonderful man. Cassie could sense the anguish Jack had felt losing his wife. Even after all this time she could still feel the sadness surrounding him over the loss of Anne.

After dinner, Cassie and Ryan sat out on the deck of the boat holding hands and gazing at the stars. "You know, Ryan, I could very easily get use to this way of life. Owning a boat and sailing through the islands is a lot of fun. And you meet very nice people at these yacht basins."

"Spending this time with Jack made me realize how much I miss my boat, Cassie. I might have to invest in another one. It would be fun next summer sailing through these islands and making my way up the Inside Passage of Alaska."

"Oh, don't you dare go to Alaska without me Ryan. I've never been there."

"Someday when we're together again Cassie we'll go to Alaska on our boat."

"It's always good to have dreams, Ryan. To me, the day we stop dreaming is the day we die." Cassie put her head on Ryan's shoulder and thought about the trip to Alaska and what fun they could have together.

Cassie felt a terrible ache in her heart at the thought that this was one dream that would probably never come true. But since Cassie always had a positive view of life she decided she would think about Alaska and other trips they might take together. Maybe if she focused on their being together, someday it would really be true.

After sitting there a little longer they got up and went to their cabin. The splashing of the water against the boat was a very soothing sound to Cassie and Ryan. They snuggled up close to each other in their bed and it was not long before the two of them fell asleep in each other's arms.

Neither of them heard Jack roaming around the boat. Jack felt like he had not had a decent night's sleep since Anne died. For some reason nights were the hardest for him. Jack also feared Ryan was going to discover the same thing would be true for him after Cassie left. He said a silent prayer that things would somehow work out for the two of them.

Jack slept until about 10:00 a.m. It had been after 4:00 a.m. before he had fallen asleep. It seemed lately, he could get along on less and less sleep.

The sun was shining brightly as Cassie and Ryan left the boat to have breakfast on shore. Then they took an hour walk along the beach. They looked forward to a little exercise since they knew they would be on the boat for several hours before they returned to Seattle.

# Chapter Thirty-One

As Jack and Ryan were untying the lines of the boat for their return from Orcas Island, Jeremy and Jane met for lunch at Anthony's Restaurant on the waterfront in downtown Seattle.

"I'm sure glad Ryan called yesterday to let us know they'd be gone another day, Jane."

"Me, too, Jeremy. From what you tell me, Ryan's brother-in-law, Jack sounds like a real character. The three of them will have a good time together."

"Yes, they will and it gives us an extra day to be together before they come back."

Jane now knew why Jeremy wanted another day with her without their friends around. The first two days they had spent together Jeremy had never even made a move to kiss her. Men had always been attracted to Jane and at first she thought it a little odd Jeremy had kept their relationship so cool, especially considering his reputation with women. However, their time together had taken a sudden turn two evenings before.

At first they had talked about Cassie and Ryan but finally decided they could do nothing about that situation except support their friends after Cassie left Seattle. Once they reached that conclusion, they began talking about people they knew and trips they had been on and never seemed at a loss for words.

Jeremy had some social engagements he could not avoid the first of the week, so he had invited Jane to go with him.

After the first night out together, Jeremy realized he and Jane were a lot alike. It had never bothered him with other women but he had a feeling an affair with Jane might turn more serious than he was willing to commit to. Besides, for the first time in a long time he discovered he was having fun with a woman just talking and being with her.

Jeremy always made sure he kept the conversation flowing while not saying anything of a personal nature. At first he could tell Jane was confused by his actions but two nights ago they began laughing about something they both had found funny. As Jane looked at him laughing, Jeremy realized they had become friends.

"Look Jane," Jeremy said as they stopped laughing. "Let me be frank. I really enjoy being with you and it seems we have a lot in common. But I am not willing to commit to anything serious. After I lost my wife, the pain was almost impossible to bear. I don't want to put myself in a position of possibly losing someone else I love and have to go through that pain again. However, I like you a lot and I feel like we could become very good friends. But I don't want you to be another notch in my belt and I don't want to be another notch in yours."

Jane was shocked by Jeremy's words. She was silent for several seconds and Jeremy began to think he might have hurt her feelings by speaking his mind like that. It seemed like forever before she responded.

"Jeremy, the more I think about what you just said the more I agree with you. I like the thought of having you as a special friend. And with no sexual relationship involved we don't have to worry about breaking up and never speaking to each other again."

"Jane, I have a feeling it will be important for us to talk in order to help Ryan and Cassie through the heartache they'll both feel when Cassie goes back to Minnesota."

Jane looked at Jeremy and nodded at his words. After their talk, the two of them realized that with any sexual tension removed from the equation they started having even more fun with each other.

Jane respected Jeremy a great deal for being so honest with her. For the first time in years she had the feeling she had found a man who would never lie to her like her husband had.

Jane's heart started to melt a little and she began to understand why it was so perfect Cassie and Ryan had become such good friends before becoming lovers. Jane had never felt she was a real friend to any of the men she had relationships with. Some she had liked more than others but she had never let her true feelings show with any of them.

She realized instinctively she and Jeremy could feel comfortable and be honest with each other. This was new territory for Jane and she knew she wound have to give some thought to this new developing relationship with Jeremy.

For now Jane decided it was enjoyable to be with each other and have fun together. When she told Jeremy as much, he agreed with her conclusion.

"I know this will seem strange at first, Jane, for both of us but I'm looking forward to having you as a friend."

Once again Jane nodded. "I never really thought about having a friendship with a man but I think I am going to enjoy our good times together even more now, Jeremy."

Having just finished a big accounting project for his boss and friend, the week before Jeremy had been under a lot of stress at the radio station. Since Ryan had taken a few days off to be with Cassie, Jeremy had decided to take some time off, too.

Jane and Jeremy went to lunch on Tuesday and then to a play that evening with some of Jeremy's friends. Although no one knew Jane very well, they came to like her and sensed something different about the way Jeremy treated her. His friends knew how badly he had taken his wife's death and were surprised at the difference they saw in him when he was with Jane.

Talking with each other about the "new" Jeremy, his friends wisely said nothing to him. They were not sure if he and Jane would ever become more than confidants but they wanted only happiness for him.

Despite his myriad of female companions, Jeremy's friends realized he was a very lonely man. Maybe Jane would help Jeremy find contentment again. It was obvious they were happy together and were very comfortable being in each other's company. They seemed to compliment each other and that often led to a healthy relationship whether sex was involved or not.

As they finished up lunch, Jeremy mentioned that he had some neighbors, the Mitchells, on Bainbridge Island who were having a party that evening.

"Why don't we go to the party, Jane? That way Ryan and Cassie will have some time alone when they get back to Seattle."

"Sounds like fun, Jeremy. I really want the two of them to have as much time alone together as possible. Let's go over to the Market and buy some flowers and wine for your friends. I hate coming empty handed to someone's house."

"That's a terrific idea, Jane. Do you mind staying over at my place tonight? I was thinking if you packed an overnight bag you could stay in my guest bedroom. Whenever Karen and Mike have a party it tends to go on into the wee hours and if we are enjoying ourselves I'd like to stay late. If you came back to the condo we'd have to take the ferry and that might involve waiting quite a long time since it doesn't run as frequently in the overnight hours."

Jane smiled at Jeremy. "You know what Ryan and Cassie are going to think when I don't come home tonight. It makes me almost want to laugh because they will be totally wrong."

"So you'll stay over at my house?"

"Yes, Jeremy, I will."

And so Cassie and Ryan came back to an empty apartment that evening. Cassie assumed things were heating up between

Jeremy and Jane and she was happy for them. Tomorrow she would find herself totally shocked when Jane told Cassie how her relationship with Jeremy was really evolving.

# Chapter Thirty-Two

It was very late when Jeremy and Jane got back to his place after the party. It was not until noon the next day before they caught the ferry back to Seattle.

"I really need to get into the office before Ryan fires me, Jane."

"You're teasing of course, Jeremy. You know he would never fire you. However, he's going to think you've been busy fooling around with me. I think you'll take a lot of ribbing about that."

"I don't know if Cassie and Ryan have plans for the evening but would you go to dinner with me if they are busy?"

"Yes, I'd love to, but I have a feeling they are going to want us to go out with them."

"You're probably right, Jane. Are you still planning on leaving on Sunday afternoon?"

"Yes, I really have to get back to Minnesota. My accountant has some papers I need to go over with him."

"We still have three days to be together. Linda and Harry are throwing that party tomorrow night over on Bainbridge. Do you still plan to go with me and stay at my house again? We could also go sailing on Saturday afternoon with some other friends."

For some reason, which neither of them understood, they wanted to spend as much time as possible with each other.

"You know, Jeremy, I'm beginning to like your guestroom." Jeremy just laughed when Jane said that.

After the ferry docked Jeremy dropped Jane off at the condo and kissing her good bye on the cheek then drove to the radio station. As Jeremy sat down at his desk, Ryan walked into his office.

"Well, I can only imagine what you've been up to these last few days, Jeremy."

"Stop leering at me Ryan. It's not what you think at all. Actually, Jane and I have become good friends. We enjoy each other's company and we've decided not to have a sexual relationship. I like Jane a lot and since she hasn't trusted men in a long time, I want to show her that not all men are like her ex. Little by little she's beginning to understand that."

Ryan's jaw almost dropped as he listened to Jeremy. Perhaps Jane and Jeremy were becoming good friends but Ryan had a feeling this could turn into a much more serious thing then the two of them realized. For now, he decided to let it go. If it did become anything more than friendship, Jane and Jeremy would have to deal with that as it developed.

"Are the four of us on for dinner tonight, Jeremy?"

"Sounds good to me, Ryan. Now, please go away and let me get some work done. The bad thing about taking time off is the way things pile up while you are away. And if I don't get busy the boss might fire me," Jeremy smiled as Ryan laughed.

"That's the truth, Jeremy. Talk to you later."

As Ryan closed the door to Jeremy's office, Cassie and Jane were having a very similar conversation.

"Jane, I can't believe you are not having a sexual fling with Jeremy. You've never missed out on such an opportunity before."

"It is rather strange for me. But I like having Jeremy as a friend. It's fun to be able to talk about things and not worry if he's going to read more into the conversation. Besides, Jeremy and I have decided that it's more important to be there for you and Ryan. I realize how devastating it will be for you to give Ryan up and go back to Minnesota."

"My life back there doesn't even seem real any more, Jane."

"Personally, I think you should divorce Jim and come live with Ryan for the rest of your lives. But, I know yours and Ryan's sense of duty would never allow that to happen."

"I'm just so thankful for the time we've been given, Jane. I'll have sweet memories forever of our time together here. Anyway, I don't want to talk about leaving Seattle. Ryan mentioned going to dinner at a new restaurant that has just opened up. Do you think Jeremy will go with us?"

Jane just shook her head. Cassie might eventually have sweet memories but Jane knew she would go through hell, first, as she reached acceptance of her loss of Ryan.

"I'm sure Jeremy will go with us tonight. We talked about dinner. I plan to leave Sunday afternoon. Tomorrow night, I'm going back to stay at Jeremy's. We have a party to go to and then on Saturday he has some friends who are taking us out in their boat. I'm not sure if I'll stay with Jeremy Saturday night but I'll definitely come back here no later than noon on Sunday. I need to leave by 2:00 for the airport."

Cassie smiled at the thought of Jane sleeping in Jeremy's guestroom. Later that afternoon Ryan went and checked on Joyce before coming back to the condo. He and Cassie decided it was foolish for him not to stay with her at the apartment. Jane would probably be at Jeremy's for the weekend and none of them was trying to hide their actions from each other.

Jeremy came directly from work to the condo. The four of them had some wine and chatted about Seattle happenings before leaving for the new restaurant Ryan wanted to try.

It was after midnight when Jeremy caught the ferry back to his home on Bainbridge Island. He told Jane he would meet her at the ferry landing the next day at noon. Jane decided to stay the weekend at his house so Cassie and Ryan could be alone. Besides, Jane liked Jeremy's friends and was looking forward to the parties and boating expeditions that were planned.

On Saturday night Cassie and Ryan went down to the waterfront for dinner before a concert. Summer concerts on the pier were a summer tradition in Seattle and after the concert they walked back to the condo hand in hand.

Before Cassie knew it, Jane was back and ready to leave for Minnesota. Jeremy and Ryan had both offered to take her to the airport but Jane decided to take a limo. With all the airport cruise traffic on weekends, Jane did not want them getting tied up in a mess taking her there. Cassie had tears in her eyes as she said good-bye to her friend. She wondered if Jeremy would not be missing Jane also.

"Jane, I want you to know how much it means having you as a friend and I'm so glad you came to visit." Jane smiled, remembering Cassie was not that excited at first.

As the new week started Cassie and Ryan fell back into their routine of going out to dinner and a couple of little daytrips. However, it was not long before the stress of their leaving each other would develop into trouble.

# Chapter Thirty-Three

It was the third week in August when Cassie got a call from Kit.

"Mom, Paul got an offer through his work to take the Inside Passage cruise to Alaska. Since we have two weeks off and the cruise is seven days we thought we'd spend some time visiting you. The cruise will be the week of Labor Day so we'll come a week from Thursday and then stay four days after we get back from our trip. Jane mentioned you have plenty of room in your place and I really want to see you. Besides Paul and I figured you probably know a lot about Seattle now and can show us the city."

Under normal circumstances Cassie would have been thrilled to see Kit and her husband but her time with Ryan was winding down so rapidly she felt a terrible pain in her heart as she told her daughter she was looking forward to her visit. Expecting Ryan to be sympathetic, Cassie was shocked when he got upset with her.

"Cassie we have so little time together. You can always be with your daughter."

"Ryan, what would I tell her? I could just see it now. Kit, you and Paul can't come visit me because I have a boyfriend who doesn't want you here."

"You make me sound so mean, Cassie."

"Ryan, I'm upset, too. I want to spend every moment with you since our time together is so short. But, I can't tell my daughter not to come."

Cassie was astounded by how angry Ryan was. He was being totally unreasonable and for some reason she could not make him understand. She could not believe they were fighting about Kit's visit. They made it through dinner without saying anything more on the subject but after dinner Ryan told Cassie he had to go check on Joyce. Cassie winced but said nothing when Ryan told her he would be sleeping at his place that night.

Cassie had tears in her eyes as Ryan went out the door. She was shocked that Ryan was making such a big deal out of Kit's visit. She wanted to be with him every possible moment since they only had six weeks left together. However, maybe it would be good for them to spend some days apart to just get use to not being with each other.

Cassie barely slept all night. She wanted to call Kit and tell her not to come but she knew she could not do that. By morning her thinking had changed. After spending a miserable night, she was now angry with Ryan.

Ryan needed to be more empathetic to her needs. She felt he was being very selfish and was ready to tell him so when the telephone rang. It was not Ryan on the phone but Jeremy.

"What the heck is going on, Cassie?"

Cassie told Jeremy about her daughter and son-in-law's visit and how Ryan had gotten upset and walked out. She also let Jeremy know she did not care if she ever saw Ryan again.

Jeremy knew she did not really mean that. He was surprised to get to the station that morning only to find Ryan in his office and in an extremely bad mood. Ryan would hardly speak to him and so he called Cassie to find out what was happening. Jeremy realized the thought of their separation was becoming too painful for either of them to bear so they had unconsciously refused to admit it was going to happen. However, reality had intruded with Kit's call to her mother.

"Cassie, you have to realize Ryan has been focusing so hard on spending every possible moment with you. He's never had a family so he doesn't understand that you have other obligations besides being with him. I'll talk to him later after he calms down a little. Please don't be mad at him."

Cassie thanked Jeremy for calling. She wanted to stop thinking about Ryan so she decided to plan some tourist activities for when Kit arrived. She knew she needed to do something to keep her mind off the situation. Even though she was angry, Cassie was not sure what she would do if she had to spend another night without sleeping with Ryan.

Later in the afternoon Cassie walked to the waterfront. Mount Rainier was out and she sat there a long time just watching the mountain. It was after 7:00 p.m. when Cassie returned to the condo.

The message machine was not flashing when Cassie got back so she knew Ryan did not tried to call her. She had not been hungry all day and had a glass of wine before finally deciding to go to bed. It was 9:00 p.m. and she still had heard no word from Ryan. She felt numb and was just climbing into bed when the doorbell rang. She was trying hard not to be upset with Ryan but was losing her battle when she opened the door.

Ryan stood there with such a sad expression that Cassie's heart melted a little. She was still mad at him but decided to let him try to explain how he was feeling to her.

"Cassie, I know you're angry with me and you have every right to be. I have been very selfish. I've never had children and I just wanted to spend every moment I could with you. Instead I lost a day of being with you. Will you forgive me?'

Cassie found she could not say anything to Ryan. She could not tell him he was being selfish when he had already admitted to it. And she could tell he had a bad night the night before just by looking at him. She realized it was too difficult for either of them to imagine what was going to happen when they had to leave each other.

Instead, Cassie put her arms around him and pressed hard against him as they kissed. There was a sadness that enveloped them as they made love that night. They were both so tired they immediately fell asleep in each other's arms.

When Jane called a couple of days later, Cassie had the feeling she had been talking to Jeremy but she never admitted to that. Cassie told her about the fight with Ryan.

"I guess I understand why Ryan got so upset about Kit's visit. I've never had children and so I can see his perspective. I know it's not logical to think that way but it is understandable. What does Ryan plan to do while Kit is there?"

"Ryan is going to spend time with Jack on his boat. Kit leaves Sunday at noon and won't be back until the following Sunday. Then they'll be here until Thursday after their cruise so Jeremy is making plans to go with Ryan somewhere those few days.

Meanwhile, Ryan and I are going away with Jack on his boat while Kit and George are on their cruise. Have you talked to Jeremy at all?"

"Yes I have. We're meeting at Lake Tahoe for the week of Labor Day while you and Ryan are with Jack."

"You'll have to tell me all about your trip, Jane, when you get back home."

The two friends said good-bye and Cassie mentioned to Ryan at dinner about her conversation with Jane.

"Jeremy just told me today that he was meeting Jane. I guess he'll be back that Friday which will give him a day to catch up on things before he and I leave on Sunday. We're going to spend some time down in California with some of our sponsors. It will be good to mix business with pleasure since it will help me to focus a little less on not being with you."

Before they knew it, the week had passed and it was Wednesday night.

"Cassie, I don't understand why I can't meet your daughter. Jack and I could just casually run into the three of you and we could all have dinner together."

"Ryan, Kit is very perceptive. There is no way I could be in the same room as you without Kit picking up some vibes between us. Remember, Jeremy's story of everyone looking at the two of us when you brought Jane and me to your cocktail party? Somehow people just assume we are a couple and I don't want Kit to guess anything about us. Not only would she not understand, but I don't want to have to explain our relationship to anyone, but especially not to my daughter."

"Maybe she would understand more than you realize, Cassie. But I don't want to argue with you about anything. I just want all our remaining time together to be happy."

"Ryan, I know we can't commit to each other and this is probably not the right time or place but I want you to know I love you with all my heart. Even though I'm going back to Jim, I want you to know I'll always love you. I've known more happiness in these few weeks with you than at any other time in my life. I feel so lucky you came into my life. I know it will be hard to leave you but the memories of our time together will make my life more bearable when I get back to Minnesota."

"Maybe you should stay here in Seattle with me, Cassie."

"Ryan, you know that's not possible. You have no intention of leaving Joyce any more than I do in leaving Jim. Please don't ever bring that subject up again."

"Cassie, I love you with my whole being and when I wake up each morning I wonder how I will ever bear not being with you anymore."

"Maybe someday we'll get lucky and find a way back to each other. But for now, I will start crying if we keep talking about this anymore Ryan. So please can we stop?"

Ryan and Cassie were up most of the night talking and making love. They would be spending three nights apart and they had not been away from each other that long since they began their relationship. Although they did not slept with each other while Joyce was in the hospital they had still seen each other every day. Neither of them knew how they would get through those next few days apart.

# Chapter Thirty-Four

Thanks to friends and relatives Ryan and Cassie managed their separation. Jeremy rounded up a few of their friends and threw a big party on Jack's boat Thursday night. Ryan was so busy talking to everyone, the sadness only enveloped him when he lay down in bed at 3:00 a.m.

Jack told Ryan how it was still hard for him to sleep at night without Anne. He was trying to prepare Ryan for when Cassie was gone but actually it made the present nights easier for Ryan since the two of them stayed up late each night to keep each other company.

Cassie was also busy. Kit and Paul kept her constantly on the go as a tour guide. Not only did they visit all the tourist sights in town but Cassie took them to some of the better restaurants that she and Ryan frequented.

Kit was excited to see her mother and was really happy to see how much calmer and peaceful Cassie appeared. She really liked Cassie's new ring and commented on how the color matched her eyes. It looked awfully expensive to her but Cassie did not elaborate.

Kit also sensed something unusual about Cassie's demeanor. It was very puzzling and Kit could not quite put her finger on why her mother seemed so different. However, she was afraid to say too much to Cassie for fear of upsetting her so she just dropped the subject.

Kit realized now how important it had been that her mother came to Seattle for the summer. Cassie needed time away from her husband and a chance to assess the direction of her life, especially now that she was retired.

"You know if I didn't know better, Paul, I would think mother's in love. I realize that's a dumb thing to believe but there is something so different about her. Now, more than ever, I realize she needed this time away from dad."

"You're right Kit. There is something different about her. It's probably just getting a break from your father. All Jim has done since Cassie left is sit in the den all day and night and watch TV. He was probably doing that before your mother left and we just didn't know it. No wonder Cassie needed a break. Remember when I asked your dad if he wanted to come out to Seattle with us and surprise Cassie with a visit? I couldn't believe he said, no. He said he would never travel again and that he liked the food Mrs. Anderson cooks for him. It's almost as if he couldn't care less whether your mother ever comes back. As long as he has a house-keeper to take care of his needs, he seems relatively happy."

"I just hope mother doesn't get sick again when she comes home. I never imagined how much I would miss her until she left this summer. I know I'm being selfish but I don't want her to leave Minnesota ever again."

"I think if Mrs. Anderson continues to come in a couple of days a week and you and Gray give her some free time like you talked about, things will be better."

Little did either of them realize that nothing they did to help with Jim would make Cassie feel good about life again. Even if they never saw each other again, Ryan was now a part of her and she would never get over losing him.

"I sure wish we had asked you to go on the cruise with us, mother."

"Kit, I really love it here in Seattle. I know people tell me the sun doesn't shine from November through April and I wouldn't like that. Even though winters are cold we still get lots of sunshine in Minnesota. However, summers are wonderful here. Look at the views I have in this condo. I could sit here for days just enjoying the mountains and water and not be bored. But it seems like I always have some new place I want to explore. I appreciate your offer to take me on the cruise but frankly I want to spend every spare minute I have right here."

Of course, she did not tell them that Ryan was the biggest reason she did not want to go with them.

"Mother, I'm glad you're happy but I hope you won't go away like this again. Gray and I are going to help you with dad and we'll be there for you from now on."

"Thanks, Kit. I appreciate your thoughtfulness. Don't worry. I won't be coming back to Seattle after I leave."

Cassie had such a sadness about her when she spoke to Kit that her daughter almost asked her what was wrong. But then Kit figured she was just worried about going back to the drab life with her dad and since Kit was so excited about her cruise she promptly forgot Cassie's joyless demeanor.

Cassie had packed some clothes and Ryan took them with him to Jack's boat. Kit and Paul had no idea Cassie would also be sailing while they were on their cruise.

At first, Kit and Paul told Cassie they could not leave for the ship until the afternoon. Their documents said to arrive between 1:30 p.m. - 2:30 p.m. Cassie explained how Jane always showed up for cruises at noon. Not only were there no lines but also their suitcases would arrive in their cabin much earlier by going at that time.

Cassie hugged them both and dropped them at the terminal right at noon. It took her a half hour to drive to the yacht club where Jack kept his boat. Ryan was on the top deck watching for her. He met her half way up the pier as she came down the dock. As soon as she spied Ryan she went running into his arms.

Jack was watching from the inside of the cabin as Cassie and Ryan kissed each other. He felt a jolt of pain go through him as he realized what was going to happen to them when they parted. But for now, he vowed to make sure this week they spent together on his boat were some of the happiest days of their lives.

# Chapter Thirty-Five

Cassie, Ryan and Jack had a great time boating. Ryan felt a little sad he could not keep Jack company during his long empty nights. Jack appreciated Ryan's thoughtfulness but told him he needed to concentrate on every precious moment he and Cassie had left.

Cassie did not want to go back to Roche Harbor. She and Ryan had too many wonderful memories of that place and she knew it would make her feel sad to go back there so soon.

Actually, both Ryan and Jack had discussed their itinerary and told Cassie what they were planning. The two men had decided to sail up the eastern side of Vancouver Island and dock in towns Cassie had not yet visited. Cassie was excited about going to some new places with the two of them.

That evening Jack threw a party on his boat with some of his friends from the yacht basin. Cassie was tired from being constantly on the go with Kit and George and thought staying in the marina that night was a good idea.

The two of them enjoyed Jack's friends but they slipped into their cabin by 9:00 p.m. They could hardly wait to be alone together and Jack had noticed how they had constantly touched each other all evening.

The two men had decided they wanted to get past Victoria the next day and Ryan told Jack to sleep in, knowing how late Jack would be up roaming around. Ryan planned to be underway by 8:00 a.m. Instead, he and Cassie awoke about 7:00 a.m. They just wanted to be with each other and hated sleeping away their time. Ryan had untied the lines by 7:30 a.m. and Cassie stood next to him watching as he sailed deftly out of the harbor, sipping the coffee she made for him.

As soon as they were in open water Cassie sat up in the seat with him. He wrapped one arm around her, keeping his other hand on the wheel to steer the boat. Cassie rested her head contentedly on his shoulder and that was how Jack found them when he woke up.

"I was just waiting until you got up to make all of us some breakfast, Jack."

"I can help you with the breakfast, Cassie."

"I really don't mind Jack. Why don't you and Ryan talk strategy while I start making some eggs?"

Cassie went down to the small galley and started frying bacon. She was just scrambling some eggs when she realized Ryan was standing behind her.

"Did you give up piloting for awhile, Ryan?"

"How did you know I was behind you, Cassie?"

"I felt you behind me."

"But I never touched you."

"What I mean to say is that I sensed you behind me."

Ryan came up behind her then and wrapped his arms around her. He began kissing the left side of her neck.

"We're never going to have eggs if you keep doing that, Ryan."

"I can't keep my hands off you. I missed you so much."

Cassie, with tears in her eyes, turned and hugged Ryan as hard as she could. As he pressed against her he began crushing her body against the counter. As their lips met Cassie felt as if she was on fire. Since she was braced against the counter, Cassie lifted her legs to encircle Ryan's waist. At the same instant they realized they were about to lose control and Cassie put her legs back down on the floor as Ryan loosened his grip on her.

"Ryan, I wonder if we were together for the rest of our lives if we would continue to feel this way about one another. Sometimes I feel like a teenager with raging hormones when I'm around you. I never dreamed I could feel this way at my age."

"At first I thought we acted like this because we haven't been with anyone for a long time. But I have to tell you Cassie I never felt this way towards Joyce or anyone else I was ever with. You certainly bring out the lustful side of me. And to tell the truth, I am very surprised at my age."

"How are the eggs doing down there?" Jack yelled at them from the upper deck.

Cassie began pushing Ryan away and looking half embarrassed, told him to go set the table. After getting the table ready Ryan poured orange juice for the three of them.

They called to Jack when breakfast was ready and he put the boat on autopilot while he came down to eat.

"I have to be honest with you two. When Ryan came down to help you, Cassie, I had the feeling it would be a long wait for the eggs."

Cassie, blushing slightly, looked at Jack and smiled. "We were up pretty early and I needed to get breakfast cooked quickly because I knew how hungry Ryan was."

Ryan shivered when Cassie looked at him with the double meaning hanging between them.

"Well, if you two were up that early you might need to take a nap this afternoon."

"I think you're right, Jack," Ryan said as he looked with a different kind of hunger at Cassie.

After breakfast, Jack continued steering the boat through the San Juan Islands heading for Sidney just north of Victoria. Cassie studied maps and guidebooks as she listened to Ryan and Jack conversing about their itinerary.

The two men discussed stopping overnight in Vancouver but Cassie told them they could do that another time. Cassie had promised Kit and George she would take them overnight to Vancouver on their return from the cruise and for now she was interested in exploring some new areas.

Subconsciously, Cassie had a bad feeling she would never come back to Seattle after she left and she wanted to visit as many different places as possible. She did not want to mention to Ryan what she was thinking because he kept talking about them being together someday. But Cassie's intuition told her that was not going to happen.

Cassie knew she had to let those thoughts go and continued with her research. Looking at Ryan from time to time, she kept wondering how long before naptime would begin. She was just about to say something when Ryan looked at her.

"You look tired, Cassie."

"Exhausted, Ryan."

"I think the two of you better go take your nap then. By the time you're finished I'll need some relief from captaining, Ryan."

"Will you be okay for a couple of hours, Jack?"

"I've sailed this boat all over the Caribbean and up to Seattle from Florida. I think I can manage a couple of hours while you're resting."

As they made there way to their cabin, Cassie looked at Ryan. "You started something in the kitchen this morning and I need you to finish it. I didn't think you would ever mention naptime."

"It's kind of silly pretending in front of Jack when he knows exactly what we are up to but it makes what is about to happen a little more exciting."

Cassie tried to explain to Ryan she did not need any more excitement than what she was feeling but his lips got in the way as they fell together on their bed. They "napped" for about two hours and finally realized it was time to relieve Jack.

Jack had some reading to catch up on and Cassie once again sat next to Ryan as he headed north to Sidney. Cassie spotted bald eagles, seals and a walrus as they continued through the islands. They skirted far enough east of Victoria

Harbor that they could not see that city and reached Sidney about 5:00 p.m. It had been a long day but there was still over three hours before sunset. They had cocktails on the deck while Ryan grilled mahi mahi for their dinner.

They went to bed right after sunset and for once even Jack went to sleep at a reasonable hour. Watching Cassie and Ryan took his focus off Anne and he fell asleep rather quickly thinking about how Ryan was going to need him when Cassie left.

The next morning they were on their way about 8:00 a.m. In Nanaimo they docked at a restaurant Ryan knew was frequented by boaters and had a big breakfast.

They continued towards Lantzville and both Ryan and Cassie spotted Graycliff, their B&B, as they continued north on their journey. They were now traveling the area they had passed through for the festival. After Parksville, they were finally in new territory to Cassie. They continued to Campbell River where Jack had rented a berth for the night at a local yacht club basin.

It had been another long day and Ryan and Cassie had another "nap" that afternoon. They also relieved Jack or sat on deck reading or watching the water and shore for wildlife. That evening they had dinner at a restaurant on shore where Cassie thought the food was exceptional. There were so many choices she would have liked to have tried. Cassie imagined she could eat in that particular restaurant several times a week if she lived in the area.

Finally, Tuesday night they anchored in the Port Hardy/Bear Cove area. That was the northern end of Vancouver Island. Cassie was excited they had made it all the way up the eastern side of the island.

In the morning they retraced their path but this time they stopped at new ports on the way back. They needed to be docked back in Seattle on Friday night since Kit and George would be back Saturday morning after they cleared customs. They passed Campbell River where they had stayed on their way north and then stayed overnight further south in the Cumberland area.

On Thursday, they headed for Orcas Island. Jack had friends who were still going to be docked there and they knew it would only take them a few hours on Friday to reach Seattle from Orcas Island.

As he knew there would be, there were several people Jack knew moored at the island and Ryan even was familiar with some of them. Orcas was where Cassie and Ryan had stayed overnight for the first time on Jack's boat when they had left Roche Harbor. Even Cassie recognized some of the boaters and they had an enjoyable evening partying between the boats.

When Cassie and Ryan finally went to bed that night Ryan noticed tears in Cassie's eyes.

"Why are you crying, Cassie?"

"Ryan, I've had the most perfect time with you and Jack. I will always remember this trip. I can't believe how fast the days have gone although if someone asked me what we did I couldn't say exactly. It truly is the journey, not the destination that is important. But this time, the destination means our trip is over and I have to spend the next four days without you which seems almost too much to bear."

"Cassie, as soon as Jeremy and I get back from California let's take a drive down the Washington coast."

"That would be fun, Ryan, but let's see how things develop. You've been gone so much you might have work piled up at the station. I don't need to go anywhere with you, Ryan. I just need to be with you. And I love Sylvia's apartment so maybe we can just stay there for a few days and roam around the city when you aren't working."

Before they knew it, they were at Jack's summer berth in Seattle. Jack seemed really happy to be back with his friends and told Cassie and Ryan about the round of parties he had planned for them that evening.

Instead, Cassie and Ryan asked Jack if they could skip the parties that night. Jack realized they were going to be apart until Thursday and knew they needed their time alone. After they docked, Jack went to the grocery store at the marina and bought some bread and chips and cold cuts.

Ryan and Cassie were in their room when he got back. He put the meat in the fridge and left them a note telling them to help themselves to the food. Then Jack grabbed a couple of bottles of wine and headed for a friend's boat. The party was already in full swing and Jack was looking forward to his evening back in Seattle. The next day Jack would discover the food he had bought for them had not been touched.

# Chapter Thirty-Six

It was 9:30 a.m. when Cassie drove up to the cruise ship terminal. She saw Kit and Paul walking out with a porter carrying their luggage.

"That was perfect timing, Mother. We just cleared customs and were going to call your cell to let you know we were waiting."

"How was your cruise, Kit?"

"Oh, Mother, it was wonderful. You can't imagine how much fun it is to sail around islands."

Cassie smiled to herself at Kit's words. She may not have made it to Alaska but she certainly knew how much fun it was to sail around islands.

Paul started telling Cassie about their previous evening in Victoria describing what a wonderful city it was.

"Actually, I took a ferry to Victoria earlier this summer, Paul."

Cassie did not say she went with Ryan and Kit was so busy telling her mother how much fun Victoria was the evening before that Cassie just let her talk.

"I thought we'd roam around Seattle this afternoon and have dinner out. There's a great seafood restaurant by the Market area. Then tomorrow we can go to church and after breakfast we'll drive to Vancouver. It should take us a little over three hours to get there depending how long the lines are at customs."

Kit and Paul both agreed to Cassie's plan.

"I've also been studying the tourist sites but I think when we get there we should take the local sightseeing tour of Vancouver just to get an overview of the city. Then we can decide which places we want to see more in depth."

Cassie was really glad they took the city tour. Even though she had tried to read up on Vancouver there were places she would have missed or not known about. She was surprised to learn there was a large underground mall downtown they might never had found. It was a lot like the hidden malls she had discovered in downtown Seattle when she had first arrived in that city.

Once they arrived in Vancouver they decided they needed to stay two nights so they did not get back to Seattle until late Tuesday. Cassie was so busy during the day she did not have much time to think about Ryan. However, nights were a different matter. Cassie had a hard time sleeping and Kit finally asked her if something was wrong when she saw how tired her mother looked by Tuesday morning.

"For some reason I'm having a hard time not sleeping in my own bed, I guess."

Kit accepted that explanation. Usually, she was more insightful but she and Paul were having such a good time on their trip that neither of them paid close attention to Cassie to realize something was definitely not right. Cassie spent the rest of that day acting bright and cheery so they would not question her any more.

Cassie was glad when Wednesday finally ended. She had another bad night Wednesday night. She and Ryan had made plans to meet for lunch the next day but she kept thinking something would happen to keep them apart. Cassie knew she should not worry about something she had no control over and wondered if she would feel this bad when she left Ryan.

At 7:00 a.m. the phone rang and Cassie, still worried something had happened to Ryan, was unbelievably relieved to hear his voice.

"Cassie, I know I wasn't supposed to call while Kit and Paul were still there but I needed to hear your voice."

"Oh, Ryan I am so glad you called. I needed to hear your voice, too. The kids are in the other room so they won't know who I'm talking to."

"Jeremy and I got back last night. It was a productive time with the sponsors and I've been in the office since 6:00 this morning getting caught up on my work. What time do you go to the airport?"

"We're leaving the condo at 10:30. Their flight is at 1:00 so that should be good timing for them. I just plan to drop them off at departures. There's no use taking them inside since I can't go past security. I should be back here sometime before noon depending on traffic."

"I'll meet you at the condo at noon Cassie."

"If you're going to meet me here I don't suppose lunch will be in our immediate plans."

Ryan chuckled at Cassie's words but Cassie did not care about lunch anyway. She had hardly eaten anything since Saturday morning when she had last seen Ryan. She had no idea that Ryan had hardly been able to choke down food either. All he could think about was being with Cassie again.

After dropping Kit and Paul at the airport, Cassie drove back into the condo garage about 11:30 a.m. She was thinking she had roughly a half hour before Ryan showed up. But to her surprise when she entered the condo Ryan was standing on the other side of the door.

"I wanted to be here when you got back, Cassie."

Looking at him, Cassie realized he had as much trouble eating and sleeping that she had.

Throwing her arms around his neck and pressing tightly to him, Cassie said, "Oh Ryan. I promise we will not spend another day apart until I have to leave. Even if Joyce gets sick again I'll sneak in the hospital and sleep with you."

Ryan knew she would not really do that but he also felt exactly the same way she did. In between kissing and scattering their clothes along the way they finally made it to their bedroom and spent the rest of the afternoon in bed. When they were not making love, they laid wrapped in each other's arms quietly talking to each other. They felt like they had been apart for months instead of days.

"Cassie, as much as I hate to leave you and this bed I am going to be sick if I don't have some nourishment. We need to get dressed and get something to eat."

"We are not leaving this apartment tonight, Ryan. Remember, when I went into the kitchen for drinks a little while ago?"

"Yes."

"Well I called for pizza and it should be here in another fifteen to twenty minutes."

And so a half hour later as Kit and George's plane landed in Minneapolis, Ryan and Cassie were sitting in bed drinking beer and eating pizza. Neither of them could remember pizza ever tasting so good.

# Chapter Thirty-Seven

The next day Jeremy brought over some papers that Ryan needed to sign. He had taken them home the night before since he knew it was easier to just stop at the condo on his way into the station. Ryan and Cassie were going to another party on Jack's boat that evening and they asked Jeremy if he wanted to come to the party with them.

Cassie was glad when Jeremy said "yes". She had not had a chance to talk to Jane and she wanted to hear Jeremy's version of his week with her friend in Lake Tahoe. When she asked Ryan what Jeremy told him, Ryan said he had not talked about it.

Actually, Ryan had been so focused on Cassie's absence he had all he could do to keep his attention on the sponsors they met.

As the three of them climbed on Jack's boat, Cassie turned to Ryan and said, "Can you believe it was just a week ago last Friday that we spent our last night on this boat after our Vancouver Island trip?"

"It seems like a month has gone by, doesn't it Cassie?"

Cassie nodded at Ryan and at that moment Jack came out from below. "I hate to say it but, Ryan and Cassie, you two look like you've had a bad week."

"Things are much better now, Jack."

Ryan went below with Jack to look at some sailing plans he was drawing up for his return to Florida. Jeremy poured drinks for both Cassie and himself.

"Okay I want to know everything Jeremy," Cassie said as she took the drink he handed her.

"There's not a lot to tell, Cassie. But I have to say the more I'm around Jane the more we seem to enjoy each other's company. Maybe I made a mistake not having a sexual relationship with her. I'm beginning to like her more than I really wanted to. It's kind of strange. We spent the whole week together on the south side of Lake Tahoe. One day we circled the lake by car and gambled a little at a casino on the north end of the lake, and we even took a boat cruise. I know we were busy every day but if you asked me what we did, it sounds like very little."

Cassie started laughing as Jeremy finished speaking.

"You know Jeremy, that's exactly what Ryan and I said about our trip up Vancouver Island. It's amazing how you can feel busy when you are together but when you try to tell someone else about your adventure it just doesn't sound like much."

Cassie wanted to ask Jeremy more about his relationship with Jane but some boat neighbors arrived and before they knew it the party was in full swing.

Cassie watched Jeremy flit from woman to woman. He was a very charming man and the women he talked to tried to cling to him. But after a little while Jeremy would move on to someone new. It was interesting watching him maneuver through the partygoers.

Cassie realized when Jeremy was with Jane, he would spend hours just sitting and talking to her like he had all the time in the world. She was beginning to think that something might develop with their relationship. Cassie hoped so for both of their sakes. As one aged, companionship and caring became a more important part of a couple's life. And, besides, Jane and Jeremy seemed to have so much fun when they were together.

Cassie noticed Jeremy would look around occasionally almost as if he was looking for someone. She wondered if

Jane had been there if he would be looking around like that. It was almost as though he was expecting Jane to enter the room at any moment.

It was after 2:00 a.m. before the party started winding down. Ryan asked Jeremy if he wanted to spend the night in Sylvia's guest bedroom. He did not want Jeremy to have to wait a long time at the ferry just to get home. Jeremy thanked Ryan but told him Jack had already invited him to stay on the boat and he had accepted.

Jeremy always kept an overnight bag in his car in case he did not want to deal with catching the ferry home some evening. There even was a small room with a bed at the station for emergencies and Jeremy had slept there a few times.

Cassie and Ryan were happy they had a weekend with no particular activities planned. There was a local concert Cassie wanted to go to and they took that in on Saturday night.

The next day they went to church and breakfast and spent the rest of the morning reading the Sunday newspaper. They walked to the park behind Pikes Place Market and spent the afternoon reading at a tree-shaded table overlooking the waterfront.

Mount Rainier was out that day and Cassie kept looking up from her book to view the mountain. It was a sight she never grew tired of. They could have stayed at the condo on Cassie's balcony to read that day but there was something fun about the vibrant feel of the Market area, especially with all the different people milling around.

The following week Ryan went in to work for a few hours each morning. They went out to eat lunch every afternoon and then afterwards walked around downtown window shopping or browsing in one of the many bookstores. Cassie knew she would definitely miss the fresh seafood when she went back to Minneapolis. Sometimes Cassie or Ryan would take turns making dinner or they would bring leftovers home from their lunch.

They went to bed early each night. They both preferred reading to watching TV. They made love every night and then would lie in each other's arms and talk. Cassie marveled that they never ran out of things to say to each other. Ryan always had radio station stories and Cassie liked to talk about various places she had researched and wanted to visit some time. They also liked to talk about the different books they read.

Cassie had finally caught up with Jane but found her unusually closed mouthed. Jane did tell Cassie she and Jeremy were talking by phone three or four times a week. Jane remarked how she and Jeremy never seemed to run out of conversation. There were times when Cassie realized how similar the two couples were even though Jane and Jeremy still had not had any sexual relations. It was the complete antithesis of the way their other relationships had been.

The following week, Cassie and Ryan took their journey down Washington's coast. They stayed two nights at the same little motel Cassie had stayed at when she first came out to Seattle and had taken her weekly trips around the area.

The motel did not have big fancy rooms like some of the chain hotels. But it was clean and Cassie liked the fact that there was a balcony to sit on overlooking the ocean as well as a gas burning fireplace. They slept each night with the little window opened so they could hear the crashing surf as Cassie had done the first time she stayed there. They walked the beach each morning before setting off on their day's adventure and then again late in the afternoon before going to dinner. It seemed an idyllic time but they were now down to their last two weeks and they felt an urgency about their time together.

The manager of the hotel remembered Cassie from her first visit and asked them if they were planning on returning in the winter to watch the winter storms as they came in.

That was a favorite pastime for many Pacific Northwest residents. The manager noticed Cassie had tears in her eyes as she shook her head "no".

When they returned to Seattle neither of them talked about Cassie leaving but Jeremy noticed how sad they both looked. At the same time they had become very in tune to each other's needs and desires. They did not even realize they began many of their sentences in the middle and most people around them had no idea what they were talking about half the time. But it was obvious to everyone that each knew exactly what the other was saying.

Since Cassie was always with Ryan she had stopped using her car. She found someone right after Labor Day who was willing to drive the car back to Minnesota for her towards the end of the month. She loaded up her personal belongings and some of her clothes in the trunk and decided to ship the rest of her things back and fly home. She would not have minded the three-day drive back but she wanted every extra day possible with Ryan.

Cassie and Ryan could tell summer was winding down. They noticed it was getting dark by 7:30 p.m. and in the summer it had stayed light until almost 10:00 p.m. One evening they were having dinner at the dining room table.

"Cassie, I know you have obligations to Jim and your family and you can't stay here, but do you think there's a chance you could come back out here next summer at least for a couple of months?"

"Ryan, I don't want you to even consider that. It's going to be so hard leaving you now that I don't think I could do it again next summer. I don't want to say never outright but I don't think it's honest for either of us to hope for that. I've been married to Jim for a long time and I need to give him another chance. If I were thinking about being with you someday that wouldn't be fair to Jim. I don't know why we were given this wonderful time together but when it's over we have to go back to our lives and responsibilities."

Ryan got up from the table and walked out to the balcony. He did not want Cassie to see the tears in his eyes. Cassie followed him out and stood facing him. She wiped the tears from his face with her hand and put her arms around him. She held him tight and pressed against him. They could hear each other's hearts beating. Up until that moment she had been almost weak with anguish over the thought of losing Ryan but she realized she had to be strong or she would not be able to leave him. As Cassie broke apart from Ryan there was a new resolve in her eyes.

"Ryan, I love you more than life itself but we have to part and I don't want to be sad and I don't want you to be sad. There are very few people who get the chance to find each other and love like we have. We need to be thankful for the time that has been given to us. Who knows? Maybe we'll find a way back to each other like you think. But if we don't, I have the most wonderful memories that will stay with me the rest of my life."

Cassie still had the bad feeling she would never see Ryan again but she did not want him to even sense what she was thinking. Somehow Cassie's talk helped both of them to cope with the situation. They both became resigned to the inevitable.

Their last week together flew by. Ryan did not go to work and Jeremy, knowing what was going on, took care of any problems that came up at the station. They spent most of their time in the condo or out hand in hand walking through Belltown and downtown.

Neither of them slept much. They would keep waking up and just hold each other. There was no longer any talk of future plans. There were times when Cassie felt as if she was dying but outwardly she tried to be happy around Ryan. She knew he was feeling the same way.

Sylvia was coming back on a Saturday and had said Cassie was welcomed to stay the weekend. Cassie thanked Sylvia but she wanted to spend the time alone with Ryan.

Her plane was leaving late in the afternoon on Sunday. Cassie did not tell Sylvia but this time she and Ryan were staying at a hotel by the airport like Sylvia had before she left Seattle for the summer. Ryan wanted to be with Cassie until the last possible moment.

Friday night, the two of them went to dinner with Jeremy and Jack. As much as Cassie wanted to spend every moment with Ryan she also wanted to say good-bye to her new friends. Everyone had tears in their eyes when they finally parted after dinner. Jeremy told Cassie not to be surprised if he just happened to visit Minneapolis. Cassie told him she hoped he would visit Minnesota and be sure to come see her as well as Jane. Before he left the restaurant, Jack pulled Cassie aside.

"I know how tough this is going to be for the two of you. Nothing any of us can say will make it any easier. But I am happy to know you'll have Jane there to support you, Cassie. And don't forget I'll be here for a little while and between Jeremy and me, Ryan will learn to cope. Take care and be happy, Cassie."

Cassie was moved by Jack's words. "Oh, Jack, you are such a wonderful man. I wish you could find some happiness in your life."

"Cassie, being with you and Ryan this summer has helped me tremendously. I'm even sleeping a little better. I won't marry again but maybe I'll find a lady friend who I can share some fun times with."

Cassie kissed both men on the cheek and hugged them tight. As they left the restaurant Cassie marveled that in a few short months she had met such wonderful new friends. She had the feeling Jim would not like or understand these men if he knew about them, but they would always remain in her heart.

# Chapter Thirty-Eight

Cassie and Ryan's journey was nearly at an end. Sylvia arrived back at the apartment late on Saturday afternoon. She thanked Cassie for taking such good care of her place. Then she told Cassie if she ever went away for another extended period again she would give Cassie a call.

Cassie thanked her but knew she would never spend another night in Sylvia's condo. Ryan was waiting in his car outside when Cassie came out the front door. He asked her about dinner but neither of them was hungry. They drove to the airport hotel and checked in.

They lay awake all night wrapped in each other's arms. They barely spoke to one another but constantly touched each other. Each wanted to memorize everything about the other. Before they knew it, noon was upon them and it was time to check out. Cassie's plane left a little after 3:00 p.m. and Ryan was planning on getting her to the airport about 1:00 p.m.

They ordered breakfast at a nearby family restaurant but when the food came neither could eat very much. They ended up leaving the restaurant with most of the food still on their plates. When the waitress asked them if there was something wrong with the food they looked at her with glazed eyes and shook their heads "no".

Ryan parked his car in short-term parking and together they walked to the ticket counter. Cassie had told Ryan he could drop her at departures like she had her daughter and son-in-law but he wanted to spend every last minute with her. After getting her boarding pass they slowly walked over to security.

Cassie wrapped her arms tightly around Ryan and buried her face in his neck. He could feel the tears streaming down her face. She finally regained control and turned her face up to his. Their lips met blindly and Cassie felt like her heart was being ripped from her body. She was too overcome with their parting to understand Ryan was feeling the same way she was.

Finally, she tore herself from his embrace and walked quickly through security. As she rounded the corner at the X-ray machines, she turned and looked at Ryan. When she saw the tears running down his face she turned back around and ran blindly down the concourse. She knew if she turned back to get one more look at him she would never leave Seattle.

Jane had realized how bad Cassie would be feeling. She planned to meet Cassie at the airport in Minneapolis to drive her home. Jane called Jim and Cassie's children and told them Sylvia had asked Cassie to stay a couple of extra days. She told everyone she would pick up Cassie at the airport when she returned so they would not have to worry about getting her.

Cassie's children were upset because they were looking forward to seeing their mother but Jane was able to soothe over their hurt feelings. Jim could hardly have cared less. "Whatever," he answered when Jane called him. Jane was glad she had not talked to Jim in person because after his reaction she felt like she could have lost her temper with him.

Cassie quietly cried all the way home on the plane. She was very thankful she had not driven because she did not know if that would have been safe considering how she was feeling. Luckily, she was seated at the back of the plane and most of the seats around her were empty. She had her row of seats to herself so she knew she was not bothering anyone.

Even the flight attendants stayed away from her knowing she would tell them if she needed anything.

Jane did not tell Cassie about delaying her homecoming. She had only told her she would meet her at baggage pickup. When Cassie walked into the baggage area, Jane gasped. Her friend looked even worse than she had imagined.

Cassie hugged Jane. "Oh, Jane, I have to go somewhere and freshen up. I can't go home looking like this."

"Don't worry Cassie. I told your family you were delayed with Sylvia in Seattle and would not be coming home until Wednesday afternoon. I had a feeling you'd need some time to pull yourself together."

"Jane, you are the best friend a person could have."

Together they gathered up Cassie's luggage and headed for Jane's car.

"Are you hungry, Cassie?"

"No."

"When was the last time you ate anything, Cassie?"

"We went out to dinner with Jeremy and Jack Friday night and then had breakfast Saturday morning."

"Cassie, I understand you aren't hungry but when we get back to my place I insist you have some soup."

"I really don't want a thing, Jane."

"Cassie, you have to force yourself. I'm not asking you to eat a lot just some soup. You need to stay hydrated or you'll end up in the hospital. How will you explain that to your family?"

That reasoning snapped Cassie out of her despair. Even though she was not hungry she had a cup of chicken noodle soup and drank a whole glass of water when she got to Jane's apartment.

Cassie thought she was all cried out but when she laid down in Jane's guestroom the tears once again flowed down her cheeks. It was many hours before she was able to go to sleep.

# Chapter Thirty-Nine

It was noon before Cassie woke up. She still was not hungry but she ate some more soup that Jane had made for her. Cassie thought about calling Ryan but knew if she did she might find herself back on a plane to him.

Cassie then called Doctor George's office and made an appointment to see him Wednesday morning before going home. She told herself she wanted to talk to him about Jim but she also needed to tell him about her summer.

For the rest of that day and the next Jane and Cassie stayed in Jane's apartment. Jane called for take-out and Cassie would choke down a little food but she cried and refused to eat on Tuesday afternoon when Jane had pizza delivered. Remembering the night she and Ryan shared pizza in bed, Cassie had the feeling she would never be able to eat pizza again.

Cassie did not want to talk about Ryan. She was so numb with grief that any mention of Ryan would start her crying. Instead, she had Jane tell her all about Jeremy.

"I just hope one of us can come away with a happy relationship from our time in Seattle, Jane."

Jane did not understand why talking about Jeremy helped Cassie but she was willing to talk about anything to keep Cassie's mind off Ryan.

"I don't know, Cassie. After my divorce I decided I would never trust a man again. It just seemed so much easier to have casual relationships rather than chancing disappointment again. But little by little Jeremy has stolen his way into my heart. I hate to admit it but I think I'm in love with him. And the bad thing is I don't even know if we are sexually compatible."

Jane's words made Cassie smile. She was so glad that Jane might have found some happiness. Cassie had always cared about her friend, and she always felt sad that deep down Jane was a very lonely person. She truly wanted the best for Jane.

"When do you think Jeremy will visit you here?"

"He's talking about coming for Thanksgiving and then he mentioned a cruise over New Years."

"Too bad it couldn't turn into a honeymoon cruise, Jane."

"First of all, Cassie, it would never happen that fast and second of all it will probably never happen period. I think that's wishful thinking on your part."

However, when Cassie looked at Jane she saw a serenity she had not seen in her friend before. She smiled inwardly and wondered if a quick marriage would really not take place in the near future.

By Wednesday morning Cassie was feeling better and knew she could handle seeing her family again. She was still in shock over losing Ryan but she knew she could hide her feelings from her family. And even if she continued crying herself to sleep each night, at least she slept in a different room than Jim so he would never know.

Jane did not tell Cassie Jim's reaction to her getting home a few days later than originally planned. She was going to let Cassie borrow her car to go to the doctor and then take her home about 3:00 p.m. That would give Cassie a little time with Jim before their kids arrived. Kit, Gray, Paul and Karen were coming for dinner and this time they were bringing the food. Jane could tell that Cassie's children were very excited to have their mother home again.

Cassie walked into the doctor's office a little before 10:00 a.m. At first Doctor George was concerned about her because he noticed she had lost weight but there was a beauty about her that had not been there before. Cassie realized she had not eaten well for almost the last whole month, knowing she would be leaving Ryan and was fifteen pounds lighter than when she left for Seattle. "Even though you're thinner, I have to tell you it's very becoming on you, Cassie. Although, I also detect a sadness about your demeanor."

"Thank you, doctor. Even if most of my clothes don't fit well any more, I do feel healthier. Probably, all the walking I did around Seattle helped."

Cassie then gave the doctor a short version of her time in Seattle and her life with Ryan. Although he did not tell her so, the doctor wished there was some way Cassie and Ryan could be together. He did not think Jim was worthy of Cassie. And he knew Jim did not appreciate all that Cassie did for him.

"If you get too depressed, I can give you some medication to get you over the initial shock, Cassie. You'll be going through the stages of grief getting over Ryan just as if he had died."

"I really don't want to take any drugs if I can help it, Doctor George. But I promise I will if things become too unbearable."

"Now, for some bad news, Cassie. I am really worried about Jim. He's still smoking and it seems even more so lately. And he has put on twenty pounds since you left. He's now about fifty pounds overweight, and that makes the diabetes worse. His circulation seems to be deteriorating and I just hope he doesn't start having problems with his good leg." Cassie looked at the doctor in shock. "Cassie, don't you dare start feeling guilty over leaving. If you had been here all summer he would have done the same thing. It was important for you to have a break from Jim and now you should be able to handle the stress a lot better than before you left."

Cassie had a momentary thought that maybe death was preferable to all the stress she was going through between losing Ryan and Jim's health. But then she realized Jim needed her, and whenever things got bad, she would have the memories of Ryan and her summer with him.

"Is there anything special I can do to help Jim?"

"Besides him losing weight and stop smoking, there is nothing you can do."

"Well, I can at least start cooking nutritionally and maybe he can lose some weight."

"That would certainly help, Cassie. But don't be surprised if he refuses to change. I am afraid your husband is on a path of self-destruction and there is not much you can do when a person is bent on destroying himself."

"Doctor, thank you for all the advice and being here for me."

"Cassie, as a doctor it's a pleasure to help people but especially when they take my advice. I know you are going to be sad for a while but you had a wonderful summer and who knows maybe some day you and Ryan will be together again."

Cassie wished everyone would stop saying that to her. She needed to get over Ryan and deal with her life, the sooner the better.

When she arrived home, Jane just dropped her at her front door. Cassie had a feeling it would go smoother with Jim if Jane did not come in.

Jim, in his wheelchair, had a bag of potato chips and a canned soda in his lap and was headed for his den as Cassie came in the door. She knew he had put on weight but she was shocked to see how bad Jim looked.

"Hi, Cassie. You sure look terrible. Guess you didn't eat much in Seattle. The kids are coming for dinner in a little while. You better go unpack so you can spend some time with them when they get here. I have a show on I'm watching right now."

And with that Jim started towards the den. Cassie could not believe he had not kissed her or anything. She felt like she was walking in after being gone a day rather than four months.

"Jim, won't those snacks spoil your dinner?"

"Cassie, don't lecture me about food. You haven't been here to take care of me." And with that Jim rolled into the den and closed the door.

Cassie stood there with her mouth opened. She could not believe how cruel Jim was acting. She walked up the stairs and put her clothes away in her bedroom.

Cassie decided she would get through dinner with her children and then call Jane and tell her about Jim. Before the summer, Cassie might have tried to talk to Jim but after the way Ryan had treated her with such loving respect she realized the problem was with her husband and not with her. It was very liberating not feeling guilty despite Jim's manipulations.

She was not sure what would happen with her life but she knew Jim could no longer abuse her emotionally. She said a silent prayer of thanks to Ryan for making her a much stronger person.

For the first time in her marriage she began thinking about leaving Jim. Maybe she was not meant to stay in this relationship until death did they part. Cassie had a lot to think about and she also wanted to get some professional legal advice to see what her options were. Maybe Ryan was right. Maybe, just maybe they were meant to be together. Cassie did not need marriage, she just needed Ryan. For the first time in days Cassie's heart did not ache. She felt her spirits lift.

# Chapter Forty

Cassie was just coming down the stairs when all the children came in the door. She had bought a new outfit after her doctor visit since most of her clothes were not fitting well. Kit and Gray both ran and gave her hugs.

"Mother, you look so different. Kit, you didn't tell me how good Mother looked."

Kit was looking at her mother in astonishment. She knew her mother had not eaten very much when she and Paul had visited her but besides the weight loss there was a beauty about her that they had never noticed before.

Just as Kit was about to answer her brother, Jim rolled his wheelchair into the foyer.

"It's about time you kids got here. I'm starving! Where's the dinner you promised?"

"What about the snacks you had two hours ago, Jim?"

"Cassie, keep out of this! You're the one who left me. You have no say in this house any more as far as I'm concerned."

Kit and Gray turned to their father in shock, but before they could say anything, he said, "I don't want you kids to start in on me, either."

"Dad, we decided it would be easier to go out for dinner rather than bringing a bunch of food here and having to cook it."

"Gray, I don't want to go out. All of you can go and just bring me some dinner back when you drop your mother off."

With that Jim wheeled back into his den and slammed the door.

"Mother, has he been like that since you got back?"

"Kit, he didn't even kiss me when I came in. He said "hi" and went to his den with a bowl of potato chips and soda. He told me to go unpack so I was ready when you all got here. I was just coming down when you came in the door. I was going to try and talk to him."

Cassie had tears in her eyes as she looked at the closed den door. Both Kit and Gray immediately became worried their mother would want to go back to Washington.

"Oh, Mother, don't worry. He's upset you went away and is trying to make you feel guilty for leaving him. I know it's not healthy for Dad, but we haven't been able to get him out of his den all summer. We don't want you to leave us again. I'm sure he'll be better towards you when he knows you're here to stay."

Cassie felt the guilt her kids were laying on her for leaving them. She sighed knowing she would have to deal with the situation with Jim for a while. She could not just walk away when everyone was depending on her to somehow pull the family back together again. She was not sure she would be successful, but she knew she needed to at least try.

Paul suggested that it was definitely time for some cocktails. They all agreed and Cassie went to the closet and pulled her coat out. Grey drove everyone to a nearby Steakhouse. Cassie realized she had become addicted to seafood while out in Seattle but worried it would not taste as good in the Midwest. She decided on the grilled cod and everyone else ordered steaks. They even ordered a takeout dinner of steak for Jim.

Cassie had a fun evening with everyone and came to the conclusion she missed her kids more than she realized. Her life with Ryan seemed so unreal, now. She had to stay in Minneapolis. She had responsibilities, and no matter how mean he got towards her, Cassie was determined she would help Jim lose some weight.

Her children dropped her off and made a date for Saturday night. Cassie took Jim's dinner into him. He barely looked at her as she knocked and then entered the den.

"Just leave the dinner on the table, Cassie. I'll eat it later. I'm not real hungry right now and I'm in the middle of my program."

Cassie noticed a half-eaten package of cookies. She knew why Jim was not hungry.

"You're always in the middle of a program, Jim."

"Don't bother me Cassie. This is my life and I like it. Now, just leave me alone."

Cassie just shook her head as she left the den. Doctor George was right. Even if she had stayed in Minneapolis this last summer, Jim would have continued in his downhill spiral. Nothing she could have done would have changed that.

Cassie went to her bedroom and called Jane. She told her all about her afternoon and evening with Jim and her kids. Jane was not at all surprised after Jim's reaction the other day. She was glad, however, that Cassie was taking it so well.

"Jane, I can't tell you how much I appreciate having you to talk to. It makes everything so much easier."

"I'll always be here for you, Cassie."

Cassie was up late that evening. She lay in bed and thought about some of the wonderful moments she and Ryan had shared. Not only did she miss Ryan terribly but she also missed Seattle. Cassie knew she had to get over her feelings of loss. It was time to move on.

She also thought about Jane saying she would always be there for her. Cassie wondered if that really would be true. Deep down inside she could not imagine Jane and Jeremy not getting together. They were so similar and liked each other so much. Now, that they were older, closeness meant so much in a relationship. Cassie knew Jane was always going on about sexual compatibility. But liking the same things and being so suitable for each other meant more than anything as far as Cassie was concerned.

Jeremy was a nice man and deep down she hoped he and Jane would get together. Besides, Cassie had the feeling the other would fall into place for them also. She would be very sad if Jane left Minneapolis but at the same time she would be so happy Jane had finally found happiness. Hopefully, at least one of them would be happy.

# Chapter Forty-One

Cassie soon discovered encouraging Jim to lose weight was a lost cause. The more nutritional food she tried to feed him, the more he objected to her cooking. They had a terrible fight one afternoon about all the snacks and cookies he was eating.

"I like that food and you can't take it away from me. I'll just call my brother and give him money to go to the store and buy me what I want if you don't get it for me."

Cassie called Doctor George to tell him what was happening. The doctor suggested she continue cooking healthy for herself and let Jim have whatever junk food he wanted.

"It's not worth fighting over, Cassie. If Jim continually becomes upset with you his blood pressure will go sky high. I don't like advising caregivers to let a patient do something unhealthy but in this case it's hard to tell which is the lesser of two evils. I hate to tell you this Cassie but you have to be prepared for trouble. Jim's health problems are going to get worse and there's nothing you can do about it."

Cassie thanked the doctor and called Jane to fill her in on the latest developments. She was so thankful she had a support system in place. Besides Jane and the doctor, Kit, Gray and their spouses were also around helping out a lot more. Sometimes, it was just spending time, talking to Cassie. Everyone realized how lonely Cassie's life was with the way Jim treated her. And the children began to realize their dad was spiraling down on a path towards self-destruction.

Cassie's life developed a rhythm. She met Jane twice a week for lunch. Then, either Friday or Saturday night would be dinner with her children. Jim rarely went with them to dinner. He preferred sitting in front of his television snacking.

Cassie always brought Jim's dinner home when he did not go out with them. On Sundays everyone went to brunch after church. Jim would always accompany them on their Sunday outings since he wanted to go to church with everyone.

Cassie had also joined a Bible study group and was volunteering three days a week at a local shelter serving lunch to the homeless. Her life was filled with activities but her nights were still almost impossible to bear. She now realized what Jack had gone through after Anne's death.

Cassie knew Jane still talked regularly with Jeremy but she asked Jane not to relay any news about Ryan. She hated thinking of him living in Seattle without her. Jeremy always kept Jane informed of Ryan and his activities. Jane wanted to know in case Cassie ever asked but unfortunately she never did.

Ryan had told Jeremy he did not want to ever hear Cassie's name either. It was just too painful. He had lost twenty pounds in the month they had been apart. He seemed to have lost all his zest for living and looked sad all the time. Jeremy was worried sick about Ryan but Jack told Jeremy he would be okay. Each day would be a little easier for Ryan.

Ryan had thrown himself into his work and the station was bringing in almost twice the money it had made previously, although the upcoming holidays were also helping the bottom line. Naturally, Jeremy was busy because Ryan was working so hard. Ryan had also bought a boat. After being with Jack the previous summer Ryan realized he missed having a boat.

As soon as Jack felt Ryan would be okay, he left for Florida. Ryan rented the slip Jack had used. He knew and liked the people who docked at that marina. It was as good a place as any to keep his boat. He still looked in on Joyce every night but he began to spend many nights on board the boat. Naturally, he had let their nurse know where he was so she could call him if anything developed.

The marina restaurant was known for its hamburgers and fish sandwiches and Ryan started eating there often since that was all he was able to choke down anyway. However, Tuesday night was pizza night and Cassie would not have been surprised to know how Ryan avoided eating at the marina on Tuesdays. Ryan had not had pizza in years but even though he had enjoyed the taste of it that night in bed with Cassie, he could not bear the thought of eating it ever again. Too many memories of their time together would come flooding back.

Most weekends found Ryan cruising among the San Juan Islands, sometimes with Jeremy along. Ryan tried not to think of Cassie but something always seemed to remind him of one of their moments together. Finally, he gave up and just let the memories wash over him. Although she was no longer there, he felt closer to Cassie remembering all their special times together.

Before Cassie realized it, the week of Thanksgiving arrived. Jeremy was flying in on Tuesday afternoon to stay with Jane. Jane was so excited she had a hard time focusing on anything else. Cassie never remembered seeing Jane so happy. Her friend was almost glowing.

Since she had a big house, Cassie decided she should have Thanksgiving at her place. Cassie was making the turkey but everyone was bringing food so Cassie did not have to do everything. Cassie asked Jane to bring pies for dessert. She did not want Jane to have to worry about cooking with Jeremy visiting and knew Jane could stop at a bakery and pick up what was needed.

Cassie told her children about Jeremy and they were excited to meet him. Jane had been a part of their lives for so long that they were happy Jane had someone she seemed to care for so deeply.

The night before Thanksgiving everyone met at a local restaurant that offered an all-you-can-eat chicken dinner on Wednesdays. It was a casual place but the family had been eating there for years on the night before Thanksgiving and it had become a tradition.

Cassie could not believe how good it was to see Jeremy again. No one in Cassie's family knew how the relationship with Jeremy had developed but they knew besides his deep feelings for Jane he was also a friend of Cassie's.

As Jeremy entered the restaurant Cassie ran and gave him a big hug as her children smiled at him and Jane. Jim, however, did not look very happy. Although there was a terrible sadness in her eyes, Jeremy noticed immediately she had the glow of a woman who had been loved and had gained a lot of confidence in herself. Jeremy also realized Jim sensed something different about Cassie but chose to ignore it. Jeremy knew it would be a difficult weekend being around Jim.

As Cassie turned towards her husband she realized she had been right about her thoughts the previous summer. She could tell Jim did not like Jeremy from the way he was acting towards him. Jane introduced Jeremy to everyone around the table and he felt very welcomed by everyone except Jim. As they were sitting back down Cassie gasped out loud and everyone looked at her with concern.

"Oh, my gosh! Jeremy, you did it."

Jeremy began to blush as he looked at Cassie. Cassie got up and gave Jane a hug.

"Look, everyone. Jane and Jeremy are engaged!"

Jane flashed the ring on her finger, and the room got very noisy with best wishes around the table. Everyone congratulated the couple except Jim.

Cassie ordered a bottle of champagne and listening while Jane and Jeremy talked about their engagement. Suddenly, a loud voice asked, "Are we going to eat soon or not?"

Jane had tried to prepare Jeremy for meeting Jim, but it was always a shock when Jim started complaining. As far as Jeremy was concerned Jim was a selfish inconsiderate man. Jeremy was aware of Jim's behavior ahead of time but it seemed so much worse when you watched him in action.

Everyone ignored Jim. By now they had learned if they tried to talk to him when he was being disagreeable he became even more obstinate. Cassie knew tomorrow he would stay locked in his den most of the day watching football. It was a relief to know she had the family room for everyone else so they could enjoy the holiday together.

Disregarding Jim's rudeness, Cassie began questioning Jeremy and Jane about their wedding plans. Cassie felt a momentary sadness knowing she was going to lose her best friend but was so glad Jane had found happiness. Cassie could not keep from smiling every time she looked at them.

The way Jane and Jeremy were looking at each other Cassie decided they had probably also discovered they were sexually compatible after all. For a moment she wished she had Ryan's arms wrapped around her once more even for just a short time. But she realized that was a selfish wish and let it go immediately.

Both Jane and Jeremy saw the flash of pain in Cassie's eyes and knew instantly what she was thinking. They looked at each other and hoped with all their hearts Cassie would be with Ryan again someday. Cassie regained control so quickly no one else at the table was aware of what happened.

"Remember, Cassie, I told you Jeremy wanted to do a New Year's cruise?"

"Yes."

"Well, we're planning a two week cruise from San Francisco through the Panama Canal and the captain will marry us just before the boat gets underway. So, it will be a honeymoon cruise and a holiday cruise."

"Jane and Jeremy, that sounds like so much fun."

"We both want a quiet wedding. It's not like it's the first time for either of us."

Dinner passed quickly and Cassie could tell Jane and Jeremy were anxious to get back to Jane's place. She knew exactly how they were feeling.

Everyone said goodnight, knowing they would all be together the next day. Jeremy and Jane were planning to go shopping on Friday and Cassie had already agreed to join them. Cassie wanted to spend some time with both of them. She knew she would miss Jane but being around Jeremy gave Cassie a feeling of being closer to Ryan even though she knew it was not real.

Thanksgiving turned out to be a fun day for everyone. As predicted, Jim stayed in his den all day, coming out only briefly to eat before returning to his cave.

Friday the three of them went shopping. Cassie left a turkey dinner from the leftovers for Jim to microwave for his evening meal. She had a wonderful dinner with Jeremy and Jane at a new seafood restaurant that had recently opened near the Mall of America.

Cassie could not believe how much her life had changed. Jim, even in his good days, would not have enjoyed the time she had just spent with Jane and Jeremy. It was different from the way she had lived before but it seemed very much a part of Cassie's life, now. Obviously, she and Jim had drifted apart and now it seemed like they had nothing in common at all anymore.

As she got in her car to go home she wished Jane and Jeremy happiness. They wanted her to go out with them on Saturday but she had wisely said "no".

"You two need some alone time now. I appreciate you letting me tag along today but you have lots of things to discuss and if Jeremy is anything like Ryan I know where those discussions will take place. Have fun together the rest of this weekend and the rest of your lives."

With that Cassie hugged the two of them and got in her car for her drive home. She had only driven a block when the tears started falling. She could not believe she had said Ryan's name out loud. She had tried so hard to erase thoughts of him from her mind. Obviously, she had not succeeded. Cassie pulled her car over to the side of the road. She cried for over a half-hour before she could continue driving the rest of the way home.

Naturally, Jim was in his den watching TV when she returned. He never saw her slip in the house, climb the stairs and close the door to her room.

# Chapter Forty-Two

It always seemed that the time between Thanksgiving and Christmas flew by with all the holiday activities. Although they had received invitations to several parties, Jim had refused to attend any.

Cassie decided she would go alone. She did not want to sit at home feeling depressed because Jim would not go out with her. There were a couple of divorced men who began hitting on her when she turned up at the parties alone, but she ignored them and they eventually went in search of someone else to bother.

She spent Christmas Day at home with the kids and a few other relatives. Cassie did not mind cooking for everyone because it kept her busy. Jane left two days before for Seattle. Their cruise was leaving on the twenty-ninth and she needed some time beforehand to get organized. Besides, she missed Jeremy and could hardly wait to be with him again.

In Seattle, Jane was shocked when she saw Ryan. He had lost weight but it was the perpetual sadness surrounding him that made her wince when she saw him the first time.

Jeremy felt so sad for his friend. "You know Jane it's ironic. Even Joyce knows there's something wrong with Ryan and has been kinder to him lately but I don't think he's even aware she's being nicer. Sometimes I know it's just hard for him to get through the day. He'll never get over Cassie as long as he lives. I know exactly what he is going through. I know it will get better for him but it will take quite a while. But look at me! Never in my wildest dreams did I think I would marry again."

"And I can't tell you how glad I am that you changed your mind about marriage, Jeremy. And I also can't tell you how shocked I am to be saying that to you."

Jeremy smiled and then kissed Jane passionately.

"It won't be long now, sweetheart."

Jane hugged Jeremy tightly. She knew how lucky she was to find love at her age.

And Jeremy was right. Before Jane knew it, they were boarding the ship and about to get married. The last time Jane had taken a cruise she had just met Jeremy and that had been less than six months ago. Before the ship left port they were man and wife.

It was soon New Year's Eve and Jeremy stood behind Jane with his arms wrapped around her as they were looking up at the moon and the sky from their balcony.

"Being on a deck of a ship looking up at the stars could not be a more perfect way to spend the holiday or our honeymoon, Jeremy."

"We could plan another holiday cruise for next year if you'd like, Jane."

Jane turned and kissed Jeremy to let him know she approved of his plans. At the same time the couple was kissing, Ryan was also on the water. The temperature in Seattle was chilly and there was not anyone around the marina. Ryan had several invitations for the evening but he did not feel like going to any parties and had spent the evening alone on his boat. He knew he would have been more comfortable at home, especially because of the weather, but felt the port was a sanctuary. He preferred being alone these days.

Ryan glanced at the sky and made a wish when he saw a shooting star. Naturally, he wished to be together with Cassie again. He thought he would go crazy if he did not hear her voice once more. Even if he did not talk to her, he had called her house. He knew he should not but he had not been able to stop himself. When a man answered, Ryan said "Wrong number" and quickly hung up. He knew he would never try calling again.

"Who was that on the phone, Jim?"

"Wrong number, Cassie."

Cassie had also been invited out that evening but she felt too depressed to go anywhere. She thought about Jeremy and Jane and hoped everything was going smoothly for them on their cruise.

Cassie finished cleaning up after dinner and looked out her kitchen window. Even though the temperature was below zero it was one of those cold clear nights. She could see the moon and all the twinkling stars in the sky. For a brief moment she wished she could be wrapped in Ryan's arms when she saw a shooting star go by. She had no idea Ryan was looking at the sky at the same time while wishing the same thing.

Jim interrupted her thoughts to say he was going to his den to watch TV for the evening. Cassie answered back that she was going to bed early.

"You aren't staying up for the New Year, Cassie?"

"New Years doesn't hold much excitement for me anymore, Jim."

"I think you're being small minded, Cassie."

Looking at Jim in shock, Cassie could not believe how cruel he sounded.

Cassie took a deep breath and squared her shoulders. "Jim, I want a divorce. I don't want to live with you anymore. I hate how mean and inconsiderate you've become."

"And I hate how rotten you've become, Cassie. You have no sympathy for me anymore. All you care about is yourself."

Cassie laughed out loud. "If I only cared about myself, I would never have come back last October, Jim."

"Well, I'm sorry you did. I have a doctor's appointment next Wednesday morning so I need you to drive me there.

Then why don't we schedule an appointment with Doug Jones for the afternoon. Do you object if we both use the same attorney for the divorce? It will save us money."

Cassie just nodded and walked up the stairs to her room. She heard Jim turn the TV on. She could not believe what had just happened and felt unbelievable hope for the first time in a long while. Maybe she could spend next summer in Seattle again after all and maybe, just maybe, she would spend the summer in Ryan's arms again.

Cassie lay awake a long time that night replaying in her mind her time with Ryan. She heard Jim go to bed and saw it was a little past midnight on her clock. She knew it was only 10:00 p.m. in Seattle. She wondered if Ryan was at a party that evening. It would be in full swing by now.

Suddenly, she felt so sad the tears began to flow down her cheeks. She would have been even sadder if she knew Ryan was lying in his bed and the tears were also flowing down his face. He wanted to hear her voice.

At least Cassie felt a sense of freedom for the first time in months. She was surprised that Jim had given in so readily to a divorce. She had a momentary thought that things were moving too easily but she decided she was due for a lucky break.

# Chapter Forty-Three

It was late New Year's morning before Cassie got out of bed since she had been awake most of the night. Jim had already had breakfast and was in his den with the door closed. Cassie had a feeling they would spend the day without speaking to each other but that wasn't new. Actually, she was relieved she did not have to talk to him.

At noon, Kit called to wish her mother and father a Happy New Year. After Cassie talked to Kit and Paul she called to Jim to pick up the phone. A little later Gray and Karen called for the same reason. Cassie decided not to say anything to the children about the divorce until after she and Jim had seen the lawyer.

Cassie fixed herself a sandwich although she was not very hungry. Then she went back upstairs to her bedroom to read. She always liked to start a new novel New Year's Day because usually her family was tied up watching the football bowl games on TV.

Cassie went downstairs about 5:30 p.m. to see what Jim wanted for dinner but he told her not to bother since he would fix his own. She shook her head and sighed. Then she decided he could do whatever he wanted. It would not be long before she would not have to be around him at all.

That pretty much became their pattern over the next three days. They avoided each other as much as possible and when they did come in contact they said very little to each other.

Cassie could hardly wait until Wednesday. She had called the attorney's office on Monday to make an appointment for right after lunch on Wednesday.

Cassie wondered what Doctor George would think of the divorce; having a feeling he would not be surprised. Unfortunately, Cassie never had a chance to tell him the news.

As Cassie sat in Doctor George's waiting room while Jim was being examined the nurse came out to get her. She quickly led Cassie to the exam room where the physician was talking to Jim.

"Cassie, have you seen Jim's leg recently?" Dr George asked gently.

"No, doctor."

"Well look. You see how black his foot is?"

Cassie looked down at Jim's exposed leg and was horrified to discover it was black.

"It looks like gangrene. Jim, why didn't you say something to someone?"

"It's not a big deal, Doc. I thought it would get better soon."

"Not a big deal? Jim you could die from this. This is an extremely big deal!"

After conferring with the doctor Cassie went back to the waiting room and used her cell phone to cancel their legal appointment. Then she called the children to tell them their dad was being admitted to the hospital. She said she would call them again as soon as she knew anything.

As she came back to the examination room Doctor George was explaining to Jim they would have to do some tests. Jim started yelling that there was no way they were going to cut off his "good" foot.

"Your foot may be the least of your problems. We may have to cut past the knee, Jim."

Jim turned pale at that notion.

"What if I don't let you?"

"If it's as bad as I think and you don't have the surgery, you'll be dead in less than a month. And it won't be pain free either, Jim."

Cassie saw tears in Jim's eyes as he turned his head towards the wall. She immediately moved to the exam table and held his hand. Although she no longer loved her husband, she felt bad for what he would have to endure and she wanted to support him however she could.

"You don't have to stay with me, Cassie."

"Jim, you would stay with me if the roles were reversed. I'll help you get through this."

Jim wondered if he would have stayed by Cassie's side if she had to go through what he was. But he was glad she would be with him.

"Thank you for staying with me Cassie. I'm afraid. But I really did think it would get better. That's why I never said anything to you or anyone else about my foot."

Cassie just nodded and continued holding Jim's hand while they waited for the hospital arrangements to be confirmed.

After being admitted, a technician took tissue samples and X-rays and a specialist came in to check Jim's foot. The specialist agreed with Doctor George's diagnosis and they scheduled radical surgery for first thing the next morning.

"We'll try our best to take as little as possible," Doctor George assured Jim.

"Whatever, doctor. I don't want to die."

Kit and Gray arrived at Jim's hospital room just as Doctor George was leaving. They looked devastated by his news.

"Are you staying here tonight Mother?" Kit asked.

"No, I'll go home soon. They gave your dad a sedative a little while ago so he'll have a restful night. Surgery's set for 8:00 a.m. and I plan to get here about 7:00. I'll pack an overnight bag and stay tomorrow night, though."

"Dad, we'll be here a little after 7:00 tomorrow, also."

"Thanks, Gray. I appreciate that. I'll see all three of you tomorrow morning before my surgery. Why don't you go home, now? I'm getting tired."

Everyone, including Cassie, gave Jim a hug and a kiss on the cheek and wished him a restful night. Cassie realized how worried Jim must be when he did not ask anyone to turn the TV on for him.

Cassie said goodnight to her children in the parking lot and said she wound see them in the morning. As she drove home she thought about her day. Before the crisis in the doctor's office that morning she had been sure that by this time tonight she would be involved in a divorce but instead she was dealing with more of Jim's medical problems. With a sigh, Cassie realized her luck had not changed after all.

# Chapter Forty-Four

The alarm went off at 5:30 a.m. Cassie had already packed her overnight bag. She showered and washed and blow-dried her hair. She did not want to have to deal with that in the hospital. The hospital had reclining chairs for the patient's family to sleep on and that reminded Cassie how Ryan had been lucky enough to have an extra bed when he stayed with Joyce at the hospital.

Jim was groggy from the sedatives he had been given. She kissed him on the cheek and started holding his hand just as the children came in the room. It was not long before the nurse came in to get Jim for the operation and both children told their dad how much they loved him.

Cassie wished him good luck. She could not say she loved him when she knew she did not. Jim winked at her and gave a "thumbs-up" sign as they wheeled him out.

It was over an hour later when the doctor came out of the operating room looking for them.

"I'm afraid I have some bad news."

The three of them looked at the doctor with fear in their eyes.

"We had to cut past Jim's knee. The gangrene had spread farther than we originally thought. We were also worried about his weight and blood pressure. Jim had a stroke just as we finished the operation. He's alive, but we won't know the full extent of the damage for a few days. However, he is paralyzed on his right side. Hopefully, with physical therapy he'll get much better but it will be several months before he recovers enough to be self sufficient."

Cassie turned deadly white and could barely breathe. She noticed both Kit and Gray were crying. It did not get much worse than this. She knew Jim would not accept his new condition well. She just hoped he would be willing to follow through with the physical therapy. She had a momentary thought that perhaps she had been granted time with Ryan last summer to help her better cope with taking care of Jim, now.

"Can we see him, doctor?"

"I'll let you see him in about a half-hour. He's in recovery, now. They'll move him to intensive care. He's heavily sedated so he won't feel any pain but he probably won't be fully conscious until some time tomorrow."

Cassie and her children sat in the waiting room until the nurse called for them to see Jim. The right side of his face was paralyzed and he looked terrible. Cassie had to choke back a sob as she looked at him.

Since Jim was in intensive care they spent the rest of the day in the waiting area and were only allowed to visit him for ten minutes each hour. None of them had eaten much during the day. Karen and Paul came to the hospital after getting off of work early. Finally, after their 5:00 p.m. visit to Jim they all went down to the cafeteria and had dinner.

Cassie suggested the four of them go home and get some sleep since Jim's condition remained unchanged. She was still planning on staying overnight in case he needed her.

The kids went in with Cassie to see Jim once again at the 6:00 p.m. visit and then went home. It had been a draining and sad day for everyone. As Cassie went back to the cafeteria to get some tea about 8:30 p.m. her cell phone rang.

It was Jane brimming with happiness over her wedding and cruise. They had returned to Jeremy's house on Bainbridge Island. Cassie listened patiently to all of Jane's news.

"I've been trying to call your house for the last two hours. Where have you and Jim been, Cassie?"

Cassie hated to tell Jane the news when her friend was so happy but knew she would have to tell her sooner or later. Jane was devastated when she heard what had happened to Jim that day. Then Cassie told Jane they had decided to go to a divorce attorney the afternoon Jim went in the hospital.

"That is the most rotten luck, Cassie."

"I know, Jane." Cassie had to stifle a sob. She apologized to Jane for ruining all her happy news. Cassie told Jane she would call her in a few days when she had updates on Jim's condition.

Jeremy came into the room as Jane hung up the phone. She walked over to him and putting her arms around his neck started crying. Haltingly, she told him what Cassie had said between sobs. "It's just not fair, Jeremy... just not fair."

Jeremy had tears in his eyes as he heard about Cassie's troubles.

Cassie went back to the waiting room with her tea. She sat in the lounge chair and wrapped a blanket around herself. She was emotionally drained from the whole day. As she closed her eyes she could not stop the tears from falling. Cassie remembered the terrible feeling she had last October that she would never see Ryan again.

# Chapter Forty-Five

Jim was in intensive care for several days and in the hospital almost two weeks before he was transferred to a rehabilitative unit for stroke patients. At first he could not speak intelligibly so he used hand signals for 'yes' and 'no'.

Cassie sat with him every day. He was getting physical therapy and they were teaching Cassie techniques she would need to follow after she took Jim home. She planned on having temporary nursing care twice a day to help with bathing and getting Jim back and forth between his bed and his wheelchair. Cassie had ordered a hospital bed and had converted Jim's den into a bedroom. Since he had spent so much time previously in the den she felt he might find comfort in there for the present.

Even though Ryan had told Jeremy he never wanted to hear anything about Cassie, one night when the three of them were out to dinner Jane looked so sad that Ryan had made a comment. He knew Jeremy was ecstatically happy and could not understand why Jane looked so sad. Jane had just gotten a call that day from Cassie with an update on Jim's condition.

Jane knew Ryan did not want to hear about Cassie but she started crying when she looked at him and Jeremy told Ryan about Cassie and her husband's health problems.

Ryan was shocked. Being so hurt when Cassie left, Ryan had been living in a tunnel vision world. He just assumed Cassie had reconciled with her husband. He had assured himself that Cassie was happy once again with her husband. He had no idea that Jim had been emotionally cold towards

Cassie from the moment she returned and had withheld any affection towards her. He could only imagine how Cassie felt being so close to a divorce and having that chance snatched from her.

Ryan desperately wanted to talk to her but knew he could not. He remembered how he felt when he first had to take care of Joyce after her accident. He had felt it was an obligation he owed Joyce.

Ryan realized that even if Cassie no longer loved her husband she would still consider it her duty to take care of him. It was one of the reasons Ryan loved her so. She was such a caring person. She had never for a moment begrudged him the time he spent with Joyce when she was in the hospital. Ryan knew Cassie would expect the same of him.

So as much as Ryan wanted to speak to her and hear Cassie's voice again he knew he would not call her. He realized how painful it would be for her to talk to him while not being able to see him.

Ryan, knowing how bad Jane was feeling, shared his thoughts with her. As much as Jane hated what Ryan was saying she totally agreed with him. She did tell Ryan she felt better now that she would not have to pretend Cassie did not exist when she was around him.

Ryan smiled at Jane and told her he wanted Jane to keep him updated about Cassie. Jeremy was happy to hear Ryan tell Jane that. He knew Ryan was on his way to acceptance and healing. He would still hurt but at least he would become a part of their world again. So, even though the situation between Ryan and Cassie seemed hopeless at least some good had come out of Jim's health issues.

Cassie would have been happy to know about Ryan. She was so caught up in the day to day issues of Jim's problems that she sometimes went hours without thinking of Ryan. But he was never far from her heart. Cassie knew she would love him until the day she died. She also knew intuitively that he was having as hard a time not being with her as she was not being with him. She hoped that as time went by he was coping better with their parting.

It was the middle of March before Cassie finally brought Jim home. This year Easter would be earlier and Cassie thought back to the previous Easter and all that had happened in the past year. She had come a long way this last year on her life's journey. A few days after Jim had come home, Jane called Cassie with news.

"I know you don't want to talk about Ryan, Cassie, but I thought you'd want to know Joyce died two days ago. She got pneumonia again but this time she couldn't fight it. She had become much weaker these last few months."

"Oh, Jane, that's terrible. I wonder if I should call Ryan."

"I wanted you to know but I think calling him would be a bad idea. Would you be willing to come out to Seattle and live with him again, Cassie?"

"You know I can't do that, Jane."

"Yes, I do. And that's why you can't call him. We finally told him one night about Jim's health problems. It was after one of your calls and we were all out to dinner. I was so sad and when I started crying Jeremy told him what was happening with you. Before that time he never wanted to hear your name. But since then he's been able to reach acceptance of the situation between the two of you and I think a call from you would set him back again."

Cassie smiled at the thought that Ryan did not want to hear her name spoken any more than she wanted to hear his. She realized he had suffered as much pain as she had. Cassie had suspected as much but felt good knowing he was feeling better now.

"Some days I think I'll die if I don't hear Ryan's voice again. But I know you're right. I wish I could tell him one more time how much I love him but for the present we aren't meant to be together."

"It's so sad Cassie but true. I am so happy with Jeremy and never realized how wonderful loving someone could be.

Since this love has come into my life I sometimes ache with the thought of you and Ryan not being together. I can understand how devastating it was for Jeremy to lose his first wife. I don't know if I can bear it if he dies first. I wish so much that you and Ryan could be together like Jeremy and me."

"Thank you, Jane, for being my friend. Even though you're living so far away it helps to be able to talk to you like this. It makes everything more bearable."

Cassie hung up and realized she had not told Jane the latest news of Jim's condition. Hearing about Ryan's wife had side tracked her. The doctor was pleased with how well Jim's physical therapy was progressing. Since his surgery he had also been eating healthier and not only had he lost weight but his blood pressure was under control again. The doctor felt if Jim continued doing as well as he was he could look forward to many more years of life.

Cassie was truly happy for Jim but as she thought of all the empty years stretched in front of her she did not know how she was going to cope. She knew divorce was out of the question. Jim needed her and she had promised to stand by his side. For now, she realized she just had to take each day one at a time.

# Chapter Forty-Six

Cassie's life once again developed a pattern. She went to Bible class on Wednesday nights and Karen or Gray came over and stayed with Jim. She also joined a book club since she had so much time on her hands. They met every Monday night and Kit or Paul came over those nights to give Cassie a break.

On Sundays everyone came over for dinner with Jim and Cassie. The kids always offered to bring food but Cassie said no. She did not mind cooking since it gave her something to do and she always made enough for leftovers on Monday when she had her book club meetings. Cassie also did some tutoring after school to keep occupied but knew that would stop when school let out for the summer.

Surprisingly, Jim kept at his physical therapy and felt stronger every day. The best thing was his nastiness was gone. Although he had no idea about Ryan, he knew Cassie had given up a lot to be with him. He was appreciative and told her so every evening when she came in to help him get ready for bed.

Cassie still had a visiting nurse come every morning to give Jim a bath and get him ready for the day but otherwise she was able to perform the evening functions.

Along with the warmer weather, spring brought longer days. Cassie felt sad as it stayed lighter later remembering her previous summer in Seattle. Those days seemed so far behind her, now.

Cassie and Jane called each other every week and Jane would catch Cassie up on all the news. Ryan was going off on his boat every weekend. Cassie wondered if he would go up the Inside Passage of Alaska like they had talked about. She would have loved to be with him on that trip. Actually, she just longed to be with him, period.

The big news was Jack had returned for the summer with a lady friend in tow. She had been a widow for three years and was interested in a non-commitment relationship like Jack. The two of them were living on Jack's boat in the same marina as Ryan. Cassie knew it would be a fun summer for everyone in Seattle.

Jane and Jeremy had also bought a condo in downtown Seattle in a brand new building. They both loved Jeremy's place on Bainbridge Island but since they were entertaining a lot and going to the theater in Seattle they decided it would be more practical to have a place to live in the city during the week for those social activities.

Every Thursday when Jeremy finished with work they would take the ferry to Bainbridge Island and then come back to town on Monday mornings. It was the best of both worlds for them.

Ryan sold the condo he lived in with Joyce. It was as if he was looking for a fresh start. Jeremy talked him into buying a condo right next door to his and Jane's. They liked living close to each other but Jane wished Cassie was also there. It would have been perfect if the four of them were living next to each other.

Memorial Day weekend arrived and Cassie remembered how she had felt getting ready for her adventure to Seattle last summer. She wondered if she could ever stop thinking of the past. She and Jim had gone to Kit's on Saturday and then again on Sunday after church for picnics as they had the previous year. It was a nice weekend and everyone was enjoying the warmer temperatures. Jim especially enjoyed sitting outside in the sun rather than cooped up inside watching television.

When they arrived home Sunday evening Cassie got Jim ready for bed. As she kissed him goodnight on the cheek she asked him if he wanted to go to a movie the next day. Jim had tears in his eyes as she was talking to him and Cassie asked him what was wrong.

"Cassie, I know your love for me died a long time ago and I don't blame you with the way I treated you. But, I want you to know how much I have appreciated you taking care of me these last few months."

"Don't be ridiculous, Jim. You know I don't mind taking care of you. And you tell me every day how much you appreciate what I'm doing. Go to sleep and I'll see you in the morning."

"I just wanted to make sure you knew. Goodnight, Cassie."

Jim's expression was so sad Cassie wondered what had gotten into him. He had been so upbeat and positive lately. She just hoped the old Jim wasn't coming back. Cassie went to bed and as usual started thinking about Ryan. She wondered what he was doing and figured he was out somewhere on his boat.

The next morning Cassie went in to wake up Jim before the nurse arrived. As she entered his room she knew something was terribly wrong. Jim was dead! There was an envelope with her name on it propped up against the lamp on his nightstand.

Cassie was paralyzed for a moment. Her initial reaction was to try and shake Jim awake. Then she wondered if she should call their children or the ambulance first. But she did none of those things. As she touched Jim's arm she realized how cold he was and knew he had been dead for quite a while. Instead, Cassie picked up the envelope that was addressed to her and pulled out the note in Jim's handwriting.

"Dear Cassie, when you read this I will be gone. I know I've thanked you many times for what you have done for me these past months but I don't want to live any more. I hate being stuck in my wheelchair and dependent on everyone. I constantly worry about having another stroke and becoming permanently paralyzed. I wouldn't want to live that way and if that happened I might not have the ability to kill myself. I have enough sleeping pills. I've been saving for this moment. Cassie, please have a happy life. You deserve it. Tell Kit and Gray I love them with all my heart. Please don't be sad for me. I will finally have some peace from this deteriorating body of mine. Thank you for all you've done for me, Cassie. Love, Jim."

Cassie was stunned. She had no idea Jim had been that depressed. He had hidden it from everyone. She called 911 to get an ambulance to take Jim to the hospital. Then she called her children. After that, she called and left a message for Doctor George. By the time the kids got to the house the paramedics and police had arrived.

Kit and Gray were crying when they entered the house but Cassie could not cry. She showed them the note their dad had left. She was very sad that Jim had taken his life but realized he had chosen a quick and pain free way to die. She wished she had known how unhappy he had been so he could have been treated for his depression. However, Jim's note had freed her from guilt, as he planned it would.

Cassie was glad Jim had finally found peace. He had never liked being dependent on others and had worked very hard after his first amputation to become self-sufficient as quickly as possible.

A short while later Paul and Karen arrived. After Jim's body was removed, the rest of the afternoon was busy with making calls to friends and relatives to tell them the news. Tomorrow the funeral preparations would be made and everyone notified of the arrangements. Cassie made dinner.

Being busy helped her not to think about Jim's death as much.

Finally, everyone went home. Cassie wanted to be alone now but she was glad they had been there for each other all day. Her children were still in shock and Cassie knew it would be a few days before reality set in. Although Cassie knew Jim hated his health problems, she thought he had finally accepted them. Realizing that had not been the case made his death a little easier for Cassie to acknowledge.

She waited until almost 10:00 p.m. to call Jane. Jeremy and Jane would have been out all day with friends and at almost 8:00 p.m. their time she thought they would be home.

Jeremy answered the phone. "Hi, Cassie, that was good timing. We got in a little while ago. I'll go get Jane."

Cassie realized Jeremy just thought she was calling to chat and waited for Jane to come on the line.

"Hi, Cassie, what's up?"

"Jane, I have bad news."

Jane was immediately silent.

"There's no easy way to say this. Jim killed himself last night."

"What?" It took Jane a few seconds to process Cassie's words. "I can't believe it, Cassie. I'm so sorry."

"It's okay Jane. I just needed you to know."

Cassie told Jane about Jim's note and how the children were getting through their grief. She also told Jane that she had not been able to cry.

"I never dreamed he was that depressed. He had been so upbeat, especially lately."

"Maybe knowing what he planned to do helped to lift his depression. It sounds like he finally felt some peace towards the end."

"I guess you're right. I never thought of that."

"When's the funeral, Cassie? Jeremy and I want to be there with you."

Jeremy, who had been listening to Jane's end of the conversation came up behind her and put his arms around her.

"We'll make the arrangements tomorrow. I really appreciate you coming and being with me, Jane. Do you think you could get here by Thursday?"

"Won't you have the wake on Wednesday night?"

"Yes. I forgot about that. I guess I'm not thinking clearly."

"We'll arrive sometime on Wednesday afternoon then. Don't worry about us. Jeremy will rent a car and we'll just come straight to the funeral home. Could we stay with you or shall we go to a hotel?"

"I would love it if you stayed with me. It seems so empty and lonely here, now. Even during the times Jim didn't talk to me, I always knew he was in the house."

"Take care, Cassie. We'll see you in two days."

"Good-bye, Jane. I know I've said it before, but thanks for being my friend."

"Bye, Cassie."

After Cassie hung up she started thinking about Jim. About twenty-four hours ago Jim had taken his life. It seemed so strange to think of him as gone.

Cassie had not thought about Ryan all day. He was, however, always her first thought the minute she laid down in bed each night and tonight was no exception. She remembered Jim's words, "Be happy," and wondered if that could be possible now.

Cassie had wanted to call Ryan but Jane had told her he had just taken two weeks off work and had sailed somewhere in his boat. Cassie wished she could be with him. However, it was probably better she get through the funeral before talking to him.

Putting her house up for sale was one of the first things Cassie planned to do. She wanted to live permanently in Seattle, and she knew she did not want to have a big house in

Minnesota to worry about. The condo definitely appealed to her.

Cassie desperately wanted to be with Ryan and she also missed Jane and Jeremy. She was not sure how her children would react to her move but knew she wanted to relocate out there.

Cassie went to sleep quickly that night dreaming of a new life that would include Ryan. Tomorrow would be a busy day with funeral arrangements to be made. After the funeral, Cassie could begin a new journey.

# Chapter Forty-Seven

Tuesday became a blur. Cassie had to make all the decisions and arrangements surrounding a funeral. She wished she and Jim had made some of the preliminary decisions before he died.

That evening, close friends and family needed to be informed by phone about the arrangements. Cassie fell into bed exhausted that night but she had a hard time sleeping in the empty house. Tomorrow night Jane and Jeremy would be staying with her and she was looking forward to the company.

Wednesday afternoon Cassie, her children and their spouses went to the funeral home for the wake. Quite a few people came to pay their respects, but one face blended into another and it was hard for Cassie to keep track of everyone who came.

Kit and Gray appeared to be doing well but Cassie knew they were still numb with shock. Seeing Jane and Jeremy come into the room she talked to them briefly since the other mourners wanted to pay their condolences. Just knowing Jeremy and Jane were in the room was comforting. Jane knew quite a few of the people there so Cassie did not worry about her and Jeremy being left alone without anyone to talk to.

Finally, the evening was over. Cassie kept glancing over at the casket. It was hard to think they would never hear Jim's voice again. Jane, Jeremy and the immediate family went to a nearby restaurant for dinner. Cassie was not very hungry and just had a bowl of soup. She still had the funeral and luncheon to get through tomorrow.

That Wednesday night Cassie kept thinking that it was only a week ago when they had been making plans for the Memorial Day weekend at Kit's. And now tomorrow, they would bury Jim. She and Jane stayed up late drinking wine and reminiscing about the fun times Jim and Cassie had in the early years of their marriage.

Thursday morning was a beautiful day. The sun was shining brightly and there was warmth in the air that foretold the summer days just around the corner. It did not seem like the right kind of day for a funeral.

This was another day during which all the faces blended together as Cassie spoke to everyone who came up to comfort her. No one was aware of exactly how Jim had died and Cassie and the children decided to keep it that way. Everyone knew Jim had suffered from various health problems and most just assumed that had caused his death, especially since the stroke.

After the cemetery service they went back to the church for a luncheon prepared by a group of women in their parish. They chose as their ministry to fix meals for funerals and Cassie gave them a large donation. She was appreciative that she did not have to deal with details like planning lunch.

It was past 3:00 p.m. when the last of the mourners left the church. Jane, Jeremy and the immediate family went back to Cassie's house. Several people had brought food for the family to the house and there was more than they knew what to do with. By 7:00 p.m. the last of the family left. Cassie gave Kit and Paul and Gray and Karen some hot dishes and desserts to take home. She did not want the food to go to waste and knew there was no way she could eat all the things people had dropped off. Finally, Cassie, Jane and Jeremy were alone.

Cassie tearfully offered her appreciation. "I'm so thankful you two came and have been here with me these last few days. I don't know how I would have made it through all this without you. Just knowing you were somewhere nearby was such a comfort."

Jane smiled. "We love you Cassie and I'm glad we could help you. Right, Jeremy?"

"Yes, definitely. You know, Cassie, you would be there for one of us if the need arose. You can always count on us to be there for you."

Cassie got up from the couch and gave both of them hugs.

"Tomorrow the realtor is coming to give me an estimate and information on selling this house. I know you just sold your place, Jane and the two of you just bought the new condo so I'm counting on your expertise."

"I can hardly wait for the four of us to be out in Seattle together again, Cassie. I know Ryan will be so excited."

"I hope he still wants me, Jane."

"How can you ask such a thing? Of course, he wants you. Actually, Jeremy told me he purposely bought a three-bedroom condo on the same floor as us in the hope that you would live with him there someday."

"Oh, Jane, I can hardly wait to be with him again. I'll start organizing things around this house and do whatever the realtor needs me to do in order to get this house up for sale quickly. I was also thinking about flying to Seattle next weekend for a few days. I want to surprise Ryan when he comes back from his trip on the boat.

"That's a great idea, Cassie."

All three of them went to bed early that night since it had been a draining day with the funeral.

They met with the realtor the next day. She suggested having an estate company handle the sale of any thing Cassie did not want. All Cassie would have to do was go through her clothes and pack any personal items or furniture she wanted to keep.

Then a cleaning service would come in and deep clean the house so it was ready for sale. She did not think Cassie would have any trouble selling within a couple of months since many buyers liked to be settled in before the new school year started.

Saturday afternoon they went to the Mall of America window shopping. They met Kit and Gray and their spouses there for dinner. Cassie did not tell her children about putting the house up for sale. She knew they were still feeling the loss of their father and she wanted to give them time to grieve.

Cassie did tell Kit and Gray she was going out to Seattle to visit Jeremy and Jane for a few days the following weekend. They thought that was an excellent idea. Cassie had worked hard taking care of their dad the last few months and they knew she needed a vacation. They had no idea that the real reason she was going was to see Ryan again.

Cassie could not believe how fast time went and before she knew it she was saying good-bye to Jane and Jeremy.

"I'll be busy this week but it won't be long before I'm back in Seattle. Jeremy, if you hear from Ryan, don't tell him I'm coming. I want to surprise him."

"It'll be a wonderful surprise, Cassie."

That night Cassie went to bed early for the second night in a row.

"I'll be back in your arms soon, Ryan," she said out loud. She looked at the ring on her right hand Ryan had given her and hoped he would move it to her left hand quickly. All night long she slept with a smile on her face as if she was dreaming something wonderful.

# Chapter Forty-Eight

Cassie kept busy that week getting the house organized. She packed up Jim's clothes to give to Goodwill. Then she started packing boxes of personal items she wanted to keep or give to her children.

On Tuesday, she met with an estate sale manager who would do an inventory and then prepare an estimate of the value of her possessions. Slowly, she felt she was getting a handle on things.

Cassie went to bed feeling good. But she woke up in the middle of the night during a vivid dream of Ryan. She thought she heard him calling her. It seemed so real and she knew she could hardly wait to see him on the weekend.

Thursday night there was a very bad storm and Cassie was glad it was storming. The bad weather would clear out and tomorrow would be a great day for flying out to Seattle.

Friday finally arrived and Cassie called a limo to take her to the airport. She could hardly believe that in a very short time she would be with Ryan again. Cassie would take the shuttle to Jane and Jeremy's new place. They had given her a key since they had made plans to meet some friends Friday night on Bainbridge Island and they wanted her to feel at home there. Jane and Jeremy would come back to Seattle to take her to lunch on Saturday. Meanwhile, Jack would bring his lady friend over to the condo tonight to meet Cassie and go to dinner. Ryan was not expected back until Saturday night.

As Cassie arrived at the baggage area she became puzzled. She found Jane and Jeremy waiting for her. She was sure they had said they would be on Bainbridge Island. Cassie went up to them with a big smile on her face. All of a sudden she saw tears in Jane's eyes and a shiver of fear ran through her body.

"What's wrong, Jane?"

Jane turned away from her as tears streamed down her face. It was Jeremy who answered.

"I'm afraid it's not good news, Cassie. Ryan's boat was caught in a bad storm Tuesday night. He called the Coast Guard with a "mayday" but his boat has disappeared, and so has Ryan. We think he's dead Cassie!"

Dead? He couldn't be dead! She realized the storm in Minneapolis Thursday night was probably the same one Ryan got caught in on Tuesday night. The last thing she remembered was how she heard Ryan calling for her in the middle of the night on Tuesday. And then for the second time in her life Cassie fell into a swirling black void.

When Cassie came to, she was lying on a couch in a small room at the airport with two paramedics standing over her. When she saw Jane and Jeremy the sinking feeling came back to her. It couldn't be true! It just couldn't be true! But as she looked at Jane she knew deep down inside it was true.

Cassie did not think she could bear the terrible ache she was feeling in her heart. She now knew what it felt like to not want to live as Jim had felt.

"Cassie, you're in a room at the airport and the paramedics are going to give you a tranquilizer. Do you want to go to the hospital or come back to our place with us?"

"I don't want to go to the hospital, Jane."

And so it was a little over an hour later that Cassie found herself getting off the elevator on the floor where her friends lived. When Jane and Jeremy looked at the door down the hallway, Cassie knew instantly it was Ryan's condo. With tears in her eyes she quickly turned and went into her friends' home.

Jack was there sitting on the couch with a woman Cassie did not recognize. He immediately got up and hugged Cassie. She could see he had also been crying. It was at that instant Cassie knew Ryan was truly dead and she realized her foreboding of never seeing him again had been right the previous fall.

"Oh my God! How will I ever live without him? I could handle being apart from him as long as I knew he was here in Seattle."

Both Jeremy and Jack, having been through the loss of a beloved spouse, hoped they could somehow help Cassie get through her nightmare. The next few days became a blur to Cassie. Most days she did not even get out of bed.

In the middle of the following week, Jeremy met with Ryan's lawyer as he was the executor of his estate. Jeremy came home that evening with news.

"Cassie, Ryan left you the bulk of his estate because he had no immediate family. With no close relatives I guess he changed his will after he met you. He also put this condo he bought in both of your names so that now belongs to you. I think he expected you'd be living here with him one day."

"I don't want anything of his, Jeremy. I just want him!" Cassie cried, running into the bedroom as the tears once again began to flow. With a distressing look at Jeremy, Jane followed Cassie into her bedroom.

"Jane, what am I going to do without him? I don't want to live."

"Cassie, don't say that. Ryan would want you to go on without him. He wouldn't have left everything to you otherwise."

"Don't you understand? I don't want his money."

"Whether you like it or not it's now yours. If you died tonight it would just go to your heirs."

Jane was worried sick about Cassie. Her going back to Minnesota in a few days was not a good idea. As much as she did not want to do it, she called Kit and Gray. If something happened to their mother and Jane had not warned them they would never forgive her.

Kit and Gray arrived the next day. Still trying to process their father's death, they were stunned when they saw their mother. Jane sat them down and told them the whole story of Ryan and Cassie. Kit immediately realized how much her mother had given up to be with their dad, particularly considering how badly he had treated her after she came back home. Neither of them wanted to lose their mother, especially after just losing their father.

Jane had Cassie's children stay in Ryan's condo which had a guestroom and a den with a sofa bed. The unit now belonged to their mother and Jeremy knew Ryan would not have minded. In Ryan's bedroom they found an eight by-ten picture of Cassie and a man taken in front of the B&B. They knew it was Ryan holding her hand and Cassie's green ring was visible. There were also various other pictures of the two of them in front of a waterfall in a forest, sitting by a lake and some small towns they did not recognize.

"So that's who gave her the ring. Remember, Gray, when I came home from Seattle? I told you mother seemed so different, almost as if she was in love."

"It seems so strange to think she was living a secret life here."

"Not quite secret, Gray. Everyone out here knew about it. And it's obvious they weren't going to leave their sick spouses. Their affair did not really hurt anyone. I hope they found some happiness together."

Cassie's children showing up forced her back to reality. She missed Ryan but knew she had to be strong for her children's sake. Cassie still wanted to leave Minnesota. She had not been able to go into Ryan's condo yet but she definitely wanted to sell her place and come live in Seattle.

Kit and Gray were not excited about her moving so far away but for now they just wanted her to care about something.

Cassie knew she had to go back to Minnesota and get her affairs settled. But there was one more journey she needed to make before going back. On Sunday Kit and Gray went back home. Cassie was staying another week and would go back the following weekend.

Cassie announced she needed a few days by herself, but that she would be fine. They were all worried about her but knew they had to let her go. She hugged and kissed her children good-bye and told them they could pick her up at the airport the following weekend.

Cassie wanted to retrace some of her journeys with Ryan, especially those throughout Vancouver Island. She wanted to savor the last memories of him and the places they had been before she could let him go. For some reason she felt compelled to take this journey.

It was almost two weeks since Ryan had disappeared. The next morning it was with a heavy heart that Cassie began to retrace the previous summer's routes.

# Chapter Forty-Nine

Renting a car for her journey, Cassie drove to Anacortes. She took the ferry to San Juan Island's Friday Harbor and then drove over to Roche Harbor. When she saw the Hotel De Haro she thought she would cry.

Entering the hotel, Cassie walked up to the third floor. A maid was cleaning the room she and Ryan had stayed in but she could see the robes hanging on the closet door and had to turn away. This journey was going to be even more painful than she had anticipated.

Cassie decided to go back to Friday Harbor and wait for the ferry to Victoria. She planned to stay downtown at the inner harbor as she and Ryan had on their first overnight trip together.

After settling in her room, Cassie went walking along the inner harbor. All of a sudden Cassie saw a man in front of her. It was Ryan. She ran up to him and touched him on the shoulder, but as the man turned, Cassie realized it was not Ryan. The tears began to fall as she excused herself and turned away.

Cassie seemed to recognize another man when she rented the car in Seattle the day before. She also thought he was Ryan, but he was not Ryan either. She realized her subconscious mind was trying to bring Ryan back and she began to wonder if maybe she would not be better off going back to Minnesota permanently. Seeing "Ryan" everywhere was just too painful.

The next morning Cassie drove to Tofino. This time it was not raining but Cassie still did not like the town. She planned to skip Lantzville and the B&B until her return from the north end of the island.

At Campbell River, she once again had dinner at the restaurant where she, Ryan and Jack had eaten. She remembered telling Ryan how good the food was and such variety she could have eaten there several times a week if she lived in the area.

Cassie made it to Port Hardy/Bear Cove by lunch the next day. This was the end of the road. She actually had made it through the whole day yesterday without seeing any "Ryans." It was still too early to stay overnight and so she went back to Cumberland. That town was almost 300 miles away and the road was two lanes and slow going but since she was not sleeping very well and with the longer daylight she decided to drive the distance.

There was not a very long drive from Cumberland the next day to the B&B in Lantsville. She had called Nina to tell her she would be stopping briefly but she did not want to stay overnight. She knew the memories of where she and Ryan had first made love would be too painful if she stayed at the B&B. She had already decided to go back to Nanaimo and catch the ferry to Vancouver. She could make Seattle the next evening, and after stopping at the B&B, she would be ready to spend time with her friends again.

The next morning Cassie was up early. In a way she was excited to see the B&B and in a way she wondered whether she should stop at all. By the time she drove into the driveway and saw Nina and Carl's welcoming wave she was glad she had decided to stop.

Breakfast for the guests was over so Cassie had coffee and croissants with Nina and Carl, telling them what she knew about Ryan's death. There were people staying in the room she and Ryan had become lovers in. Cassie was glad the room was occupied. She knew she would totally break down if she even took a quick look.

After chatting with the couple Cassie asked them if she might walk down the steps to the sea before leaving. As Nina nodded her head yes, Carl spoke up.

"Going down to the sea is fine, Cassie, but first I want to show you something."

Following Carl to his garage, Cassie was puzzled as he took a shovel from behind the door. Next to the garage was a small fir tree. Carl began digging near the tree.

"What are you doing, Carl?"

"I have to tell you, Cassie. If I didn't know Ryan was dead I wouldn't be doing this. He always believed you two would come back here someday."

"I know. He told me that too, Carl. It's strange because my intuition said that was not going to happen. That is one time I wish I'd been wrong."

As Cassie looked down at the ground, Carl pulled a wrapped package from the hole he had dug. It looked about the size of an eight-by-ten picture frame wrapped in heavy brown paper and tied with string.

Carl cut the string for Cassie. As she unwrapped the package, she saw bubble wrap underneath. As she unwound the bubble wrap, Cassie did indeed see a picture frame. In the frame were handwritten words on a piece of paper.

As she looked closer, the writing was in the style of a poem and appeared to be Ryan's handwriting. Suddenly, she remembered that morning before they had left the B&B. Ryan had talked about assisting Carl with a project.

"You helped him do this, Carl?"

"Yes, I did, Cassie."

"I remember how secretive Ryan was the night before we left here. He went to get some wine and was gone a long time. He was buying all this wasn't he?"

"Yes, he got everything the night before and then we buried it in the morning before the two of you left. Read it, Cassie."

Cassie read the words that Ryan had written:

Darling Cassie,

My heart knows some day
You'll find a way
To read what I have written...
There are no words to express the love I have for you, Cassie.
If you are reading this then I know we have found our way back to each other.
Here's to the memories we already have and to the memories yet to come.

I will love you forever, Cassie.

Ryan

Cassie looked at Carl as the tears ran down her cheeks.

"Carl, I'm going to walk down to the water now if you don't mind."

Carl just nodded at her as he wiped a tear from his eye.

Cassie walked down the stairs clutching the frame under her arm. She knew now that Ryan had been thinking of the future when he wrote those words. Cassie sat on one of the fallen logs and stared out to sea for quite awhile.

Cassie thought about the memories that now would never come. She still could not believe he was gone from her life forever. She felt she would never get over this terrible pain she was feeling.

The tears were streaming down her face as she climbed back up the stairs. She could not help remember the time the rain lashed at them during their upward climb that first night they made love. Cassie saw the flag and knew she was close to the top. She also knew she was close to ending her journey. As she reached the top she saw a man standing by the hot tub. I sure hope it's not another Ryan, she thought to herself.

But it was! Only this Ryan looked different. He looked like the real Ryan. She knew she had to have lost her sense of reality. This Ryan had been leaning on the outside of the hot tub but now he was walking towards her. As Cassie stared at the man coming towards her, she dropped the picture she had been holding and heard the glass shatter.

"Ryan?"

"Yes, Cassie."

"But, Ryan. It can't be you!"

Cassie felt herself reel as Ryan put his arms around her. He smelled like Ryan and he sounded like Ryan. He took his hands and wiped the tears from her face.

Cassie looked at him with questioning eyes. As she looked at him she saw his lips come crushing down on hers and she knew instantly it was Ryan.

When the kiss ended, Ryan took Cassie's right hand and removed the ring he had given her, transferring it to the fourth finger of her left hand. He also picked up the picture she had dropped.

"I guess we need a new frame, Cassie."

With their arms wrapped around each other he supported her as they slowly walked back to the B&B.

# Chapter Fifty

It had been a month since Ryan and Cassie had found their way back to each other. Ryan had bought another boat and they were sailing up the Inside Passage of Alaska for their honeymoon. Cassie was looking forward to seeing many new places she had never been to.

Cassie still marveled that Ryan had come back to her. At first she felt a little guilty about marrying Ryan so soon after Jim's death but even Kit and Gray were glad she had found Ryan once more. The children and their spouses all liked him immediately and just wanted Cassie to be happy after her sad years living with Jim.

They had a small wedding with a few friends and Cassie's children, in the gardens at Roche Harbor. Ryan had leased a seaplane to take the wedding guests to and from the wedding and had rented the entire third floor of the hotel for the wedding party. Naturally, he and Cassie had stayed in their old room.

After they left Carl and Nina at the B&B, Ryan told Cassie the story of the night he almost died. The storm had come up so quickly he did not have time to get to a harbor. Somehow, a pin in his motor had loosen and fallen off and he had not been able to steer the boat. That was when he called in the "mayday."

The boat was being tossed around by the waves and Ryan knew he was in terrible trouble when he spotted the shore. There were numerous island outcrops that could rip the bottom out of the boat, and the closer he got to the land, the more worried he became. Finally, the unthinkable happened. He felt the bottom of the boat scrape against a rock. Knowing it would not be long before the boat began sinking, he knew his only hope was to get to shore in the dinghy. Hypothermia would set in quickly if he ended up in the water and he was determined to not let that happen.

As he climbed into the dinghy to push off he slipped and hit his head on the edge of the boat. As he was knocked unconscious he remembered crying out for Cassie. Ryan's story had Cassie shivering when she realized she had heard him call out to her that night. When she told Ryan tears came to his eyes.

When Ryan regained consciousness he found himself in a small cabin on an island. The owner, Gregory, told him he had watched Ryan's boat sink after he fell into the dinghy. Gregory had waded out to get the little boat as it came close to shore. The dinghy had also scraped against the rocks and was leaking.

Gregory was somewhat of a hermit. A supply boat stopped at some of the islands in the area every two weeks and that was how Gregory stayed in contact with the outside world. Unfortunately, it had just been there the day before and Gregory had no phone or means to get in touch with anyone.

Ryan's cell phone had gone down along with the ship's radio when the boat sank. Ryan found it hard to believe in this day and age someone could live in an area so close and yet so far from civilization. He had worried the most about Cassie thinking he was dead. He did not want to chance trying to take the leaky dinghy back to the mainland so he had to wait until the supply boat showed up again.

As soon as the boat returned he called on the radio and arranged for transportation back to Seattle. Both Jeremy and Jane had turned white when they opened their condo door and saw him standing in the hallway. They told Ryan about Cassie's husband and her journey back to Vancouver Island.

He could not believe her husband was dead and that they could be together again. Ryan asked Jeremy to call Jack and his friends and let them know he was okay.

Ryan then chartered a seaplane to Nanaimo and rented a car for the drive to the B&B in Lantzville. He knew Cassie would show up sooner or later. Carl and Nina were also shocked when Ryan came knocking at their door. Ryan could not believe his good luck that Cassie was already there although she had just left for her walk down the stairs. Carl told Ryan he had given Cassie the package, but Ryan did not care about anything except holding Cassie in his arms again.

Cassie was so excited that she and Ryan had been given another chance together. This was one time her intuition had been wrong and she was eternally grateful it was so. Sailing near several islands, Ryan was looking at some of his nautical maps as Cassie came up and whispered in his ear.

"I guess we better look for the next available marina, Cassie."

"I hope it's nearby, Ryan. I'm ready for a nap."

Cassie moaned as Ryan drew her to him and his lips descended on hers.